ROSE BULLET

ROSE BULLET

A Romantic Thriller

AMRISH SHAH

tara
India Research Press
Flat. 6, Khan Market, New Delhi - 110 003
Ph: 24694610; Fax: 24618637
www.indiaresearchpress.com
contact@indiaresearchpress.com

2021

ISBN 13 : 978-81-8386-179-3

Printed and Bound in India for
Tara Press-India Research Press

To my Father, Gopal, who taught me how to conquer death.
And my Mother, Pratima, who showed me how to conquer with love.

A soul mate is the true lover who not only touched your heart,
but also held your soul for you, while you searched for it elsewhere.

1

The sun is a red glow as it crawls up over Punjab. The air is thin and the breeze busy caressing the faces of those who have left their homes to beat the traffic. The peach sky, drenched in the colours of dawn, promises a dry day. The smog makes the otherwise serene morning a tough master. Is this a promise or a threat? Morning dew-drops frame the windows of the cars parked by the road and the choking dust of yes-terday's storm is now a distant memory. Time flies here, and yet everything seems to be in a state of inertia.

The little town of Jalandhar is preparing for *Karwah Chauth*. The women in Punjab wake up to eat before the sunrise and then fast through the day, praying for their hus-bands' long lives. *Karwah Chauth* changes everything. Every street isdrenched in colours and light. For an entire day the city allows itself to be transformed into some-thing new, something that will fade away with the next dawn. The women are high-spirited as they pray that their beloved, but absent husbands return safely. This coun-tryside that has seen furious battles, from the legendary days of the *Mahabharata* to the Mughals, from the freedom struggle to religious riots, when men have left home and never returned. The women, dressed in their brightest clothes and jewels, come to-gether to celebrate their good fortune of having a living husband, because life can change from heaven to hell for the victims of cruel karma.

A man enters a phone booth. He is neither old nor young, neither tall nor short, neither thin nor fat; dressed in brown trousers, a cream shirt and brown shoes. He doesn't wear glasses, a wedding ring, turban or bag.

Once in he putsin a coin from his pocket and punches a number.

When the last man has left the boss closes the freezer and repositions the two cold drinks dispensers in front of it. He looks around, puts the tables back into place and turns the lights off as he goes to change. 'It was a quiet night, brother. Have a good day!' he cheerfully greets the watchman who has just arrived for the day shift.

On an empty road just outside town a man in a blue tracksuit is running alongside the mustard fields. Nothing better than a morning run when the sun is merciful and the mint breeze fills the lungs with energy. His fists are tight and his gaze is alert. He looks serene but there are frown lines on his eyebrows. He wears a talisman, a stone ring on one of his index fingers that catches the sun. His body language is confident and his feet on the tar a rhythm that indicates panache. He runs without a care in the world, listening to music and thinking of the day ahead. He takes this road every day, has done for years, because nature is beautiful and there's nothing like starting the day with an adrenalin rush!

Not far from where he runs, on a winding road, a Skoda is devouring the asphalt at every turn. The driver is in control. What he sees around him pleases him and, at least for the ride, he can shut the world out of his steel shell. His lips are watering with the thought of the best *kheer* in Punjab that his mother cooks.

The stereo blares and the AC is set to 18 degrees, cold enough for him to feel his goose bumps; but he likes the chill. Soon he will be a millionaire. Yes, glorious morning!

This road was built years ago, tearing down a part of the forest to cover the ground with asphalt. As he drives over a bridge he sees that the jungle is slowly reclaiming the land, creepers falling from the trees touch the ground in places and the roots lift the tar in others. From his windscreen it seems as though the forest's open mouth is about to close again. Suddenly a car appears in the distance, coming from the opposite direction. If the music wasn't so loud he would hear the sound of wheels screeching up the hill, but he's lost in his dreams. And when the oncoming black car hits his he looks more confused than afraid. *What? This was a beautiful morning . . . I had plans for my future, I am destined to inherit a fortune from my ancestral property, and now I may not be alive. It's absurd, ridiculous, outrageous even! I can't die in a car accident . . .* his half-open eyes read as the car drops into ditch below.

Rajveer, the runner in the blue tracksuit, diverts from the main road and sprints on a dirt road. He crosses a small wooden overpass with a rivulet flowing underneath. The smell of mustard is like the gravitational pull of his earth. His ankles get slightly wet as he runs through the moist grass and his nostrils open to the scent of green. He feels stronger, rejuvenated every time he strays from the main road. The lure of adventure, of the roadless travelled, the search for the unknown, brings him to such lonely spots. He leaves behind the sound and the images of a buzzing city, today more than ever, the city that has come alive with the preparations for *Karwah Chauth*.

Back in the town the sunrays wash the windows of a rundown building. Its glass panes reflect the morning sky with its pink clouds. All the windows are closed, except for one.

There stands a man with a country made gun. He smokes slowly, breathing in deeply and listening to the cracking sound of paper and dried tobacco leaves burning-betweenhis fingers. Under his feet a mat of cigarette stubs covers the floor. He has waited for a long time for his prey, but the time is not yet. He's a man-eater of a kind. The city is his forest and the gun his claws. He knows he has to lower his head beneath his shoulder blades like the tiger, hide in the grass and sense the change in the surrounding.

A man enters an ATM booth. Although he is an Indian he's trying too hard to fit in. He intoxicated with the thoughts of the upcoming festival, the cheerful mood of the people on the streets, the swarms of children looking for sweet-stalls while the adults rehearse the music they will perform in the evening. He's from a different land, where festivals either don't take place or are celebrated more sedately, in a hall, where the music stops playing at midnight,a country on the other side of the ocean where Indians congregate, sharing the life andmemories of a home far away. The man is dressed like an Indian, moves like an Indian, buthe smells of Singapore from a million miles away. Those who notice his expression can detect a grimace of disgust mixed with the excitement of walking on his motherland.

The AC in the ATM booth is soothing; it reminds him of his second home in a foreign country. He needs to buy a gift and impress his newly wed wife. *Can't wait to touch her, to wrap her in my arms for the whole day, she smells like jasmine...*

He takes the money, new banknotes that will be changed into filthy ones as soon as he buys breakfast, and puts it carefully in the Indian Rupees section of his large wallet. He holds his arms out wide as if to hug the world. The only city that comes to his mind is where his job has taken him, Singapore. But at the same time, behind the closed lashes, he imagines all the marvels that come with a festival in Punjab, his young wife and the extended lovemaking. He opens the glass door and hears a sound, like a firecracker. At first he doesn't pay attention to it, but a few seconds later, as he feels his shirt glued to his chest, he looks down to discover a pool of blood. His blood oozes out of his chest like water from a tube-well.

He falls on his back and his shock turns into an incredulous grin with his final breath. *She must be dressed in her favourite* Patiala salwar *so divine. Has she eaten her fruits?*

People start to gather around his corpse. No one dares touch him. They all know that a gunshot in the heart from somewhere far away was no mistake. It means that this man had to die, and no one wants to disobey the order of the killer.

Rajveer breathes heavily as he runs in his pristine white shoes. He passes through a few villages on the outskirts of the town. His routes are often random. As he runs a moon-faced woman observes him. She stands on the roof of a beautiful mansion with mustard flowers in her hair. She woke up in an empty bed that brisk morning; her husband was apparently out working the previous night. She got out of the bedroom, still unsure whether she was worried or furious, asked her maid to makeher a cup of *chai* and stood sipping it at her window. She looked at the reflection of her green bangles in the morning light. The woman was preparing for *Karwah Chauth*. Friends would come home to greet her-her husband's family and her own-to see what a good wife she was and what a successful marriage she had made. But where was he? There are a lot of things that a wife isn't supposed to ask, but her husband should at least be home every night. He had deliberately not come home and she knew it. He would come at nine and apologize for having to work all night. If she dared speak he would throw his white lies in her face-that his hard work allowed her to sit at home all day being served by maids and worrying only about what to wear.

As she walks slowly across the roof, watering each plant meticulously and humming a song from a movie, she doesn't notice a shadow behind her. If she had she would have screamed, but the shadow, shapeless and deathly silent, creeps behind her and gets a firm grip on the two ends of her *dupatta*. Before she knows she is choking on her tongue, her eyes poppingout. A few minutes later her slim body drops on the delicate mustard flowers, the cupstill in her hands.

The thud breaks her green bangles, scattering glass splinters on the floor that quickly turned bright red. Just a few days ago the same floor was decorated with *rangoli* that included her name entwined with her husband's. It was their anniversary.

But Rajveer doesn't know what has happened just a few hundred metres from him. He is submerged in his run, *High and Dry* by Stereophonics blasting inhis ears and a rush of adrenalin pushing him to go an extra mile.

He reaches a lake. Its surface is tranquil, reflecting the few teasing clouds that have gathered above it. He feels every molecule of air go down and cool his heated body. He jogs to relieve the pressure from his muscles. He stands still, trying hard to cut off the voice inside his mind. Rajveer, like any other young professional, is bombarded with several distractions work, pleasure, social media, news. The more the voices and vices the greater the clutter and confusion. The mind is flooded with information, mostly noise, but Rajveer is a fighter. *I need to change my imprints.*

As Rajveer bends down he sees a stone. Grey. Flat. Round. It is exactly like the ones he used to throw in the lake when he was young, with his friends. They would throw the flat stones and see how far they went, how many 'jumps' they made. Those were the *golden years*... he thinks.

He looks around, as if to check if he's being watched, picks one stone and throws it. He needs to work on his focus. His body bends right as he pulls his arm back to give it speed, his elbow bent at a ninety degrees angle that will straighten to one hundred and eighty as soon as he lets the stone go.

Tok. Tok. Tok. Three bounces.

The stone reaches the other side of the small lake, hits an iron pole, changes its trajectory and dives straight back into the water. The stone against the pole has made a shrill sound that echos in the forest and Rajveer is afraid that it may have attracted the attention of someone strolling by.

He feels like an idiot. A grown man throwing stones in the lake!

What he doesn't know yet is that the shriek of the stone hitting the iron pole covered a more dangerous sound-the sound of a bullet shot in the vicinity.

But the citizens are oblivious; the festival has got everybody in a cheerful mood. No one thinks about death because people want to sing, play music, eat sweets and wish each other. As he jogs back Rajveer notices the first groups rehearsing their versions of the legend of Veeravati. On the other side another group composed only of women practices the ritual to the moon that they will perform tonight, to ask the moon, their planetary representative, to ensure the wellbeing of their husbands. Some women are buying their red *lehenga sarees* to impress the moon while their husbands are probably busy earningmoney for their children's honeymoon.

Rajveer shakes his head as if to stop thinking of the rituals that these ignorant women perform every year with the belief that their voices will be heard. But every year, even if their previous prayers weren't answered, they go back with the blind belief that this year they will get them what they want.

Year they will get them what they want. He looks at them with pity. He knows that at least in Jalandhar the lives of people are in the hands of men rather than the gods.

Inspector Kawaljeet, middle aged, slim, hawk-eyed, digs his fingers into his tiffin. Aheap of plastic folders with details of the dead victims cover his oversized desk-the victims' photos from one open folder staring into his face. He sings to himself a Bol-lywood classic-'*tujhe dekha toh yeh jaana sanam, pyaar hota hain deewana sanam*' as he plucks out a *gulab jamun* and nibbles on it with great affection. The police station is deserted. He swivels his head around to spot his subordinate. Looks like the men are praying for their wives' loyalty. Adultery is the new festival in town. He wipes his hands clean, gathers all the folders and prudently stacks them into a box file labelled in red-NRI Missing/Accident. As he pulls down the flap to the cardboard box he mutters under his breath, *Wahe Guru.*'

2

A breezy daybreak, a paved path to a blazing career and suddenly all her choices have melted away. Life can just as easily turn into a destiny unknown, she is convinced. For the twenty three year old Jannat, occupied with the busy life of a journalist and a doting boyfriend, decisions seem complex, even when they are all about a future full of adventure, a future that's brimming with news to roll out.

She gingerly looks at the Heathrow airport lounge, as if it was infested with Martians.

What have I gotten myself into? Can't this day just be a dream? Jesus, can't I start my day all over again? I promise myself I won't make the same mistakes again. Or will I?

January in London is mean. All those sweet, caramel-scented memories of the holidays from the citizens replaced with gloomy days and the threat of a never-ending winter.

Life goes back to normal, people take return flights home, wrapped in their coats and long scarves they hurry from terminals, often popping into coffee stations to grab a shot. Are they seeking or running away from a life they had once envisioned?

Jannat, always curious for answers impossible to find, looks out of a window in the waiting room overlooking the runway. She ponders about the world, the country and the city that she is living in and the one she is travelling to. *India, seriously? Wasn't it better with Andy? The more we are different the more we are the same*. Why is she here? Why not Scotland? Why England? London is a melting pot for people of different races, varying ambitions and diverse objectives. Yet they thrive together as if they share the same purpose. *I guess ambition is your enemy, ambition is your friend.*

My mother used to tell me that I had an overactive imagination. Andy said that too. I can't help it. She catches sight of a newly wedded couple, hand in hand, and she can think of the fingers, those that fitted into hers. *His skin odour was alcoholic*. She gives a sigh of help less irritation: the 8.06 pm flight from Heathrow to Indira Gandhi International Airport, New Delhi, can test the patience of the most-seasoned traveller when delayed. The deserted designer stores, post-Christmas, look like a movie setting. *I hate shopping.*

She watches the airport janitors and baggage porters like a tracking shot in a film. There is something comforting about the sight of strangers for once; they look as be wildered as she is. *Thank goodness!* The pre-mixed orange and soda fizzes over the lip of the can as she brings it to her mouth. Tangy and cold, the taste of her final argument with Andy last morning. *Pig*!

Leaning over her chess-top dining table she absent-mindedly holds a mug and pours hot green tea into it. The mug has a handwritten signature (Preet), with a message scribbled in red marker ink. She is nervous, irritated and at her wits' end. *What happened Preet? Did I miss something?* She slams two slices of bread into the toaster and sits at the table. She flips through the morning paper, too angry to register the news. She just needs to have something in her hands to shut the storm in her mind.

As she sits at the kitchen, clad in her white dress, high heels and a simple hairdo, she looks like an intellectual cover girl in a feminist magazine. The mole on her upper lip makes her stand out. Jannat Gill also has what every single Indian woman would want a very successful boyfriend whom she has chosen and who adores her to the point that he proposed after merely one year of dating. He just went out, bought a ring an expensive diamond ring that would make any girl jealous-took her out to dinner, hid it in a fortune cookie and proposed to her in front of the whole restaurant. He rushed into disaster. He wanted to settle down with a typical Indian homemaker, who would assist him to write his own fortune.

Andy walks into the room, fixing his tie. He's sharp-featured and sure of himself. He hasn't slept all night and his face carries the signs of insomnia, but he gets rid of the worst of them with a generous cup of black tea.

'Hey, no need to take your anger out on the toaster . . .'

Jannat takes in a deep breath.

Ever since Andy made his intentions clear with that masquerade (*who the hell proposes in a restaurant in front of perfect strangers?*) she has had to rethink their relationship. She already knew Andy. An English citizen of Indian origin like her he was more traditional than her, but the proposal was the last straw. She felt the intention that underlay his romantic gesture contradicted his claim of being in love with her. *Is he a chameleon? If he thinks he can lock me up in a house and make us breed like rabbits he is a snake!* She had re-peated these words to herself for a few days, and then, when he started talking about the wedding, she burst into speech. She needed time to commit, probably lots of it. It was not just about her mood swings, she was genuinely not ready. He was looking for a partner for life. A fight followed and by the end of it, as the two of them stood in opposite corners of the room, their mouths foaming with rage, it was evident that there would be no wedding. Every drop of love was turning sour. In the battle between love and pride, pride wins most often.

'Andy, the property manager called. He's dropping off the new lease papers to my office later today-the agreement is in my name. You need to drop off your set of keys on your way to work.'

They both look at the clock on the wall. They are running late, but after the umpteenth fight last night they needed to get some sleep this morning. Now there is more time for talking.

'So that's it? Jannat, is this what you really want? Can't we . . . '

'Look Andy, don't make it any harder. My career is my first priority, you . . . '

'Getting married doesn't mean dying, Jan. We live in England, not in tenth century India. Priorities change. You are in your twenties already;

don't you want children? I could be your last chance . . . Before you find somebody else who is worth it, you may be passé . . . '

'Andy, leave. Spare yourself the embarrassment.'

'Oh! Because I'm so old-fashioned right? Because I want a family? And then they say that men can't commit. I am try . . . '

'Andy Puri, are you willing to give up your job to look after the children? I'm happy to have babies, but I'll be back at work the next day. If you are happy to bea stay-at-home dad I can think about marrying you. Right now journalism is my priority. It's no secret. I told you the day we met.'

'You are being ridiculous. Where have you seen a man who looks after children? I have nothing against your job. You could keep writing from home, a blog . . . '

'OK, get out. Now!'

'You think you can influence the world, become an Arianna Huffington. It's not a cakewalk Jan.' Andy's arguments are like fists striking the brick wall. There's nothing he can do or say to change her mind and he realizes he has gone too far to win her back. Frustrated and sad he takes his coat and walks out and slams the door shut.

She can still see herself alone in the room, feel

all the emptiness of Andy's absence. The terrible English light filters through the clouds and enters the kitchen. A tear rolling down her cheek reflects the only ray of sun that entered her house. *To fall in love is routine; to stay in love is a bloody miracle.* A stinging smell attacks her nostrils . . .the bread . . . She turns around and sees the thick smoke coming out of the toaster.

Someone's phone rings in an incongruously upbeat song. They are slow to answer and it jingles on and on around her. She can feel her fellow passengers shift in their seats, rustle their magazines, tap at their computers, dive into their mobile screens. She tries not to look up and continues to read the free magazine she was handed on her way into the airport, but the words blur in front of her eyes, nothing holds her interest.She takes another sip; the can is already half empty. She steps out towards the ladies room, carrying her expensive bag that contains all things important, her iPhone and her iPad Mini.

Inside she stares into the mirror. 'Do I look like a mess?'

She tries on a pair of earrings on as she hears the door open again. 'Andy,' she sighs, and hopes that he hasn't remembered something else to say to her. But she hears him walk in, open the drawer where he had put the ring after she had refused to wear it, pop the box open to check if it was there and close the drawer again when his eyes fall on the lipstick lying on the table. He picks it up and scribbles on the mirror on top of the dresser. *You will never find true love*, Jan. He walks away with a curse dancing under his breath. Jannat is not certain how they got to this point. All of a sudden Andy is exactly like all the Indian men she had come to know-patronizing, decisive, stubborn and chauvinistic. He wanted what all other Indian men wanted and only coated it with some nice ribbons and curls of English icing-the sex before marriage, the bars, the movies-he acted as if he were liberal, sophisticated and careless, but the fires of tradition burnt within him. 'Maybe it just me,' she reprimands her inner voice. Before marching out she wipes the lipstick wax off the framed mirror and rubs it against her lips. She stops to gather her wits and picks up the same lipstick to jot something on the mirror. *I will find true love.*

3

'Are you okay?' the cleaner enquires as she hears a soft cry. There is no answer.

'Need help?' Still nothing, just sniffling.

Jannat feels restless. She pats the thumping of her heart away. *This is it. I don't want to think about any of it, anymore.*

She steps out of the restroom. The journey stretches out ahead of her, eight to ten empty hours to fill. She lifts the can to her mouth again, but there is not a drop left.

Getting on a plane has always been a warm experience for Jannat. She's travelled abroad earlier to prepare special reports; as an exchange student;

on a holiday; to attend a language school and for job interviews. She has grown to love the smell of air freshener and coffee, the puzzled expressions of first-time travellers and the nonchalant expressions of business travellers who didn't care if they were in Taipei, Bogotá or Paris. She used to love all these things, but everything is different today. *Can't there be a switch where I can take control of my mind?* Yesterday morning, some thirty hours ago, she was burning toasts and blaming Andy for not having been able to finish her article.Now she's here business class seat at least the journalism job doesn't skimp on luxuries . . . she feels comforted.

'Ladies and gentlemen, welcome aboard Flight BA143 from London to New Delhi. We are currently third in line for takeoff and are expected to be in the air in approximately seven minutes. Thank you for choosing British Airways. Enjoy your flight.'

Jannat takes a deep breath. It's not that she can't wait to get to India to start her assignment-*India is great, just not for me*. She just wants to lean back in the soft, sagging velour chair, feel the warmth of the sunshine streaming through the window, and feel it rock back and forth and back and forth, the comforting music from her stereo. *Or I would rather be here on the plane, looking out at the clouds, finding the truth-who am I, rather, where do I go?*

Soon her thoughts sway like a blazing pendulum ticking between life and death.Between this morning and yesterday.

She glances at her rose gold watch. The *World Weekly* building rises in front of her, shimmering in green glass. This is the haven for which she has given up marriage. *Also the hell where I'll get my head chopped off if I don't finish the bloody article before Bloody Mary comes in*, she thinks as she blows her nose in the elevator. *Should I just go back home and report absent? Maybe she'll be more lenient if I tell her I just broke up with my boyfriend and I am coming down with a terrible flu? Probably not, she'll still chop my head off!*

Bloody Mary, the nickname borrowed from Queen Mary I of England, is May Edwards, editor-in-chief of the magazine, the most feared woman in the UK, maybe Europe. Anna Wintour, the famous editor of Vogue, is a sweet granny compared to her. It is said that the Queen herself shivers when she hears that the *World Weekly* will feature an article on the royal family. Yes, and I work for her. Great for my career, a little less great for my sanity.

As she walks into her office Jannat sees Shelley, May's personal assistant, on the phone. She is evidently talking to May because her hand trembles while taking notes. 'Yes Ma'am.Of course,Ma'am . . . ' Jannat hears her say. If that chick played a little less Sudoku and worked a little more she wouldn't be so damn scared all the time . . .

She walks away from May's office to her desk. As if Shelley has heard her she jumps to her feet, runs to May's office and replaces the yellow mug with the purple one, checks if everything is in order and sharpens an undisciplined pencil that is untidily resting on the table. She leaves the room just in time to greet May.

May comes in with her usual aplomb, her silver hair shining, her red lipstick contrasting with the black suit onto which, today, she has put a shiny chinchilla fur, grey like her hair and so soft its touch is like stroking a feather. She strides with her deep blue eyes fixed onto a point far away that only she can see and misses Shelley who is waiting for her by her desk like a good soldier. She doesn't even listen to her finish her sentence and takes her fur off with one hand and drops it on the desk.

'Good morning, Ma'am. Your cafe latte will be delivered at 9.55 am. Your 10.15 appointment is on schedule. And . . . ' Shelley doesn't let the beautiful fur fall on the desk; she snaps to collect it and then stands anticipating orders before going to put the fur in the closet.

'Get me Jannat. Now!'

Shelley puts the fur in the wardrobe and runs

to the intercom. 'Ms Jannat Gill, please come immediately to Ms Edwards'office.'

The call is heard through the whole office. The old witch, she wanted everyone to know I'm late with a deadline! Ready Jan. She's going to snap your neck like a praying mantis . . .

In less than two minutes Jannat gets to the door of May's office. She breathes deeply before knocking and looks at Shelley.

Shelley's expression reminds her of beaten dogs; this can mean nothing good. The fact that Shelley looks at her with her liquid eyes and that tremulous smile convinces her that today is not promotion day. Jannat knocks on the door without further thought. When she hears a dry and imperative 'come in!' she knows it's over, there's nowhere to run, nowhere to hide.

Her heartbeat increases when she sees Shelley crossing her fingers. Poor creature, she's trying to be nice and her kindness makes people want to beat her. Her appearance is so unfortunate with that horrid ginger hair and freckles; why did Bloody Mary hire her? She's so keen on looks, it almost seems if you are not gorgeous you're not allowed to work here. And then there's Shelleywho without that mask of makeup could be featured in a scary movie. She's just procrastinating. When she hears May clear her throat she knows she can't makeher wait another second. Jannat's anxiety releases a mixed bag of fears. *Which one is going to win?*

Jannat enters the office. The room is vast and nicely furnished. It's pretty clear that May spends most of her day here and wanted to make it comfortable. She has Persian carpets, designer furniture and a view of the city. Behind a door there is a spacious bathroom with a closet. May doesn't let many people into her office; if you are called here it's either because you are a top exec, in which case you are invited, or because you are a journalist who is late with a deadline, in which case you are likely to see this office for the first and last time.

Jannat has rehearsedwhat she wants to say.She's going to look repentant and claim full responsibility for missing a deadline. She is ready to start speaking when she gives way to a storm of sneezes. As she opens her mouth to speak she can only grimace as she tries to hold a sneeze and then, as soon as she lets the guard down, there they come, one after the other . . .

At first May is unimpressed. She keeps flicking through the mock-up of this week's *World Weekly* until she comes to the centre page where Jannat's article is supposed to be and where the pages are blank. It is a pure white crisp pulp between the vibrant colours of fashion advertisements and a piece on the financial crisis. Only then, as she stares at the blank pages, does May seem to notice Jannat's presence in the room. She looks puzzled and disgusted by her sneezing. The first thing she does (after shrinking her pupils like a predator caught in the light) is snap up from the chair, grab an antibacterial spray and start disinfecting the room. She walks around like a lunatic, spraying until she comes face to face with Jannat. In fact, May, after having run around the room, has now found the perfect spot to di-rect her clinical poison-her. The cough is added to the sneezing and, before she's almost choked to death, Jannat gets up and looks at May.

May wakes up, as if she had been hypnotized, and regains her composure. As if nothing had happened she leaves the half empty spray bottle on the far corner of the table and goes back to her chair, her throne rather, and looks intensely at her insubordinate reporter. May is poised as she looks at the two blank pages in centre of the magazine mock-up. Jannat is sure that May's silence means she should talk first, but as she gath-ers her ideas and takes a deep breath May addresses her politely, 'Tell me dear, do you speak Russian?'

'No, Ma'am . . . I . . . ' answers Jannat with a puzzled look on her face.

It could be one of two cases-she's either giving me a piece on Russia to reward me for something

I have done (and I must have done it without knowing I was doing it) or I'm being sent to Russia as a punishment, which is more likely. Bloody Mary is sending me to freeze to death in a gulag . . .

'Very good!'

Good?

'Because I don't speak Russian either. And I was wondering if English isn't your language. I woke up this morning struck by the doubt . . . Maybe she speaks Russian and I gave her a deadline in plain Queen's English and that's why she didn't get it . . . '

Ah I see, we were just trying to be sarcastic, weren't we, Bloody Mary?

'May, I can explain, I was . . . '

'Excuse me. We're not at a cocktail party, Ms Gill. I would prefer you address me appropriately,' snaps May in a voice that seems to be emerging from the bowels of the earth. It's a demon's voice.

'I'm sorry, Ma'am. I can explain, give me . . . '

'Please do. Do so in less than a minute as I have a full schedule today and I, unlike those who work for me, do not intend to miss my deadlines.'

May sits back, clearly faking interest for what Jannat has to say, and her mind is set on her next meeting. She is like the fastest Ferrari at Le Mans and her mind works at the speed of a flying jet. A job at this magazine is like the pot at the end of the rainbow; the line of applicants stretches around the block. If May decides to fire me today ten of the best journalists in England would kill to fill my blank pages.

'I'm so sorry. I've not been well at all this morning. I had terrible writers' block . . . '

'Ah! A wonderful excuse invented years ago by a useless, procrastinating git who had the audacity to think of himself as a writer. Writer's block is a drunk man's excuse for committing suicide, doesn't work, and continue!'

'Things haven't been great at home and it has affected my work. I'm terribly sorry, but I promise to have the piece ready by midday, I will . . . '

'It's a little too late, don't you think? I'm enjoying this conversation so much I give you the benefit of one last excuse. Be more creative, amuse me please, it's part of your job, Miss Shakespeare in brief! And you might want to sound remotely convincing so that I am not tempted to fire you.'

'Fine. I missed my deadline. Big deal. But I've had sleepless nights and endless days. You picked me because I have a master's degree from Oxford and I was the best in my graduating year, I'm a hard worker and you know that. *The Economist* knows that too, I refused . . . '

'Miss Gill, threats are in such bad taste, don't you think? You can . . . '

'Ms Edwards, if I wanted to work for *The Economist* I would have taken the job a long time ago. It meant more money, less work and more flexible hours. If I'm here it's because I want to be here, not because I'm forced to take your crap for lack of alternatives. If you give me time until midday I'll hand in the article, if you fire me you'll get someone else to write it and I'll get another job. I don't need to hate you or fear you, my life is too complicated as it is to take notice of your mood swings.'

The words just flowed out of her mouth, she wasn't in charge of her own mind and unaware of what she was saying. Even her recollection of what she hasjust said is blurred; a sense of fear surrounds her. The only thing she remembers is the sight of May's pupils and mouth widening synchronously. *Here goes my job. Now that I have to pay the rent on my own it's exactly what I need! Well done, Jan!*

May takes a few seconds to regain her composure. She lets her eyes go back to a nor-mal size and breathes a couple of times. She would not only fire Jannat but also make her walk on her knees back to her desk. However, all she said is true, she knows the girl has received better offers elsewhere and she knows only too well that, as undisciplined as she may be, she's one of her best reporters. Nonetheless, this audacity has to be punished.

On the other side of the desk Jannat is strangely calm. She expected an outburst and screams so loud that the very foundations of the building would have crumbled. Neither the rage nor the screams have come and Jannat feels like she might have touched a soft spot. She looks at May with a grin. Jannat one May zero.

But May has been a hostile fox for as long as anyone can remember. She is smart. She was taken by surprise, but with a few minutes to recruit her forces she comes in, deadly.

'Very well, thank you for that wonderful insight into your psychologically balanced life.' She opens a drawer and extracts a thick folder tied with a string. It is evidently the work of various interns who did some background research.

'Deadline: 1 February 5 pm. Subject: Contract Killing. Location: North India, Punjab. Oh, and you leave tomorrow, you have a British passport, right? I don't want you to miss even one day of useful research!'

'Are you trying to get me killed? You know how . . . '

'Of course not, but if you don't want to go I can ask someone else to do so and you can clear your desk by lunch time, after you have delivered the article that you are late for. Let's focus, Jannat. Wait, let me help you with logistics . . . ' and she buzzes Shelley.

'Yes, Ma'am.'

'Get Jannat Gill on tomorrow's flight to New Delhi please. And my latte has gone awfully cold now, thanks to an unscheduled meeting. Re-heat it, or better still go fetch me another one . . . This time decaf . . . I feel I've had enough buzz to last me the whole day.'

May smiles at Jannat and goes back to the mock-up. Her cunning eyes are glued on her next prey for a cover story: Kate Moss posing for a Burberry fragrance.

Jannat is stunned. This is happening. Is she hallucinating after her breakup this morn-ing? May has clearly ended the conversation with her. She's not even kicking her out of the office, she's ignoring her. 'Ms Edwards, please . . . I understand you are angry but this is way too soon, way too random, you know it too . . . '

May doesn't lift her eyes from the magazine. 'Get on that plane, Gill, or ship out. Your choice. You rightly reminded me that you have alternatives and the list of people who want to work here could fill the whole London phone directory, so it's your call, I don't . . . '

'But . . . '

'I believe you have to pack. I believe you also have to finish that feature . . . Twelve fifteen. Last chance, Gill. The issue goes to print at three.'

Jannat is looking for something to say when May's phone rings. The ringtone is the classic Bond theme. 'Sir Connery, how delightful to hear your voice, Mr Bond! I know, I'm unforgivable. I've been away for work.You give a chance to young people and then you have to nanny them . . . But I promise I will not miss your dinner! I can stay late for cigar . . . ' She glances at Jannat; it's an order to leave the room.

Jannat can do nothing else but walk back to the door, open it, walk through it and close it behind her. Jannat chokes on her breath.

'That bad?' asks Shelley without lifting the eyes from her Sudoku puzzle.

'A lot worse . . . '

Now she wants to get me murdered! And she has a whole month to burn my bridges with magazines from here to Timbuktu. This way she'll keep me on the leash forever! Should I simply resign?

4

Argh! Jannat sits back in her cubicle trying to put her mind to the article she has less than two hours to hand in. Once the article is finished and handed in-not her best piece of work and definitely not in the running for the Pulitzer-Jannat takes a couple of hours off to go home and pack.

Shelley has called her in her obnoxious nasal voice to inform her that her ticket was ready for an 8:30 pm flight tomorrow. As soon as she gets home she realizes that something was missing. She rolls her neck. Andy must have come this morning to take away his stuff . . . His scent lingers in the room. In a way it's comforting for Jannat to think that at any given moment Andy, with his beautiful, strong features, could walk in, hug her and tell her that everything is going to be all right. She would perhaps readily accept the ring, get married and have twins. *Split personality?* She sighs. Who cares, he's not coming back. Most of all, I'd rather be shot dead doing something I love rather than sit at this very table with my steaming cup of green tea and wonder what the world needs to know?

Now that Andy has taken away his books, his clothes, his tidiness, and his selfishness, the house looks a lot more like her-scented candles, pink roses and books on Budd-hism scattered all over the place. Of course she's not as tidy as him and if she weren't leaving this house would look like a cave in less than a week . . . But hey! My life starts again from this point. *If I get killed in India someone else will have to clean my mess and if I don't, well, I'll be so happy to have made it back alive that I won't mind cleaning. This is my house, my life. From this moment onward there's a blank page on which I can write what I desire.*

She lights an incense stick to sooth her nerves and takes her mug to the bedroom. She throws clothes on the unmade bed. *Tonight I'll sleep in this bed for the last time, for a month at least, and when I come back I won't have seen Andy for a month and the bed will still smell of him. Andy, Andy, Andy, let's get him out of my mind and pack, shall we?*

Jannat takes out the big suitcase and tosses it

on the bed, the only one she has that isn't a sloppy backpack, and fills it like Andy taught her, albeit with a lump in her throat first the shoes, each one wrapped in its own plastic bag. 'Shoes are dirty, Jan-nat, you can't throw them in with underwear and everything else that you put in direct contact with your skin.' Then the jumpers and the trousers. She looks down. Oh bollocks . . . She has to take everything out because she was packing her suitcase for British weather. She has nicely folded seven jumpers and two woollen dresses, but it's unlikely that I get to wear all of them, right? Okay, two jumpers, denims, long skirts, tee shirts and shirts. Her mind spins like the Ferris wheel in the visible skyline. Now toiletry. And as she walks to the bathroom she sees her long white dress abandoned on the armchair. It must have been there since the Christmas party, buried under Andy's clothes. She takes it and presses it close to her body, considering if it's worth taking or not.

Ah come on, they must have at least one place where I can go party, lounge or have dinner, at least once. I could use Tinder, dinner date with a hot Bollywood star, dance at a bar. There is always a first. But this is Punjab, May I hate you. She flings the dress on the Oakwood dresser. 'Oh sweet Jesus, am I going on a work assignment, to get drunk after a break up or to find a guy on the rebound!'

She wraps her arms around herself talks aloud, 'The mind loves to fly in a thousand directions till the pilot puts it back on track, the truth being that often the pilot is missing in action. Jan, you can do it. Is the flight on time?'

She takes another sip of tea to mellow her throat and then collapses on the bed, listening to the Tibetan bells playing in her stereo. She notices the photo of her grandmother. She takes it, cleans it with the sleeve of her shirt and holds it in her hands. Her breath slows down as the reminiscence takes centre stage. She closes her eyes for a minute when her phone rings.

The soft tune of *Sound of Silence* reminds her of her last phone call from her friend some months ago.

That day her phone had rung the whole morning. She was, as usual, late with the delivery of an article. She heard it but decided not to answer and finish the task instead. At lunchtime, after she had emailed her article, she picked up the phone from her handbag and checked on who'd called her so many times. As she did she went through a mental list all of those who could have needed to speak to her urgently.

Three missed calls from Preet. *Okay, not too bad. She probably wants to go out shopping or watch a Salman Khan movie. After her marriage she's practically locked herself in the house.* Jannat called back feeling a lot more relaxed and ready for a girly chat. But when Preet picked up the phone she was in tears, gasping for breath and couldn't even speak. Her words died in her mouth, drowned in saliva and tears.

'Hello? Hello Preet . . . What's up? Is everything okay? Preet, talk to me . . . what's going on?'

When Preet finally caught her breath and found the strength to put a few confused words together Jannat found out the problem was with her husband. She'd had a tiff, a difference of opinion. It sounded urgent yet commonplace. 'Okay listen, don't panic. I'm sure it's just a phase. Don't take any rash decisions. Preet, listen to me. You have to remain positive. I mean, it happens in every marriage, you know that.Come on, even I know that!'

'Listen, why don't we meet at Starbucks? Yeah, the same one as last time. How about in half an hour? Okay, see you then. Take care, babe!' Preet had stopped crying, she had pulled herself together and it seemed to Jannat that everything was in the process of getting back on track.

Looking back Jannat also remembered thinking, 'Women who make their lives revolve around their marriage are bound to be sad.'

Jannat had gone to the café, she had ordered a tall cappuccino and waited at the same table where they always used to sit, but Preet hadn't come, not that day or any other day. When Jannat tried to call her phone was off. She thought she might have fallen asleep, forgotten about the appointment or got caught up in a fight with her husband . . .

A few days later Jannat had forgotten about this episode. She had assumed that everything had gone back to normal and that it was a casual fight between husband and wife. She didn't particularly like Harry and knew Preet herself had grown fonder of him when she discovered that he was the sole heir to a rather large financial empire, but he didn't seem like a bad person. He loved Preet. The way he looked at her at their wedding would have convinced anyone that the newly wed Randhawa couple was going to last forever.

The cry of a small boy onboard brings her attention back. Jannat opens the tray table with a clenched jaw and spreads her things on it. There's nothing like a long flight to catch up with research.

Jannat lowers her head in despair. When they took off there was no one sitting next to her. Then how has this person materialized? If he thinks he can start a conversation he has just made a huge mistake. She raises her head, a cold and forbidding expression on her face. Her angry eyes fall on the friendly and chubby face of a steward who looks at her and smiles. He is pushing the beverage cart and speaks cheerfully like all flight attendants. 'May I interest you in some refreshments?'

Relieved the guy isn't here to stay Jannat first orders vodka with orange juice and then stares at the pile of documents with a stickey note from May, 'Please read. It's in English.'

'Actually, a cup of black tea . . . No sugar please.'

'Yes Ma'am.'

Jannat works diligently through the flight. Every now and then she sips water. She glances through the research material. She learns that a major British news agency carried a report claiming that at least a hundred non-resident Indians are killed every year in Punjab alone. Most of these victims are women. Contract killing is seen as a solution to several problems-lover's tiffs, a need to remarry or property disputes by several Britons and global citizens. Since the beneficiaries of the crime are a thousand miles away they are never caught. And those who commit the crime on their behalf belong to shadowy crime syndicates with their complex networks. The number of victims has risen to a few thousand over the last decade itself. The contract killing business was rampant in North America between the 1920s and 1950s. In India the nexus between crime syndicates, politicians and the police is sufficiently powerful to keep matters in the dark. Even the local media knows nothing about its leading operators.

Jannat is sickened by what she reads but is also morbidly attracted to the topic. She discovers the duality of a flourishing state like Punjab and its people of origin. How can you think of killing someone you love or are supposed to love? How is it that you are so determined, but most of all cold-hearted, not only to think of it but to look for someone a million miles away, someone you have never seen and who you'll never see, to do the killing for you? She's reading about people in the UK who allegedly send their wife 'on holiday' to India where she gets killed. About NRIs hiring local Indian assassins to bump off their kith and kin for property. Everyone knows it's a gunfor hire. Sometimes they make it look like a robbery gone bad or an accident, but more often than not they don't. She is surprised to learn that it's not only women who get killed. Contract killing is a way to undertake honour killing. Killers can be hired for a very reasonable price (considering the cost of living in London an Indian professional killer would certainly not be rich in England). These are individual hired guns that have escaped the law. Apparently people know exactly when a contract killing has taken place and why. Why don't they speak out? Perhaps it's understandable that a small farmer in Punjab prefers to keep quiet about a killing rather than be killed himself. This is live and let live with a cruel twist. Apparently some very influential men control this syndicate and have been active for the last few generations. *Have I made the mistake of my life by taking this on?*

Jannat is exported back in time when she had come acrossHarry's face, swollen with grief, on the front page of a London expat magazine. And the headline read: 'London's NRI Loses Wife in a Tragic Accident in Punjab'. Jannat had bought the magazine and read the article, feeling shaken. *What happened?* Preet called me a few days ago. We were supposed to meet for coffee, she bailed and all of a sudden she's dead at the other end of the world? This is impossible, clearly a mistake!

But when she got home she found a message from Harry on her answering machine.

'Hey Jannat, it's Harry, Preet's husband. I don't know if you heard. I mean, I would prefer not to give you this news over the answering machine but . . . anyway, Preet went to India for a holiday and she died there tragically. I don't know what to say! Well anyway, there's a prayer meeting tomorrow at the Chelsea Centre. I've invited all her friends. Well okay, see you tomorrow morning, maybe, good night!'

Harry's message was very confused, he had evidently been drinking and his breathing was slow and heavy as he spoke. Jannat was deeply perplexed. *Holiday? India? What's going on?* But when she went to the prayer meeting the next day Harry looked the same, as if nothing had happened. He smiled politely at the guests and shook hands as if they were gathered for a community service meeting. Jannat was nursing her shock and her grief left no room for suspicion. She would have liked to ask more questions about the accident but her phone rang as soon as she finished writing her condolences on the register. Of course it was Shelley telling her that Bloody Mary needed to speak to her 'as soon as she could decide whether she still worked for the magazine or not', and so she had to run.

Days had passed. While Preet's memory stayed vivid in Jannat's mind Harry's face faded away. She never called him to ask about the accident or if he was fine. Although she wouldn't even admit it to herself, Jannat could not help blaming him for what had happened. The 'holiday' and the call Preet made that day were linked in some way. No one decides to take a holiday alone a few months after getting married. Not a holiday so far away, at her parents' house. *Am I overreacting? Why am I getting so suspicious? My investigative self and me.*

Jannat lifts the tea mug that Preet had gifted her. Wow, the mug has her handwritten message, so real-'Go find yourself, Jannat'. She opens her eyes at once. She gets up from the bed and grabs the magazine report on Preet's death to put it in her bag. Before dropping it inside she holds it tight for a moment. 'I tried calling your parents but the numbers I managed to get from people here were all disconnected. I know you'd love me to go and meet your family since I will be in Punjab. I promise I'll try my best.' A tear rolls down her cheek. Right now she misses Andy more than ever. To-night more than ever she's debating her choice. On the one end is her open suitcase that makes her miss the man who went with her on all her previous trips, the man who she loves, or at least loved, very dearly. On the other there's the magazine open on the page about Preet's death. She had a husband who had kindly suggested she leave her job and she rushed to India. But Harry reminds Jannat of Andy, selfish. She's alone, angry, sad and in the end very disillusioned about Andy, about her future, about this unwanted adventure in India.

She had a couple of hours to kill before she reached the airport. She made herself a nice mushroom soup and got into bed with a book-*Fifty Shades of Grey.*

Screw you, Andy. Erotica is what she takes a fancy to when she is lonely. As a teenager she used to hide under the bed and read Anais Nin's erotica, though her favourite was *Delta of Venus.* She fondles herself to relieve her stress. 'Don't know when I will get my next share of fantasy.'

The plane goes through a little turbulence and the seatbelt sign lights up. Jannat gets breathless for a jiffy. Her vision is hazy. A strange thought enters her mind. *What if death is the beginning and life is just one glossy commercials before the main show starts?*

All right, I have all the signs here that tell me that it's time to get some sleep. Let's close this nasty stuff and maybe try and watch a TV show. Jannat looks out of the window.

The bumpy ride takes her back to the valley of the shadow of death. *Why can't I see anything?* Ever since she lost her mother in her childhood she cut herself off from everybody; out of this seclusion grew her fascination with the valley of the shadow of death, a space but no space. The uncertainty of life is shrouding her mind in gloom. Death by thought.

And then she loses her dear friend Preet. Has she developed commitment phobia because she is afraid of losing her loved ones to death? As she puts away her papers a slip of paper falls on the floor of the cabin. She bends down to pick it up. *Did I just jot this down?* It's a note in her handwriting of all the people who have been killed and the contact details of their families. She needs to strengthen her nerves because she is a journalist and this is her job. 'Passion transforms you first and foremost and then the rest of the world,' words of her ripened college professor, Steve, clear her doubts. He was so cool. He patted me with so much longing. I did throw in a hint once but he didn't respond. Ah, he was consumed by his passion. And what is my passion? Her shaky hands place the sheet on top of the pile. Her stomach vibrates with uneasiness. She needs to bury May and surge ahead. Pleased with herself she lies down. The business class seats are indeed comfortable, and with a little luckthe children two rows down will be asleep soon. Her forehead displays a fresh array of wrinkles. However she is unable to sleep, she keeps thinking about a handwritten note in the margins of an interview taken from a local newspaper. The thoughts are burrowing into her brain like a worm. In one of the cases a woman shopping for souvenirs was killed by some thugs on a motorbike who shot her right in the face. They didn't take anything, even though she was a Canadian and proud to broadcast her wealth through expensive ac-cessories and jewellery. *Bam*. One lethal shot. It was later revealed that she and her husband were to travel together to Punjab but he was held back at the very last minute and she ended up going alone.

To her family of lawyers based in Canada this seemed strange and they started working backwards, trying to find a reason for the husband to want the wife dead. They learned that he had made some risky investments that hadn't been as fruitful as expected thus forcing him to rely on his wife's money, which was of course his money too but for which she wanted a detailed account. They also discovered that he could not produce such an account because some of the expenses were a little shadier than he would have liked to be known.

Of courseno one could prove that the husband had contracted for the killing of his wife. The fact that it's still a 'family business', where one calls a brother or an uncle, the uncle calls his uncle or his brother and so on, makes these transactions untraceable. You can pay in advance or after the job is done. If you don't pay the men who did the job for you will do the same job on you, killing a member of your family until you decide to pay. But it's not only this that keeps Jannat awake. No, she's a journalist, a good one too. She has travelled the world and reported from really filthy places. These are the demands of the job. They are scary the first time, revolting the second time and routine the third time. *But this is different.* There's something about this story that has a personal connection with her own life that she can't figure out. *Some kind of calling?* She turns her little light off to finally try and get some sleep before they land, but her brain just will not stop.

Exhausted she picks up the bag lying at her feet and rummages in it to find something to read till she can fall asleep. Strange, I thought I was too late to buy a magazine at the airport, but I must have done it without realizing it . . . Or maybe it's Shelley who put it in my bag as soon as it came out of the printer.

As she fishes the magazine out of the bag Jannat realizes it's not the new copy of *World Weekly* but an old magazine with the article on Preet's death. When she had first picked up the magazine she read the article three times but never actually looked at the rest of the magazine. Tonight she decides expressly to skip that article and read the rest. Jannat is too tired and sad to think about Preet now. If only she could get drunk now she would, but she's going to be in India in less than four hours and she can't afford to begin the assignment intoxicated. As much as she wants to avoid the article she does come back to it eventually. Preet smiles from the centre-page of the magazine. There's a photo of her and Harry the day they got married and several pho-tos of her alone at her graduation and on holiday. The small article praises Preet for being the perfect example of what a good Indian wife should be like: devoted to her husband, educated and able to entertain guests. It talks about a simple life, a simple family and a simple bond between husbands and wives with values. Of course the magazine, mostly addressing a public of wealthy British, Indian and Middle Eastern housewives, does not mention the feminist groups Preet joined when she was at the university. It doesn't mention her difficult beginnings, moving to London from India and having to get accustomed to new customs, a new language and the climate. And it only briefly describes Preet's involvement in the campaign against early marriage in India. *This smiley doll is not my friend.* Preet was so different.

She was so opinio-nated. But this stupid magazine only talks about her beautiful house in Chelsea, about the white horse her husband got her for her birthday and of her dream of having a family. They say she liked knitting, a good afternoon tea with 'the girls' (who the hell are these girls? This journalist is describing the death of Charlotte from *Sex and the City*). Unfortunately she was killed in an accident before Harry could join her and now he would have a ceremony in London with all her friends who loved her so much and so on and so forth. Two words stick to Jannat's forehead like pins on a board: husband and holiday. She remembers that call. Preet was crying her heart out. She was definitely in no mood for a holiday. In fact she had mentioned the word divorce a few times and it was Jannat who had to calm her down, telling her that all marriages go through some sort of trouble at some point. Besides, who takes a holiday alone shortly after their wedding? The what ifs invade

Jannat's head, and as the peach and golden light suffuses the clouds she knows she won't sleep tonight. Right now she feels like she won't sleep again until she has sorted this out. But then she reminds herself, 'Sometimes it's best to jump into the vortex of existence with a leap of faith and let the universe do its job.' Ah, my fixation for reading adultery.

5

The Indira Gandhi International Airport greets Jannat with all its Indianness. Of course it's a major international airport for one of the most powerful countries in the world, but at the same time, unlike other, more sterile airports, it carries the heavy burden of its culture and past. It's noisy, chaotic and invaded by a variety of different odours. There are of course duty-free shops and souvenirs, but everything here has a different spirit. The London airports are cheerful only at Christmas. Here the airport is flooded with colours, lights and people. It's amazing.

However Jannat's sleep has been disturbed. She was unable to rest for more than a couple of hours. She had bad dreams and woke up several times. She acknowledges the beauty around her but doesn't register all the details as she would in a restedtime. She's in no mood for a conversation and silently follows the yellow cardboard signs to Gate Number 4.

A kind flight attendant hands Jannat the slip of her boarding passwith a smile. 'Please, Ma'am, take a seat.The flight to Amritsar will start boarding in half an hour.'

'Thank you. How far is Jalandhar from there?'

'A little over two hours by car. Make sure you take a prepaid taxi or they will try to rip you off . . .'

'Thank you.'

She raises her eyes for the first time to look at the face of this nice guy. His sparkling teeth shine out of his dark Indian skin. He smiles at her.

A cluttered magazine stall makes her feel at home. One particular cover page grabs her attention a scrawny mother with an ill-fed daughter in tow struggles with a pot of water on the parched lands of the Kutch desert. The tagline: Save water,save a life.

Jannat spots a Starbucks on the other side of the alley and, after having checked her watch that still displays London time, decides to go for a nice cup of French Press coffee for a change.

I hate jet lag . . . And it gets so much worse as I get older . . . Oh God, is it morning? Night? Afternoon? Please shut down all the lights. Let me sleep!

The queue at Starbucks is long and messy. She sits down on one of the stools at the counter to wait for people to be served and leave. A Punjabi lady walks by her with a tray filled with fried foods and milkshakes. Whoever is going to finish all that food is definitely born to eat. Jannat gradually begins to lose her patience. We live in a strange world, there are people dying of hunger but there are more that are dying of gluttony. She closes her eyes for a moment. *I don't want to sleep. I just need to shut out all these voices and lights from my head for a moment. I feel as if it's about to blow up.* She considers whether her sanity is worth a cup of coffee; the smell of it, hot, steamy, aromatic, works its way into her nostrils.

Ah genius! They spray coffee scent in the air to make you want it . . . great marketing strategy!

But as she opens her eyes thinking, 'Okay, Starbucks, you win, I want it now!' she finds a paper cup right under her chin. As she sees her reflection in it she is surprised to look at a puzzled Jannat. She doesn't remember ordering it, and yet here it is, just as she wanted it, black, no milk, no sugar.

She finds a man sitting next to her. He sips his own coffee with the most peaceful air in the world. He's in his mid-fifties and wears a white linen suit.

He has white hair and a thick French beard. He is old enough to be her dad, but he is definitely charming. Dark, with a long face and a smooth complexion. *Ayurveda, I guess.* Jannat stares at him enjoying his coffee with his eyes closed. When he is done drinking he clicks his tongue and opens his eyes. They are of a deep green that stand out against his dark skin. *Yes, definitely a handsome man. 'He has something of the guru, like one of those ancient souls . . .'* thinks Jannat still looking at him. He looks back at her and at once she's self conscious. What could he possibly think of her?

'Ehm . . . I'm . . . I mean, I'm sorry, I guess . . .'

'Ha ha, there's nothing to be sorry about. I'm Mr Acharya, very pleased to meet you.'

'Jannat Gill.'

'First time in India, huh?'

'How'd you know . . . ?'

'I can tell . . . In fact I can tell a lot of things . . .'

'Mmm . . . Thank you for the coffee, this is yummy and definitely much needed after a night flight . . . What kind of things can you tell?'

'For instance, you've just been let down by someone . . . I'm suspecting the end of a love story . . .'

Mr Acharya's tone is that of a wise man.He tells

her what he knows as if he is giving her a recipe for butter chicken, without pompousness or self celebration. And she really likes that, she likes his soft voice; his choice of words gives his sentences a different cadence. Anyone would have just said break up.

Most of all she likes his accent. Jannat can tell that he speaks good English, but his accent is so exotic and raw.His R's are so definite; they fight their way into his mouth and come out as they were initially thought of, like strong, rough letters.

Jannat's eyes widen, her eyebrows rise. She purses her lips and nods, impressed, trying not to display how fascinated she is with this man as he continues.

'Life is about timing, you can love or hate the same person but at different times. Strangely, it depends upon your state of mind.'

Jannat is startled into guilt.

'But true love is as rare a sighting as Halley's comet. Perhaps you are moving towards finding it. Love is enigmatic.'

'Okay . . . You have my attention now,' Jannat is spellbound.

Acharya smells his coffee like a connoisseur. Jannat can smell his coffee.

He sips it with fervour, like a tiger tasting blood.

'I can also sense that a mission that will become close to your heart has made you travel thousands of miles for the first time. You are afraid but shouldn't be. This is an opportunity, not a threat. Just go . . . '

'Even death is an opportunity, I can sense,' Jannat shudders.

'True that. Death is the real ride. Life is simply a lesson on how to fasten your seat belts.'

'All right, I'm genuinely freaking out now. You don't even know me . . . how . . . how do you know all these things? Are you . . . ' 'Our faces are the biggest giveaway. It's a map to our mind.' Jannat bends towards him in awe like a teenager would with her favourite professor. 'Can I seduce you even though you are my father's age?'

'I'm a face reader, beware,' he says, smiling.

'Face reader . . . Wow, that'sinteresting,' responds Jannat, slightly disappointed.

This man is a charlatan who saw what gate I came from and which one I was going to and must have picked up some information about me. She clutches her wallet with clammy hands since it houses her passport and cards.

'That's usually the reaction I get. But you

shouldn't be so quick to doubt. It's a skill that has been passed down over a couple of generations in my family. Speaking of family, you're the only child, yes?'

Jannat nods, he can't have possibly made this out from something she was wearing or said.

'I thought so . . . And deep within those dark eyes of yours is a little girl still trying to come to terms with her not-so-happy childhood. Is it your parents? Were they divorced?'

'Yes, when I was barely three . . . '

'I think that the child inside you keeps suffering. But like they say, what doesn't kill you only makes you stronger, right?'

'Yeah well, I'll drink to that! Cheers!'

'So where are you headed now, Ms Stronger Gill?'

'Please call me Jannat. I'm off to Amritsar and then a cab to Jalandhar from there. And what about you, Mr Acharya, Mumba . . . ?'

'My flight to Kerala is delayed for a few hours. I've got a conference to go to. Life coaching . . . '

'You sound like a man on the move. It must be nice, so much . . . '

'Yeah sure, with a limping right foot. I had

an accident, fell down a staircase and damaged a leg for life. Anxiety is evil. It's my doing. I believe in destiny and I feel it's also why even the airport prefers to call the place you go to your destination. It's the place where you go because in the big design of life you were supposed to land there.

Do something, meet someone . . . each of us here today is on his or her way to fulfill something that has been meant to happen because we have constructed the path to it. Some people will find a job, some love, some will find a life, some will die and some will change their *kismet,* that's the . . . '

'*Kismet* huh? You make it sound so romantic. I'm not sure what mine holds for me . . . ' The question lingers in the air like the steam of the coffee. All the sounds around them fade into oblivion. When two likeminded souls meet it creates a universe of its own at least for a stint.

Mr Acharya looks intensely at Jannat's face as if the answer to her question was right there, hiding among the microscopic wrinkles at the sides of her eyes. He is indulging her. She is drawing herself within.

Acharya signs off, 'You can create or obtain anything that you desire provided you have trained your mind to attract it.'

From across the alley the airport manager at Gate

Number 4 announces the boarding call for the flight to Amritsar. Jannat is woken up like the princess in the fairy tales and smiles at Mr Acharya as she gathers her stuff from the counter and under the stool.

She's back to her polite self, a woman on a mission, possibly without emotions but now with an easy breath. 'Thank you so much for the coffee. And for the insights, of course! I am . . .' 'The pleasure is mine. Go with the flow and trust the universe,' he digs his hand deep into his trousers pocket and smiles as he finds it. He removes a visiting card from a steel cardholder.

'Here, take this. You may want to stay here during your trip to Jalandhar. The hotel manager knows me. They'll take good care of you. The city can be a difficult. It's nice to go home at night to a pleasant environment.'

'Thank you again . . . This is perfect! You . . . '

'And since you're going to Punjab, enjoy your KBK report research!' 'I'm sorry? K . . . '

'KBK is the *Kabootar Baaji Khulasa* . . . Punjab is filled with dodgy travel agents making false promises to send people abroad. Since you're there on your real mission that could be covert, you may as well do a *khulasa* on these guys too . . . it will keep you safe . . . ' 'Not a bad idea at all. I'll keep that in mind!'

Mr Acharya stands up and shakes her hand with a firm but gentle hand. 'First find the Truth. Then understand the Truth. Then question the Truth.'

'I know you what you mean . . . I wish . . . '

A cluster of passengers comes between the two.

'I envy your life. It all seems so structured yet so poetic, so . . . '

'Envy needs a spellcheck. Anyway life is too short, so here's the secret ask yourself what is most important to you and then have the wisdom and courage to build your life around that.' Jannat, lost in thought, scratches her cheek. Then it starts to sink in. Slowly, almost at the pace of stillness. Mr Acharya walks alongside Jannat for a few steps. She notices his obvious limp. Must have been a bad fall. He holds her hand like a father lending warmth to his daughter.

'Whatever we achieve, we are only intelligent ants in the broader vision.'

Jannat feels weak in the knees but her heart is overflowing. They say goodbye in absolute serenity, just their hands waving out to each other in communion. The eye contact remains steady. She thinks of him differently, definitely not as a father figure. She is smitten. *Why?My obsession for old wise men? Professor Steve, I hate you!* And then she hurries to her gate.

She rushes to her next destination. Her head is high and her legs swear of balance.

6

The arrival of her flight at the domestic terminal of the Amritsar airport is not poetic at all.

Jannat hadn't noticed so many people on her flight. Perhaps the economy class was more crowded, but still . . . How is this possible? This is the whole of bloody India . . .

Seeing people in an empty room, in the heat and with flies everywhere shocks her to the extent that she is ready to get on the same plane she just exited and go back to her grey, boring but familiar England.

She hears a sound similar to that of a bird being shot. She has never heard it before, it doesn't remind her of anything. Her mouth turns dry.

When she sees all those who were patiently waiting with herrunning to one side of the room, the first thing she thinks of is a terrorist attack.

She senses a tremor in her stomach and wishes she knew this place a little better.

Two words of Punjabi might help too, to ask someone about safety procedures. She is standing close to the conveyer belt, which is right in front of the door. An undefined mass of people run towards her children, fat mothers squeezed into their colourful saris, old men-dropping what they were eating or the paper cups from which they were drinking. A horde is about to run her over. Like any prey, terrified and not knowing what to do, Jannat takes a step back waiting for the crowd to mash her under their own feet. So much to save a few seconds, as if the world is coming to an end.

But nothing like that happens. The people disaggregate and fight for a position as close as possible to the big open mouth that will start spitting out their suitcases in a second.

They say that when you know your enemy you are less afraid. Well, they are wrong. *I'm never going to be able to find my space in this shapeless crowd; some overweight kid will crush me . . . Is this where my grandparents came from? What happened? How did they come to England straight from this Indian* mela?

The passengers, formerly grouped in a flock have indeed created a firm wall that cannot be broken. They are coming from the capital with bags full of goods that can't be found here and they are not letting anyone get near them. *The scene would be quite comical if I wasn't watching it a million miles away from the belt, waiting for a regular sized blue suitcase. It's hard to spot it in London, and someone else always mistakes it for his before I can get hold of it, I imagine how easy it's going to be now.*

She waits with her arms crossed, there's really nothing she can do about it. The looks on people's faces are what amuse her the most. The flight had mainly families on it there's first a line of men, who are the arms, and right behind every man there's a woman, the brain.

'*Puttar,* that one! That one! Come on!' The tone is somewhere between an encouraging cheer and an imperative order. Some hold their babies who sleep, careless about the confusing, and munch on something. A little girl, seemingly forgotten by her parents, is dancing around an imaginary dot, watching her skirt create a wheel around her waist. Sometimes she stops to regain her balance and her eyes look tired and confused, but then she shakes her head and starts a new spin. In a flash Jannat is transported to England. Her grandmother would walk her to the local park and recite her mother's poems while she would play in gay abandon. The grandmother would read Jannat her mother's diary where she had penned her poems. Her mother, Krishna Gill, was a gifted poet. She was also a curator at the Centre for Indian Arts. She had a great taste in the arts and a greater flair for language. Jannat pulls out her mother's diary that she has carried with her in her bag.

Her favourite lines are scribbled on the first page-'Your power to influence the universe isn't fuelled by intelligence but by intention.'

Jannat notices some women of her mother's age but much more ethnic. She turns the page to read the next thought, 'Live a life driven by the most powerful thoughts that can make death tremble at your doorstep.'

Mamma must have definitely penned these beautiful thoughts for me. Jannat feels flattered. She manages, quite magically, with tingling limbs to grab her suitcase. She gets up. She feels like a gladiator who has just defeated a pride of lions in the arena. But then she lifts her eyes to see the immigration counter. There's a sign indicating the line reserved for foreigners. *Oh no, please, I need a bed so desperately!*

'Excuse me,Sir . . . ' she addresses a policeman who wanders around the terminal.

'Yes, Ma'am? How do you do? How may I help you?'

'Oh, how kind you are . . . this is a warm welcome indeed . . . Well, I was wondering if those people, I'm sure by mistake, might have walked into the wrong line . . . You see? International passports only?' and as she points with her finger to the yellow sign she is overcome by the sad realization that this guy has blurted out all the English sentences he knew on his first interaction. Period. Now he looks at her, lost, as if they were at school and she had asked him to solve an Einstein equation.

'Never mind . . . thank you . . . ' she says as she walks away.

'Thank you, Ma'am, welcome to India. India is great!'

If she weren't this tired she would definitely burst out laughing. It's on occasions like these that she regrets not having a travel companion.

As she exits she observes that the airport portico is a mess. People run every everywhere.

The semi sterile smell of the airport is brutally slain in the aromas of incense, jasmine flowers, samosas, fried food and urine.

The smoky air is unbearable and the screams of people on the other side of the fence, who are waiting for their families, for a business partner, for a tourist, with their cardboard signs lifted up in the jungle of hands, makes Jannat want to walk right back inside. Paradise lost, paradise gained.

Gosh this is so cold. Why is this so cold? This is India for God's sake! Jannat dreams about what she will do when she gets back to England. She'll go straight to Bloody Mary's office to strangle her with her bare hands. That will make headlines for *World Weekly*.

A short chubby cabdriver with a suspicious-looking face, which forces Jannat to think that the cab is evidently only a side business, approaches her. 'Madam, welcome to Amritsar. Madam, taxi? Best taxi in Amritsar, A/C and non-A/C, two-in-one, Madam. Party music, Honey Singh? Where? Golden Temple? Manali, Malana just tell, I will take. Fast and furious . . . ' 'Hotel, Madam? Good rate, A/C, TV, hot water, cold water, no water,' another voice emerges from the crowd.

She's not exactly the typical Englishwoman. She has more Mediterranean traits, mixed complexion that never gave her away when she is in Morocco and Spain, but here all eyes are on her.

Shivering in the cold and tired to the bone she pushes the cloud of drivers that has gathered around her.

'Madam, I have new taxi. You came for shopping, no? Wedding shopping? Husband shopping?'

'Please, just back off . . . ' *I just need to find . . . There it is! A pre-paid counter, brilliant!*

'A taxi to Jalandhar, please.'

'How many suitcases and where in Jalandhar madam, please?'

Good question . . . Couldn't that Shelley worry about a room too? Instinctively her hand pulls out the card Mr Acharya gave her in Delhi. *Is it going to be safe? Who knows who he really is, what his friends are like* . . . This place may not even exist, but if it does and it's as nice as he says it is, I finally have a place where I can open my suitcase, take a shower, sleep and organize my work . . . But if it's not I'm on my way to getting raped and possibly lose a kidney . . . What if Mr Acharya is an organ trafficker in disguise, he was so smart?

'Ehm, Ma'am . . .'

'Yeah, you are right . . . Amar Hotel, Model Town, Jalandhar City.'

'Very well, taxi 2396 over there. Let me call the driver to come and pick up your luggage.' 'Thank you . . . '

After a ride that seems to take eternity, barring the delightful mustard fields that are reminiscent of Bollywood movie posters, the cab enters the city of Jalandhar. Jannat is too tired to look outside and take in the details, but the first impression is good.

She expected some sort of dusty village and what she finds instead is a rather large city with a relaxed vibe, not the hectic impression she got of Delhi. *Yeah, I think I can spend a month here without going mad.*

The cab pulls over in front of a nice hotel. It is not magnificent. It may have seen better days, but the colonial style throws Jannat back into a book she had read when she was in high school. Kim by Rudyard Kipling. Kipling's description of government buildings, so white and so spotless, reminds her of this place.

Everything about this place is magical-the tidy lawns, the white marble fountain, a few pigeons nestled in the building ducts, the marigold flowers that have been discreetly sprinkled at the side of the steps, the doorman with a thick moustache and a colourful turban, the sparkling brass door handles, the immaculate traditional Indian uniform of the man who is taking her suitcase and the special Punjabi footwear of the staff!

Time has stopped here. The developing India with skyscrapers in every town is somewhere out there. Here there's only the whiteness of the building, the click clack of the water in the fountain and the bright steel railings that light her path.

The interior of the hotel is even more astonishing. Jannat has shed her tiredness and looks around herself in disbelief. Again, nothing is magnificent, but everything is beautiful. There's a crackling fire in the large chimney and several crystal bottles rest on a low tray for the convenience of guests seated in the lobby, the armchairs are soft and comfortable and there is no temporary vibe to it.

Jannat is instantly grateful to Mr Acharya for the tip. If she can find his contact address she will write to him immediately. Perhaps the manager would know of him.

'Good day, Ma'am. My name is Ashutosh Rai and I'm the manager on duty. Mr Acharya called to warn us that a friend of his would arrive today. Anyone who is a friend of Mr Acharya is a special friend of ours.'

'It's my pleasure indeed. This is an exotic place . . . ' she says as she hands him her passport.

He fills a form and hands it to her to fill in the information that wasn't on her passport. Including her profession.

'Excuse my audacity but I read on your check-in card that you're a journalist from London . . . ' 'Yes . . . I hope you're not holding that against me! I'm here on an assignment, I will stay for a few weeks in Punjab but I won't cause any . . . '

'Oh no, Ma'am, on the contrary. We would be honoured if you would accept our invitation for a ball we are hosting tonight to celebrate the prestigious business community of Jalandhar. They are our preferred clients,' he says with a meek smile.

Jannat is tired and needs a shower terribly, but this man is so kind. *This is my first day, I need friends.* His voice is definite and his words crystal clear. *And who knows, I can get a lead at the party. It is the business clan.*

'Okay, sure, I'd love that. One thing though . . . I had a really long trip and terribly need a shower and a couple of hours of sleep . . . '

'Of course, Amir will take you to your room and I'll arrange for a chauffeur to take you to the venue at 8 pm. The place is called Dhillon Farms. Luxury and style, Punjab at its best,' Ashutosh concludes with the smile of a Sufi saint.

7

Jannat collapses on her bed as soon as the door closesbehind her, pulled softly shut by Amir. She watches her breath as she senses the presence of ethereal serenity within the four walls. The room reflects the hotel lobby. There's wood everything, marble flooring, spotlessly clean, with carpets on the floor that have a Kashmir design. The oil painting on the wall portrays a young Punjabi girl spreading her arms in the middle of mustard fields. The colours are muted but her expression swears of liberty. *Irony, truth or duplicity?* The bed smells of clean laundry, a similar scent to that of her grandmother's laundry when she went to visit her during the long summers in Devonshire. The bulb screwed in one of the wall lamps is flickering. She switches it off. Even the moon has dark spots.

'The beds are high enough for you to empty your suitcase and slide it under the bed. The wardrobe can accommodate your clothes and your paraphernalia. We want our guests to feel at home,' said Amir as he left the room. And it's true: being here, in this very room, makes Jannat want to move here for good. The subtle smell of incense and the nice mustard marble bathroom with steaming hot water and soft towels has already made her forget the chaos at the airport.

She takes a shower and crawls into bed. She has dreamt about this moment for the last twelve hours and yet there's still that little worm munching on her brain. She rolls into the immaculate sheets a couple of times. The room has the perfect temperature for her to enjoy her duvet and also walk around in her thin pyjamas.

Okay, I cannot sleep . . . Am I worrying about the ball?Come on, Jan! I work for the most feared editor of the whole UK, I can't worry about meeting journalists here . . . in the back of the beyond . . .

And yet there's something that doesn't allow her to sleep.

Jannat gets up and flips the screen of her laptop open. The sticker with the Free Tibet slogan, a memory of the old university days, is nearly faded. Every time she replaced her computer in the last few years she peeled it off and stuck it back on. She bought it with Preet at a sit-in for Tibetan monks . . . Ahh, Preet!

Jannat opens her blog and writes furiously, then she reads what she has written, cor-rects a few mistakes, cuts a few sentences that were clearly too long and publishes the article. She ends her post with a quote, 'Fighting the battles of life and love is not about how well you fight, it's how well you are prepared.' The light in the room is bright, it's the middle of the day outside and she feels as if it's one of her sleepless nights. She looks at the bed she has just rolled into and decides against a second try.

Oh, damn the jet lag! I'll tire myself to death and then come home for a good night's sleep. It's the only way of beating it. The ball is going to be boring. I might meet some absurd natives. I'm going to be the sleeping journalist from England. I hope there's no dancing involved. In India people dance inside temples too.

She unlocks her iPhone and goes through all the information she has noted down on the plane. Yes, there's everything I need for today.

Ready to dive into what brought her here Jannat picks up the phone and dials 0. She asks for the manager, Mr Rai. He picks up the phone and asks her in his soft voice, 'Did you sleep well, Ms Gill? Are you ready to order lunch?'

'Yeah . . . I mean no. Would it be possible for you to arrange a cab for me?'

'Of course, Ma'am! Where to?'

'To a village named Nangal. It's not too far my GPS says?'

There is a long pause. 'Of course, Ms Gill. The taxi can be here in twenty minutes.'

'Perfect! Thank you, Mr Rai.'

The cab brings Jannat back to the India that frightened her before. The cab driver has not stopped chewing (and spitting out) *paan*. The windowpane on his side is stained with tiny red dots and streaks. He chews, rolls the window down, spits and rolls it up again, smashing his tainted spit all around.

Jannat lets out a sigh, several sighs in fact, hoping that he would understand that she's annoyed, but he goes on without paying her much attention. *Does she even exist for him?* She decides to concentrate on the world outside.

The winter clouds dim the light of the sun.A thin layer of mist lies on the dusty road and Jannat is surprised and saddened to see the barefoot children smiling and waving at her. She wonders how these little girls can wear such torn and patched cotton shirts and pants without freezing to death; it's not quite as cold as in London but there's a strong chill in the air. She herself is wearing the thick jacket she usually wears to go to work in London and she regrets having left her gloves at home.

She mentally checks what she has brought with her. How the hell did I not think of checking the weather? But then again, who on earth is sent halfway across the planet on a mere twelve hours' notice? I better find a good laundry soon because with the few winter items I have there will have to be a lot of washing . . .

'Slow down please . . . '

The cab driver has (unexpectedly) understood and has slowed down the car until it stopped. Jannat rolls down the window and hands out some can dies and chocolates she has in her purse. It was her comfort food. She pillaged Andy's stash-he wasn't coming back.

The children's eyes widen to the point that Jannat fears they are going to explode. They eat the candies and chocolate and then lick the wrapper.

If I had more I'd give them more. It's such a pleasure to make their day! The cab starts once more and, after a few minutes and a number of questions to passers-by and old men warming their bones at a *chaiwalla*, it finally pulls over in front of one of the victims' houses.

For a moment Jannat is unsure of what to do. There was no telephone contact and she couldn't tell the family she was coming. Her English self would turn back and leave, but she has come so far for this, she can't leave now.

She takes a deep breath and gets out of the cab. She reads the name on the gate. It's a worn out wooden name plate-Baljeet Kaur She walks into the compound. It's a typical Indian compound. Some elderly women are sitting outside, chatting and drinking hot ginger tea. As soon as they see Jannat walk in they stop talking but no one gets up to greet her.

She joins her hands, *'Namaste ji. Sat sri akaal.'*

'Sat sri akaal. Who have you come for?'

'I am a journalist from London. I am here for some information on Kuljeet.

I want to interview the mother, Baljeet.'

The woman doesn't seem to like the idea of an interview, but one of her friends, a chubby lady with a warm smile, excited to have a foreigner to talk to, hurries to get her a glass of water.

'Please take a seat till I return,' gestures the first woman, clearly the oldest in-charge of the house.

Jannat sits down obediently, holding the glass. *Tap water on my first day here is a little t*

The chubby lady who had gone inside walks out again, pulling a man by the armbefore introducing herself. Jannat notices a photo on the wall. She checks her phone. It's the same man from her research-a collection of online articles, this one refers to a suspicious accident where the man's Skoda was pushed off a cliff by a runaway car. The picture of the smashed Skoda is like a burnt piece of metal sharing print space with the victim's picture.

The man who has just come out doesn't have a friendly face. He looks like the vic-tim's father and, as Jannat smiles and greets him, he cuts her short with a grunt, 'I think you are knocking on the wrong door, we have nothing to say, please.'

'But Kuljeet Singh was your son, I guess he was murdered recently, I know . . . ' 'Listen, young lady, please leave. We can't help you . . . '

The ladies have gathered together. They seem to know this angry tone only too well and Jannat understands that the man is in no mood for an interview. She nods and stands, ready to leave, but with a parting shot. 'No problem, but your revelations can save a few other lives.'

The cab driver walks in, scratching his belly. Jannat has been inside long enough to establish a conversation; he might as well walk in for a cup of tea. He evidently doesn't expect this scene and is a little taken aback. The man reaches him in two long strides and with a finger pointing at his nose screams at the potbellied cabbie, 'Take her away and make sure she doesn't ever enter this town or else . . . '

The driver turns on his heel as if he had just received an order from an army general and runs to the car, opening the door for Jannat and almost hurrying her in. She bows her head, defeated.

The ride back is sadder than the previous one. Women carry pots of water for the evening cooking; the cattle are on their way back to the barn; farmers, tired and hungry, wind up their work with a sigh; kids rushing back home with their guardians; the sun goes down and casts a gloomy light over the passing townships.

The landscape from Nangal to the city is transformed from a dry sandy suburb to the busy commercial heart of Punjab. At once Jannat feels the weight of defeat on her shoulder. All her acquired communication skills are not good enough. No wonder she had a huge showdown with May.

Are they all going to be like this? What if they are and I have to spend a couple of weeks chasing ghosts in these suburbs? I could have been in Kabul instead. This can't be right. I want to right a wrong. I'm the good guy, on the side of justice. I just want the truth. Why are they so scared?

She's angry with the big Punjabi landlord who ordered the cab driver to take her away, but in a way she also understands him. Why would someone who has gone through so much pain be willing to talk to a journalist about it? This is not Madonna's new boyfriend or a yacht party on the French Riviera that people can't wait to tell you all about. This involves suffering, pain and loss. Who is she to dig their hearts and offer them for £ 2.30 a copy to a bunch of hungry readers? Subscribers who will leave the magazine on the coffee table until the next issue comes out? Why does the world need to feel the pain of an old couple's massive loss, in a tiny Indian town, which may not even exist on the map? Welcome to the ruthless world!

With these thoughts on her mind Jannat gets back to the hotel and goes to There is no other truth and there is no other lie.' her room. She has totally forgotten about the party and the first thing she does after kicking her shoes to the two opposite corners of the room is to power up her computer and update her blog before she loses her trail of thought.

Kindness is the elixir of life, the only vial of strength that will make death tremble right at the doorstep when it comes for you. There is no immortality and if it does exist then it lies in the spirit of the self that fortifies with every moment spent to brace another soul. There is no other truth and there is no other lie.'

As soon as she raises her head from the screen with a refill of chi, noticing the shiny lights of the city pierce the night, she closes her eyes to rest. The room situated on the acute corner of the building is filled with silence that can scare the devil. A few minutes of abyss.

8

The phone rings incessantly in Jannat's room. Only the very last ring wakes her up from her hypnosis.

'Good evening, Ms Gill, this is Mr Rai. I called to remind you that the car will pick you up in one hour. Also if you need me to call in a hairdresser or a beautician, you are so . . .'

'Thank you, Mr Rai, it won't be necessary. I'll be down in one hour.'

Jannat puts the phone down and lets herself fall back on the bed that, she only notices now, someone made while she was away. *This hotel is fantastic. I never want to leave . . .* Half an hour later she forces herself out of bed, takes a shower and wears the white dress she had thrown into the suitcase, mostly because she didn't know where to put it.

Thank God I took it. If I had found a hook to put it back in the wardrobe I would have done it and I wouldn't have had a dress for tonight. I wonder how formal it will be. I mean this is not exactly New York.

Her image of India is still unclear. She doesn't know that the party will gather the elite of Punjab and that her dress, as nice as it may be, will be a simple dress compared to the display of wealth and grace from the other female guests. India surprises and how!

Jannat gets seated in a private cab and a few minutes later makes her entrance into one of the most spectacular places she has ever seen.

Dhillon Farms is something like an old palace turned banquet venue surrounded by a luscious park. When the car approaches the mansion, driving slowly through the two rows of lights on the elegant lane, Jannat feels lost for a minute. *It's like going to a party at Buckingham Palace and what am I wearing?*

A plain dress... what was I thinking, why did I not enquire! Why did I not wonder why Mr Rai wanted to send me a hairdresser? This is why, because these women here have pineapple-shaped hairdos and I have natural, untidy, long pin up curls . . .

Mr Rai seems to be reading her mind because as he helps a breathless Jannat out of the car he says, 'Ms Gill, do not be intimidated. These people are looking forward to meeting an international journalist like you. And, with all due respect, you look stunning, I really . . . '

'Thank you, Mr Rai, much appreciated . . .' she responds as she stumbles out of the car. She meticulously adjusts her white wedge sandals.

She enters the large room with its red drapes tied in golden ropes and sees an indistinct crowd of people, all very elegantly dressed. For Jannat, who has always been a rather hippie student and has only recently refined her tastes, this is the most elegant place she has ever been to by far. The humungous crystal chandelier in the centre of the hallway dazzles her for a moment with its bulbs all lit up. The high ceilings and the four corner pillars give it a palatial look. The wooden interiors remind her of a Scottish castle that she has visited in her college trip.

I need a drink! She nods to the waiter walking around with a tray of champagne glasses but he doesn't seem to respond to the call. Mr Rai graciously introduces her to the most influential families of Punjab and under her amber skin Jannat blushes.

She is then introduced to a local journalist. *Ah! Let me do some digging.* But he turns out to be a

Dalai Lama follower. Jannat feels so home with his revelations about the monk that she is flushed pink all over her cheeks.

Why the hell am I blushing? Less than forty-eight hours ago I dared to give a piece of my mind to May Edwards, the terror of London, and now I blush in front of these unknown strangers just be-cause they are all wrapped up in dazzling clothes and jewellery? Nope, rationality doesn't seem to work . . . I'm about to hyperventilate... One, two three, drink!

And she thinks this as the waiter passes two inches from her. Jannat is talking to an older lady and doesn't want to turn but she nonchalantly extends her arm and tries to reach for the glass when her hand hits something. Something soft and warm. *Shit, I just grabbed the waiter's hand.* Jannat turns her head mechanically and sees that she is indeed holding a hand, but it's not that of the waiter, who, embarrassed, stands between her and a handsome young Punjabi man. Jannat feels her ears turn red, unsure what to say as she stares at the hand. It's a beautiful brown, soft hand, with a sun tattooed on its back and crowned with a *kara* in gold on the wrist. She lifts her eyes to find the man smiling at her as he slowly releases her hand and lets her have the glass.

She straightens her spine and looks more attentively at the man who nods, encouraging her to take the glass from the tray.

'Please,Ma'am, you should have it, I insist . . .'

'Well, let's just say I have it because I'm thirsty... But thank you!' The sentence was meant to be a little more gentle, an icebreaker, but in fact it sounds more like she wants to cut the conversation short, which of course she didn't . . . *This guy is the first person who isn't a million years old I meet, I could as well give him a shot . . . Ouch, big mouth!*

But the man doesn't seem to take notice of Jannat's abrupt response and extends his hand in a friendly manner. 'Rajveer Khanna, nice to meet you. I'm a businessman . . . ' 'Jannat Gill, I'm a journalist . . . '

'Right, from the UK, I would guess from your accent?' 'Yes, and I could guess from yours that you are from . . .'

'Ha-ha, funny, I like a sense of humour in a lady. And I'm afraid it's not common.' The journalist, who she had a conversation with a few minutes ago, is on his way out. 'Dharam Singh, *aapse milkar badi khushi hui*, all the best, *mein aapka* Dalai Lama *wala interview zaroor padhoongi,* internet *pe.'*

'*Shukriya* Jannat,' he walks away.

Rajveer raises his eyebrows. '*Hindi zabaan saaf hain aapki*, internet lessons?' '*Bebe ne bachpan se hi hindi pe zor diya hain. London mein reheti hain lekin aaj bhi keheti hai chahe Mars pein ghar bana lo, Jannat, lekin apne vatan ki mitti ko kabhi alvida na kehna.'*

Rajveer chokes on his drink. He blows out a loud gush of air. *Wow.*

She smells him. *Woody fragrance.Impressive. Encounter by Calvin Klein.*

There is something electric between them; they don't know how to define it. They just met so they would never admit it, but the truth is that there's an attraction they can't fight. *A coup de foudre* as the French would say? *Love at first sight?* Is it too fictional? But if they believe that a person whom one has just met can change one's life, well, they ought to be each other's person. They can't define it as love, they don't know if they truly like each other yet, but somehow they both felt like ships that have entered safe ports after years of wandering.

Ah, finally. I've been looking for you my entire life. Where was she every day of my life? Why wasn't she the first woman I thought I loved? Why wasn't she every woman I ever made love to? His brain keeps spitting out these thoughts disregarding his rational self.

Jannat's brain is no less active, and in spite of her focussed self her subconscious can't stop sending signals-her palms are starting to sweat, her tongue is dry and her eyes more sparkly than ever.

I can't let him think that I'm the kind of girl who falls for the first guy she meets. This is definitely a strong rebound, but there's something different about him, something I can't define. It is drawing me in, intoxicating me with every word he utters. Is it his body scent, is it jetlag or is it his killer eyes?

As the two warm up to the conversation another waiter passes by with a new tray of glasses. This time Rajveer helps himself to one and smells the wine, but his gaze is on her. She bites on her lower lip. Holding the iced glass Rajveer looks around at the guests at the ball. The room is filled with the most influential businessmen, politicians and motley characters of Punjab. As he pierces all of them with his dark eyes some smile back, some raise their glasses and some simply acknowledge the presence of a new woman in town whom Rajveer noticed first, as usual.

As his eyes return to Jannat she has just finished her glass of champagne and doesn't let the waiter escape before she has taken a second one.

'Impressive, I must admit!'

'You're easily impressed. I need to beat the mother of a jet lag!'

'So what brings you to this far corner of the earth? Business or pleasure?'

'Strictly business, are you kidding me?' The

last part of the sentence, again, wasn't supposed to sound rude, but once again she has managed to be ruder than she would have wanted. She's really tired and tries to articulate the statement ' . . . except tonight, of course, tonight is great! The manager of the hotel I'm staying at very kindly invited me to this ball...this may be the only chance I'll have to relax. From tomorrow it's all work . . . '

'Is it a big story you're working on? If you don't mind me asking, what is it about?' Jannat shuffles her feet while her eyes blink rapidly. The subject she is actually researching is delicate and this room is filled with the very people who could organize a contract killing. They have the money for it and, with all this business and all this wealth, some obviously also have motives. She beams a knowing smile as though re-collecting something. Her chest thrusts out.

'It's an interesting story on the KBK report. I believe it's a pretty relevant chapter of 21st century Punjab history, it's . . . '

'Really? I've never heard of KBK . . . is it . . . '

'*Kabootar Baaji Khulasa* Report, it's been repo . . . '

Rajveer bursts into a roar of laughter so loud that some people in the room look their way out.

'Seriously. It's almost a household custom here

in Punjab to send a member of the family for greener pastures overseas. Through any dodgy agent, it so . . . ' They burst out laughing together, but soon they are done and before a little awkward silence arises between them the fancy orchestra plays a Latino dance track. Rajveer takes the opportunity of stepping closer. 'So the music is following you?' 'I hope it's just music and not the demons of my past?' she confesses. 'With music on your side even the demons will dance to your tune,' he whispers. 'I am not sure if this is . . . '

'The beauty of this moment is unparalleled, feel it!'

Rajveer gestures Jannat onto the dance floor but she stammers, 'I may be rusty, not good at . . . ' 'That's for me to decide,' he answers in a soft husky voice.

The smooth movements of both dancers force the rest of those who attempted a less traditional dance to leave the floor to them. Neither Jannat nor Rajveer want to embarrass anybody but they are just into their tango, lost in each other's eyes. It's not sexual, or better, not only sexual. There's more to it. The old spinsters will probably think it is just attraction, but between these two there is something else, something more, something deeper.

El tango es un piensamiento triste, que se baila. The tango is a sad thought that is expressed through a love filled dance.

Life and death flirt as their feet pause abruptly. The breath is fearless yet the heart beats with a sense of impending doom. Their minds linger on the choice, to surrender or to demolish.

Have I made love to her in the parallel universe?

Is he the guy I am in love with in the world next doors?

The spirits of two individuals unite. The touch is so comforting, the scent is so familiar and the bodies are balanced in perfect sync. On the last note of the tango the orchestra stops abruptly, as a tango should stop, like a slap.

On the last note their legs are wrapped in a maze of limbs that can't afford to leave each other. He has taken her, in the few minutes that they danced the tango, to a different world, a world that is only theirs, where only they can live and which exists only because they want it to. They belong together now, or at least that's what they feel as soon as the guitar stops playing. But as the room fills with voices and other sounds their minds begin to analyse the experience and raise the usual questions that prevent love from springing up naturally. *Is he a player? Is she just interested in a quick escapade? What does he think of women? Has he had many? Would my family like her? Is she a slut? Is he wicked? Is she drunk?*

And just like that everything falls back into place and the spark of love that was about to start a fire and burn the building to ashes is momentarily lost. The mind plays chess with its own master and often checks and mates.

The two tango stars walk back to their table, feeling the eyes of the entire ballroom on them. The scented air is loaded with tumescence. There is awe, there is envy and there is jealousy in the eyes of the stunned audience. Mrs Bansal and her daughter Diljeet look at them with hatred. Mrs Bansal knows all her husband's money will not straighten her daughter's nose and make her look prettier.

She will always be an ugly rich girl whom men will court only for her money, hoping to get a mistress the day after the wedding. For this reason alone had Mrs Bansal forced her husband to refuse the one or two suitors who made a move, and for the exact same reason she brings Diljeet to every possible party. Diljeet, on her part, is twenty five, sees all her friends getting married and having children and would settle for any man just to be married. She has always had a soft spot for Rajveer, but even she, despite all her money, knows he's totally out of her league.

Jannat is sitting at the table massaging her heels. It's been a while since she wore such high heels.

Dancing a tango in them is not exactly relaxing either. She can feel her pulse accelerating. 'I never thought a Punjabi man could do any dance other than the *bhangra* . . . especially not the tango . . . '

'But my *bhangra's* definitely better . . . '

'Really? I would love to try it sometime.'

'That's great, because I know just the perfect occasion for your first *bhangra* experience. Come over to my place for the Lohri celebration on Saturday.'

'Lohri?' asks Jannat with her tongue tangled.

'It's a ceremony to celebrate the coldest day of the winter.'

'Oh, that's nice. I wish we had something like that in England. Winter there is so cold, there's no difference between a day in October and a day in February . . . I'll try, I can't promise anything.'

'What do you mean? All days are the same here too, and there's not much difference either . . . ' 'I know but a feast like . . . '

'Yeah, that too.'

'Mr Rai, you've been most kind but I must leave now. I've really got to get some decent sleep . . . ' 'But you've not eaten, Ma'am. Please have something . . . '

'Seriously, all I want is to sleep. Do you mind asking your driver to take me back to the hotel?' 'Please, may I?' cuts in Rajveer.

'I'm sorry?'

'I mean, if you're okay with it, I could drive you back to your hotel. I was leaving anyway.' 'Yeah, sure, I'm cool. Is that alright, Mr Rai?'

'As you wish, Ma'am. Mr Khanna is a gentleman. One of the few left, unfortunately.' 'I have no doubts . . . Shall we?'

As the two approach the entrance Mrs Bansal goes to greet Rajveer. 'Why does a man whose nights are busier than his days have an early night tonight? Could it be because of the beautiful young lady, a fresh catch for the evening?'

Rajveer is evidently not at ease around this bitter old lady but manages to hide his discomfort. He looks Mrs Bansal straight in the eye and smiles. 'Mrs Bansal, I didn't think I'd be so lucky to see you here. This is Jannat Gill, a journalist from London. Jannat, this is our MP's better half, Mrs Bansal and their daughter...I'm sorry I forget your name . . . ' 'Rude but sexy . . . How could I not forgive you?

Hi, I'm Diljeet.'

'Nice to meet you. As he said, Jannat Gill.'

'Come on, stay. What's the hurry? The night's

still young my friend!'

'My friend here is jet-lagged and I need my beauty sleep too. After all, I have to live up to my sexy tag, haven't I?'

He asks Jannat for her hand so he can escort her with pride. She gently lifts it. Rajveer notices a black strap on her wrist.

'Friendship band, nice touch.'

'Survival band, adventure.'

They leave without saying goodbye under the flaming eyes of the mother and the adoring eyes of the daughter. Two proud pairs of shoulders glide side by side and disappear into the darkness beyond the front door. The room subsides into the mundane.

9

Rajveer zips in his black SUV and it melts into the darkness. He rolls down the window and apologizes loudly, 'Sorry. I suffer from mild claustrophobia. I was very naughty as a child and my dad would lock me up in the toilet each time I played a deadly prank. Some things remain with you till your last breath.'

Jannat looks out at the stars shining outside and rolls down her window. In the ice-cold night the stars are bright and yellow. Jannat has never seen them so close. She's tired and yet excited. She knows it's that last adrenaline rush before falling fast asleep; it's no foreshadowing of something beautiful about to happen, but she's determined to enjoy every last drop of adrenaline in her body. She fixes her breathlessness with a deep breath. Rajveer parts his legs as he checks her out subtly. Although she is tired and a little tipsy Jannat appears sexier than she is, with a flushing complexion. Her dress creases to show a hint of her alluring cleavage. The curves of her upper body are highlighted in termittently by the passing cars as is Rajveer's chiselled face.

Rajveer breaks the silence. 'It was great to have you around. I never knew a Jalandhar evening could be so exuberant.'

Jannat strokes her throat and speaks in her slightly inebriated twang, 'The more you chase it the more it will allure you . . . so stay calm. Joy tiptoes into your senses like a rat and nibbles your ear's like nobody's spirit.'

Rajveer is spontaneous. 'Cheers to that Miss Shaky-sphere.'

Jannat sneezes and Rajveer closes the window for her, pressing gently onthe centralized key. He also turns the heating on. 'Someone is getting a cold here huh?'

'N . . . no, I'm just, achoo . . . I'm just terribly allergic . . . '

She holds her breath, rummages through her purse, but of course, she was meant to go to a ball, not a safari, she only has the key to her room, her credit card and her phone.

'I don't have any tissue, do you happen to . . .'

'Yes, in the glove compartment . . .'

Jannat opens it and extracts a large box of tissues. As she pulls it out she grasps a piece of cloth or canvas along with the box. She pulls at it thinking it to be a piece of cloth to clean the windshield, but as soon as her hand is out of the glove compartment the canvas falls at her feet with a dull thud. She opens it to see what could have been wrapped in it to make such a noise and is surprised and terrified to see a pistol.

Thoughts rush her mind... He's locked the doors so I can't get out of the car. He hasn't noticed though so I can still pick it up and. Should I take it in case he tries to attack me? Should I put it back? Oh God, I don't even know anybody with a gun. Andy shouted at me once because I got a water gun at the beach, he said shooting is always an act of violence. Oh God, what do I do now? Well Mr Rai knows I'm here. If I don't get back to the hotel tonight . . . Wait, they are friends. Mr Rai is probably waiting for him where they've agreed to take me. This is entirely Mr Acharya's fault... Wait, he's in it too . . .

'Are you okay?'

'W . . . what?'

'You okay? You needed tissues but then you

spent the last two minutes with the box on your lap, tissues in your hand and a lost look...so I was wondering if there's something wrong . . . '

Instinctively Jannat's eyes drop to the floor where the polymer framed pistol lies between her feet. Rajveer's eyes follow hers and he sees the pistol.

'Oh that? No worries, here.' And he pulls out of his lateral compartment a bunch of papers and hands them to her. 'Here are the permits; it's a Glock 17. I can carry that pistol, it's certified for personal safety and the pistol is registered. I'm probably the only one in the whole of Punjab who has bothered to go through the whole process.'

He keeps talking as he puts the gun back in the glove compartment as if nothing has happened. But something has happened, Jannat knows, and this is why she's quiet all of a sudden.

Rajveer tries to break the awkward silence once more. He is unnerved by Jannat's gasping, a bead of glow rolls down next to her ear. He needs to act now. 'Look, I understand. You think it's crazy, but it's really just a safety thing . . . a precaution . . . '

'Somehow, to me, carrying a weapon always means one is summoning death . . . One's own or perhaps someone else's . . . '

'Life is a dressing room, prepare to fight like a

warrior, death is the arena where gladiators fight to master their spirit.'

'So you could be inviting death earlier than it is meant to be, Raj.'

'It doesn't bother me, Jannat. It's an exhilarating sense of power. All I know is death will come once for sure and I hope for a good cause.'

'Like the martyrs . . . '

'Sort of.'

Jannat cannot resist, 'So you like power that can cast the shadow of death.' 'I live for power. I believe like our warriors of the past that power is passion, a purpose . . . power can change a single moment from life to death and death to life.'

Jannat is not pleased. ' . . . With a weapon, that is cowardly. True power comes from within. It's greater than all the armed power in the world.'

Rajveer rolls his eyes. He doesn't want to upset her with his beliefs on a night that has been enigmatic otherwise. 'I accept the evil with gentle hands and a steely heart.'

'The evil inside you will destroy you first and then the rest.'

They are both silent again, each absorbed in their thoughts. A ray of moonlight strikes Rajveer's *kara* for a second. The whole car seems to shine with the light diffused by the bracelet. She notices also, for the first time, a ring on Rajveer's forefinger. There's a red gemstone in it and it reflects all around the roof of the car. Jannat considers this a good topic to restart the conversation.

'I know the *kara* is a symbol of the Sikh faith. What's the significance of the ring?' 'Well it doesn't mean much to me but it certainly does to my mum. She got it custom made from this gemology guy who convinced her that wearing it would promote my longevity, strength and all that jazz . . . '

'Really?'

'I wear it because it makes mummy*ji* happy. Frankly I think when your time's up, it's up, ring or no ring . . . '

The car pulls over. Jannat finds herself in front of the colonial entrance of the Amar Hotel. She almost feels sorry because the drive was so short. This Batman of a character is indeed interesting, if for nothing else then because he keeps a gun in his glove compartment! And his dark SUV can easily pass off as the Batmobile of Jalandhar.

Rajveer stops the car in front of the entrance and gets out to open her door, but as he extends his hand for her to lean on her sandal gives away and she nearly trips. Rajveer is there to catch her.

She hobbles her way up the marble steps and

cannot help but think of the freshly made bed and her flower-scented bedroom.

She turns around suddenly. 'The heel of my sandal broke. Too much drinking, I mean dancing. I thank you very much. No, I'm serious. I needed it . . . I . . . never mind . . . You are a born saviour!'

'Well. Some would say natural born killer. It depends on the point of view, I guess . . . '

'Is that a hint . . . or is that a hint?'

'Well . . . I was wondering if you'd like a little tour of Jalandhar. You know, the authentic kinds, not the one you get in pre-paid packages.'

Jannat stands on one foot and a frozen heart. 'Thank you, but I'm really busy with work. Tonight was fun but I'm going to be locked up here or doing interviews the whole time. KBK. Good night!'

'Good night . . . Jannat,' he whispers as she walks away. He clasps his left hand on his chest as he waits for her to turn and smile. She disappears in the silence of the night. He stares into space. His hands are clenched. His chest is leaning on the steering wheel.

Rajveer is all they say he is. He's a charmer, he is a cheat and he is what other men would want to be but don't dare be. And yet his dreams, deep down, are very ordi-nary. Most of all he wants to fall in love, be passionate about a girl who is more than just a pretty face. And this Jannat could have been a good woman to fall in love with if it hadn't been for that stupid gun.

The morning light shines outside Jannat's window. She's fast asleep when a knock on the door wakes her up. She rolls between the crisp sheets. The weather outside makes her want to spend the whole day in this comfortable bed and order several cups of tea. She feels like a woman in the mood for some easing. Every now and then we want to satiate the void inside us. And then out of nowhere someone arrives and fills it up with absolute ease and we experience wonder. The knock on the door was soft, as if it was someone who didn't want to disturb her, probably Mr Rai. She decides to get up and see what the matter is. She opens the door and a blade of cold air strokes her legs and swirls into the room. No one is in sight.

As Jannat lowers her eyes she notices a silver tray on the floor with an envelope on it. The envelope has her name written in beautiful handwriting. She picks it up; the paper is thick and expensive. She opens it and extracts a small card that reads, 'Authentic Punjab adventure planned for you, I'll be waiting for you outside your hotel at 10.30.'

This can be no one but Rajveer.

Jannat smiles as she closes the door and crawls back into bed. She glances at the clock on the wall and is astonished to see that it is now ten. *Ten o'clock? How did I sleep so late? I can't have gone to bed later than 10.30 last night... Shit, I've got to get dressed!*

The day they spend together is possibly one of the most magical Jannat has ever spent. They go around the bazaar, looking at shops that seem to emerge from the *Arabian Nights*-fabrics so vivid, shoes called *mojdis* with gold and silver embroidery, women out shopping dressed to kill, watching some extreme bargaining, smelling the spices that wrap the whole market in an invisible scent and tasting freshly-made *jalebi-sandrabdi*. Jannat expresses her awe at the robust mixture of the old world and the new age lifestyle. She finds Rajveer a perfect metaphor for that. After the personalised city tour Rajveer takes her in his SUV and drives on the highway that cuts across the fields of yellow mustard. The colours are magical, shading from light yellow, almost green, to a brownish yellow.

Away from the mushrooming glass jungle the countryside is reminiscent of the Punjab fabled to be paradise. The smell in the air is pungent and fragrant, promising a good harvest and an even better tasting of the finished product.

When he stops the car Jannat gets off to take photos of the children running across the fields with their kites. They are still stuck in a time that doesn't match with the rapid urbanization of India. The colours, so flamboyant and so brutal at the same time, amaze her. Everything she has seen so far seems to have emerged from a dream she has never dreamt. This is a reality more fantastic than a dream. It's absolutely amazing. She has no words to describe it if not through her photographs. But she knows believing is the biggest part of magic. She believes she is experiencing a paradise of sorts. Maybe it was memories of this place that inspired her grandmother to name her Jannat.

For lunch they stop at a *dhaba* by the side of the road. Rajveer orders for both, '*Paneer matar* with *makki di roti*.'

As they wait for their food a boy comes to serve them a glass of fresh *lassi*. The boy could be in his early teens but it's really hard to tell. She fishes a Big Ben key ring from her bag and hands it to him. He looks at this marvel that he never seen before, there's even a glitter at the very top of it that shines in the sun. The boy is bedazzled and has no words to thank Jannat.He considers that perhaps she has given it to him to clean. Jannat has to ask Rajveer to explain that it's a present, one that he can keep it. The boy is absolutely overjoyed. And as Rajveer feels the warmth radiating in Jannat's body he understands that, as happy as the boy is, she's surely happier than him. *It's unusual to find a woman like her, especially around here. Women here are always so focused on a good marriage, money and jewellery. She is so different. It's even hard to understand for someone used to living here like me. How can she be so genuinely good-hearted?*

After lunch they take the car again and drive to a farm. On the way Rajveer stops at a jaggery factory to let Jannat taste freshly made *gur.* Then they get back into the car and drive to the farm. Jannat's eyes widen when she sees how many different animals are on the farm; it's the kind of outing she would have liked to have but has never experienced.

'This is amazing . . . When I was young we lived in the city centre and I was allowed to go to the park only if I had an adult with me, my mum or my nanny. So I didn't get many chances to experience nature. In standard four me and my classmates thought that berries grew on trees . . .'

'Hahaha, that is funny . . . '

'Yeah . . . Well I'm catching up now, right?'

'More than right and as a matter of fact you are catching up right now . . . look what's here . . . '

'Wow, a cow!'

'Yes, but look under the cow!'

'Well it's a bucket . . . '

'And what is the bucket used for?'

'I don't know . . . sand castles?'

Rajveer gives a hearty laugh. 'Yes, but in this case they are used to collect the milk; this lady here would love you to help her milk the cow.'

'What me? Milking a cow? I'm can't, I mean . . . It's probably the first time I've even touched a cow . . . '

'Well then better start soon! I'll be here snapping pictures!'

And so Jannat does as she's told. She kneels down and, despite the first few minutes when she's not exactly at ease, she pulls and the warm milk springs out. It's a marvellous sensation and Jannat would never stop the drumming in her puffy chest.

The day of adventures continues as Rajveer planned it. They eat freshly roasted cobs, sip ice-cold beers by the riverside and ride scooters through a nearby village and its fields, feeling the long grass whip their legs. They munch on fresh sugarcane and wash their feet in a natural fountain. She gathers moments and not things for a change. She floods her Instagram account with pictures, doing things and seeing places she never dreamt existed. Rajveer bounces on his feet all day. He finds himself looking at things in a light that he never has since his early childhood. What has changed today, Punjab or his own limited perspective?

At the end of the day Jannat is exhausted and, as Rajveer drives swiftly across the mustard fields bathed in the golden light of the sunset, she stares outside at the mil-lions of colours that glow brilliantly. Now that she thinks of going back . . . she'll flip open her computer, take her iPhone and start researching about . . . well about death, there's no other way of putting it. It seems impossible that this day, so magical and so full of 'real-life Punjab', has taken place in the very same context where these people pay to have each other killed. It didn't cross her mind during the day but now her gaze falls on the glove compart-ment. *Is the gun still there? Why does he have it? What side is he on, that of the killers, the victims or the supremely indifferent?*

All these thoughts tangle inside her head, like colourful threads that create a knot she can't free herself from. In the driver's seat Rajveer concentrates on the road but notices Jannat's sudden silence. *Why? Is she missing someone? Has he done something? Is it still the gun?*

He was going to drive her back to the hotel, but the drowning red sun is such a turn-on and the day has been so exquisite that he may as well top it up with another splash of romance.

10

The night is cold but the wind is gentle as they drive past small street stalls where fires are lit to start cooking *parathas* and *dal* for the evening meal. Passers-by linger in front of these stalls, exchanging a couple of words with the owners, only to enjoy the warmth of the fire and smell of rich fried food before hurrying home.

Rajveer drives his sleek SUV, black as the night, gliding amongst folks in somewhat sinister peace. Inside the car they seem invisible. But Jannat has just had a memorable day and cannot notice these things. She looks outside with the eyes of a child, wide, round, hungry, taking in every detail. Rajveer stops the car in front of a fort at the top of a hill.

They get off the car. Jannat finds herself in front of the ruins with several entrances to a maze. She runs her hands through her hair, the night is dark and cold, is this a good idea? Where are they? But Rajveer gives her a reassuring look; his long eyes prompt her to choose her entrance. Jannat presses her lips together.

'Come, I'll show you something. They call this the maze of destiny. Pick your en-trance.' Unable to say no Jannat enters, avoiding any eye contact. She crosses the first door-way in front of her and is suddenly thrown back a hundred years. The walls of stone are cold and grey, but the darkness around her makes the sky above her look bright. Those stars . . . so big . . . ambassadors of hope.

Before she knows she's out of it. The maze is only a prop, a skillfully made artefact for young men to charm young women with the beautiful view of the town underneath.

She feels a flutter in her belly. Rajveer reaches out for her hand. She is startled. She can feel the tremble in his hand.

'Raj?'

'Sorry, there was a rat that just passed by. I am petrified of rodents. I just . . . '

'What . . . '

'They are filthy as hell. I faint if they touch me, I'd die . . . ' 'Well . . . '

'My bad,' Rajveer shoots back with a shaky laughter.

Jannat bites the inside of her bottom lip. Right below the cliff there is a graveyard, old and run down. Jannat almost overlooks it. She only notices it because in the bright light of the moon she can see a darker patch, a new grave. The white tombstones re-flect the starry shimmer. Jannat feels a lump in the throat. The thought that someone who was alive a few days ago is under the ground now gives her the chills. *Fear cannot avoid death but it can block the wonderful experience called life.*

Rajveer is confused. *Why did he get her here on a whim? Is he getting too smooth for comfort? Is he sending her the wrong signals?*

Jannat surfaces from her foggy mind. She brushes the negative thought away and glances again at the carpet of lights that is spread as far as the eye can see.

'*What if our life, like a film, is already recorded and simply projected backwards?*

This is the line that made my boyfriend fall for me.'

'I am jealous, Jannat.'

'You are good with words, you should work with May, my cruel Boss.'

'I am good with love too, any candidates?'

'Not me, I am out of the race.'

'Me too, love is death, you lose your "self" in the bargain.'

'The universe was created with the energy of love and that's the truth we go to once we die.'

'This can't be coming from you, Jannat.'

'My mother, she was a poet, she wrote amazing thoughts in her notebook.'

'So it runs in the genes . . .'

'Yeah, even the restlessness. Death is a seductress.'

'Oh, Jannat! Like everything else in life death is also impermanent, it comes and goes, so why think, just fly?'

'So finally you've flown me through all of Jalandhar!'

'I always keep my promises, in life and death, in heaven and in hell.'

This last reference reminds Jannat of what she just saw below. She rubs the back of her neck.

'Talking about death, does this graveyard speak

of some deep dark secret of the people of Jalandhar? Is there a . . . '

'Well my motto is don't tickle the devil, Miss KBK, let him be . . . '

'Runs in your genes it seems.'

She looks at him rather grumpily. They both laugh, brushing away the thought of the graveyard and of death. Their loose limbs plod in silence. His arms silently go around her waist. She shudders with his warm touch. He is going to take me down.

Outside the hotel Jannat sees Rajveer leave. She is waving him goodbye, ready to finally take a shower and go to sleep when he lowers the window one last time. 'Don't forget, Saturday night. Lohri at my place. I've got to go to Delhi for a couple of days but I'll be back . . . '

'I'm really sorry but I don't know if I'll be able to. I've just got so much work and not much time . . . Places to visit, research to . . . '

'I have a feeling I'll see you right here on Saturday evening at 5 pm.

Give the devil his due, Jannat!'

'Well don't bet... I'll see what I can do.You know where to find me.

Anyway the question is, how do I find you?'

Rajveer gives her a flirtatious look. 'I don't know what Englishmen are like, but for Indians, Punjabis in particular, chivalry is still important. I'll find you!'

Jannat enters her room and smells a different fragrance. The scent of her rose-tinted thoughts is floating in the air. 'Every now and then we look for something to fill the void in us . . . and then out of nowhere someone appears and fills it with absolute ease! This is how we experience wonder...wonder, the enchanting breath of the universe . . . '

Jannat switches on her laptop and logs onto her blog. Her fingers are swaying with the scent of mustard across the keypad. The music in her soul decides to peep out.

'When you confess with your breath and not just words
It is love
When you caress him with your eyes and not just your hands
It is love
When you touch her soul in every corner and not just her body
It is love
When you feel his presence more than you feel yours
It is love
When you smell her and not your own perfume
It is love
When love loses, surrenders to pure free flowing energy
It is love
When one spirit holds the other in tenderness
It is love.'

The burgundy walls are wet with vapour. Jannat smothers a cushion between her silky legs. Poetry makes love to the body, Jannat feels relieved.

The next morning as she is finishing her breakfast Jannat is approached by Mr Rai. 'I trust your stay with us has been pleasant so far, Ma'am? Is there . . . '

'Absolutely; it has been amazing!'

'I'm really glad to hear that. I came to inform you that your cab is here. Do you . . . '

'Thank you, Mr Rai.'

As she walks out a dressed monkey welcomes Jannat. At first it's funny to see a monkey dressed like little Abu in *Aladdin.* Then a woman approaches her. She looks very different, very unlike any Indian woman she has seen so far. The first thing Jannat no-tices is a cap (baseball? NBA? Some American sport anyway). The woman wears a khaki shirt and tight black jeans. The first two buttons of her shirt are undone and Jannat can see *Bajrang Bali's* photo pendant disappearing between her breasts. Her chest is thin and her skin is fair, her arms are bare and as she approaches Jannat it's clear that the monkey is with her. It's a friend.

'I'm Chamkaur Choudhary taxi driver. I am unique, not just in Jalandhar but inall of India. Where would you like me to drive you, young lady?'

Jannat is still impressed and a little intimidated by Chamkaur's blunt and yet friendly introduction and only manages to stammer, 'Ludhiana.'

Chamkaur notices that Jannat cannot take her eyes off the monkey. She is not sure if this exotic looking lady is happy about the little one or plain scared.

'She is my sweetheart. Her name is Jhoomri. It's a nice name, right?

She is like a house on fire. Jhoomri, say hello to the NRI beauty?'

Jhoomri extends her furry hand to Jannat to shake. Jannat shakes it reluctantly. Pleased with her diplomatic skills and with the good behaviour exhibited by Jhoomri Chamkaur claps her hands, ready to go. 'So, whereabouts in Ludhiana?' Jannat stares at Chamkaur, unable to refuse or object.

'Fatehgarh village.'

Jannat gets in the car and is amused as Chamkaur picks Jhoomri up and places her on the front seat, fastens her seatbelt and proceeds to spray a generous amount of deo-dorant on herself and the monkey. Jannat stares as the monkey sits quiet, like a well-behaved child, looking around as Chamkaur does this.

'Are we ready to go? Is there . . . '

'Here comes the ride of your life!'

Rajveer is stuck in traffic at the Karnal Toll Gate in Delhi. He plays with his ring to kill time, then takes the cell phone lying on the passenger seat and goes through the pictures he has taken of Jannat during their outing in Jalandhar. He smiles at her face, innocent and unaware of being the subject of his photographs. Minutes later the traffic is cleared and Rajveer's car is sliding through the streets, approaching the suburb of Chanakyapuri, the residential area for the diplomats of the capital.

Rajveer sits on an expensive couch in one of the mansions in the high walled compound. He seems to be completely at ease and not intimidated by this extreme display of wealth all around him.

On the sofa opposite his sits MP Bansal, beaming with anticipation. His fat face is constantly sweating and his cheeks glow in the morning sunshine. A grimace of disgust crosses Rajveer's face. Downstairs he can hear Mrs Bansal and her ugly daughter getting ready to go out and he is extremely grateful he didn't bump into them on his way up.

Rajveer picks up the small briefcase at his feet and hands it to Mr Bansal who had his arms stretched towards Rajveer even before he picked up the parcel. He hands it to the MP, unwilling to make unnecessary conversation.

'The colour of money is the best aphrodisiac Raj, it's getting more and more expensive to be a politician.' He laughs vulgarly. Then in a split second gets grim like a hangman.

'How much is it? Five crores, thank . . .'

'No,Sir, its three. I have cut two for your assignments . . . I gave you a bulk deal, we had . . . '

'Oh . . . so you don't even spare politicians, huh?'

Rajveer smiles as he gets up and straightens his trousers. 'Sir, do politicians ever spare anybody? Business is . . . '

The MP laughs wholeheartedly and walks to his desk, the phone has started ringing and he needs to take the call. Rajveer smiles and disappears before Bansal has a chance to turn around. Bansal goes back to his phone call ' . . . yes, Sir . . . all of them . . .the job is done . . . Time to talk more business . . . we are the reigning emperors of our constituency.'

Meanwhile Jannat is having a harder day than the previous one. Her head is pounding. Wherever she has stopped someone offered tea, and as soon as they found out who she was and what her agenda was they have taken it back and chased her away. It has really been a day of failure. She is unsure if it's because these people don't understand that she wants to help them or they know what might happen if their stories go public.

The truth is that she has spent the whole day driving with Chamkaur from one place to the other and achieving nothing at all. This is disheartening.

She unlocks her iPhone and checks the names of the families she has already visited. She had hoped to do a couple of interviews a day-they would ask her to stay for lunch, they would become friends and they would share photos and other substantial material evidence.

None of that has happened and she's almost running out of witnesses and victims' families three days into her search. What happens to her assignment? May is waiting to crucify her at the first sign of failure. Getting fired for not being able to deliver is definitely not cool in the print media.

She presses her forehead against the window and a tear rolls down her cheek. She's helpless in Punjab, her only three acquaintances are a Rambo-like female cab driver, Mr Rai and that businessman, Rajveer, who has taken her out and given her a fantastic day but keeps a gun in his car. Should I start from the gun? In the end it's the first re-levant thing I saw . . .

He said he needs the gun for protection. Protection against whom?

What does he do or has he done for someone to want him dead?

And suddenly her mind flashes to Saturday, Lohri. She's going to have free access to his house and to his family. How could she not discover something there?

11

Chamkaur stops the car in front of a dhaba on the highway lined on both sides with mustard fields. Jannat looks at the yellow flowers and her mind goes back for a moment to the day before-such sweet memories.

The driver turns around and tells Jannat to stay in the car.

Well, where else am I supposed to go? There's nothing around here . . .

Nothing except some truck drivers sitting at the tables outside the *dhaba* enjoying a meal, a drink or playing cards.

Chamkaur walks straight into a phone booth. She doesn't look at them. If she had looked she would know that there are people she knows playing cards at the corner table. She doesn't look but they notice her. A woman driving a cab in man's clothes doesn't go unnoticed around here . . .

Meanwhile Jannat is in the car, bored and unsure what to do next. Finding out more about Rajveer could be an idea, but he's most likely carrying a gun just to protect himself from . . . anything really . . . She's not sure he has been threatened and even if he has been, why will he spill the beans to her? Business is business. In the end his family has had a successful construction business for three generations. Everyone knows them, why on earth would he risk his life and the lives of his family by sharing any information (if he has it!) on contract killing?

She's pulled out of her reverie by the sound of glass smashing. It's not a broken glass. This is bigger. A car crash?

Jhoomri is excited and jumps about in the car. Jannat isn't sure what she's supposed to do.She can't see anything seated here. She gets out of the car at once and goes to look in the direction of the phone booth. She just remembered the small cabin is made of glass. It's the only thing made of glass.

As she walks past one of the big Tata trucks parked in front of the cab the scene before her eyes is terrifying-four men have smashed the glass of thebooth where Chamkaur was using the phone. She's trapped inside the metal skeleton with a man on each of the four sides. There's no way out.

Jannat doesn't know what to do. She would call the police if only she had saved the number . . . But these people want to hurt her, they are going to be fast, there's no time for police here . . .

As she stands there, thinking, she sees Chamkaur kick one of the thugs in the crotch. The man bends over in pain, leaving a little space for her to leave the phone booth. Fast as lightning she pulls out of her breast pocket the deodorant that Jannat saw her spray on Jhoomri before and sprays it in the eyes of the three thugs who are still standing.

They start screaming and calling her names which Jannat doesn't understand.Chamkaur uses all her might and kicks one of them hard in the belly. The other two also collapse as she holds their heads and bangs them against each other. 'Powerful instincts,' Jannat observes.

Chamkaur runs to the car, fast, screaming to Jannat and Jhoomri to get back in. The man she kicked in the belly is right behind her. He's evidently the oldest, more used to solving things the hard way when something goes wrong. Jannat can see that he's in pain, but he runs. He wants to get Chamkaur and there's nothing that can stop him.

Jannat fetches Jhoomri just in time to get back in the car. Chamkaur follows, she's breathless but she's not going to let this thug take what she risked her life to get.

When Chamkaur finally reaches the car and takes the driver's seat she breathes deeply. For a moment the world is still and soundless.

Then, with a grimace of terror, she lifts her head up as something cold strokes her neck. The window! Shit! The window!

Jannat had opened the driver's window when Chamkaur left to freshen the air in the car. The thug, not too far from Chamkaur, has reached the car and pulled out a revolver, pointing it at them.

'Oh shit! What the hell's going on? Chamkaur?'

But Chamkaur is as terrified as her and there are very few things she can say to calm Jannat.

'Madam, just don't react. He is just trying to scare you. Stay calm. I will take charge.'

Why the hell did I expect her to be cool or have an answer ready? Of course she's worried. She's being chased by this brute and now has a gun pointing at her brain . . . She needs to calm down.

'Bitch . . . you sprayed into my partners eyes . . . you kicked me hard. You are going against Thakur.

Now I will take you to Thakur, he will straighten you to hell.'

Jannat thinks aloud, 'Oh Jesus, there is going to be more terror, I should have . . . '

The thug, having heard a voice in the back, picks up a stone from the ground and, without moving the gun from the driver's head, smashes the window on Jhoomri's side. Without the pale sun reflecting off the car window he can finally see what's in the back, and he must admit this is more than he could expect. He's an ugly customer. One eye has been sewn shut after some previous injury, so he rubs the single eye from which he can still see. He looks vicious to the core. 'Before I shoot you in the chest, drive quickly to Thakur's den. You know the way, you sly rat, I will . . . '

The sight of the neatly dressed Jannat is a gift he didn't expect but which he is willing to share with his friends. He looks at her, his mouth watering and his one eye burning with desire. He whistles to call his friends, but they are still trying to get rid of the deodorant in their eyes and they take turns at the *dhaba's* washbasin. They are temporarily blinded.

The scar-faced man looks at Jannat and is almost happy he can enjoy her all by himself. The grip on the gun loosens but it's still too strong for Chamkaur to move.

Chamkaur looks at Jannat in the rearview mirror. 'We have found his weak spot, now let's use it,' her eyes seem to say to Jannat who is still frightened but also relieved to know that there's something they can use to beat him. Besides he's outnumbered. He's alone and they are two. And a half.

Jannat recalls all the erotica she has read. What a shameless way to use it. She promptly starts to touch her thighs. She rolls her beautiful hand slowly on her legs, stopping at the zip of her tight jeans, just to tease, and then going up onto the very tight black leather jacket. The man cannot take his eyes off her. She bites her lower lip and arches her back, pushing her chest forward, and her breasts nearly explode under the shiny jacket.

She keeps her eyes closed; these things are easier to do if you don't see the face of the stinking brute in front of you.

The man takes all her movements in, as if he was learning a lesson, and, as soon as Jannat starts unzipping her jacket revealing a fair-skinned, full, perfect chest, the man can't take it anymore. He loosens the grip on the gun trying to reach Jannat with the other hand.

Chamkaur is faster than him. As soon as she feels the cold pressure of the barrel move from her neck she spins around and takes it, pointing it at the man.

'You stinking prick! You want flesh? Now lick your own.'

The man panics, he's not used to this turn of events. He usually takes what hewants without asking and he's never had to run for his life. But this time it is exactly what he has to do. He turns around, bends away from the damn barrel and runs for his life.

Chamkaur is not willing to drive away and let go, even though it is what Jannat would beg her to do. She calmly gets out of the car, lifts the gun and aims at the man.

The world stops for a split second; the air is filled with gunpowder that pricks her no-strils and the sound of a bullet out of a gun, nothing like she had ever heard before, absorbs every other sound.

The world starts anew. It's like a bomb. You open your eyes and see how the world has changed; in Jannat's world there is a man on the ground, ten metres away from her.

As they drive past the man lying on the floor Jannat notices he has only been hit in the leg, Chamkaur rolls her window down and pulls out the gun, aiming at the head this time. Jannat holds her breath. She doesn't know if she can face the fear of the sound and smell of the shooting twice in a day. The man turns around and looks at them, joining his hands to beg Chamkaur not to kill him. Chamkaur stares at him threateningly. She wanted to simply warn him. She closes the window and throws the gun in the glove compartment, leaving the man on the ground, choking on the dust left lingering in the air by the wheels.

They drive in silence for a while, until Jannat gathers the courage to simply ask, 'What the hell was that?'

Chamkaur's phone rings. She it picks up, pretending not to notice Jannat's question, or probably using the timing of the phone call to make up a reasonable excuse. Jannat is gasping for breath, she feels choked in her throat. *Am I in the midst of a gang war?* The little monkey has regained her place in the passenger's seat like it's just another day in paradise. Jannat curses under her breath while sitting right next to the shattered glass that lets in the icy air. Conspiracy Chamkaur?

'Namaste, Sirji. I tried to call you from the phone booth so that I am not traced by your moles. Since your cell was off I spoke to Inspector Yadav from the PCO. Sirji Raja Thakur and his gang tried to attack me. He sent four bastards. But I took care of them and packed them off. My information is bang on. Raja has hidden a large amount of heroin in the dry well behind his Phillaur farmhouse. Raid it right now. *Jai Hind*.'

Two minutes earlier Jannat wanted to ask Chamkaur to be dropped off, now the scenario has changed. 'So you are a police informer.'

'I've been ten years in this field. I drive a taxi for a living and I work as a police informer for self-respect. Sounds very *filmi*, right?'

There's a minute of silence at the end of which both Jannat and Chamkaur burst out into hearty laugh. Jhoomri, unaware of what the two just said but feeling a lighter, more cheerful atmosphere around her claps her hands.

'I was a good-for-nothing village girl, the tomboy of the hamlet, playing football with the boys and drinking cheap beer in the afternoons. One day I kicked the football so hard it broke the windscreen of a police jeep passing by. The sub-inspector on duty reprimanded me. He was handsome and available and I was too smart for a woman in a village.

We got arrested in love. It was fireworks instantly. Two young passionate Punjabis. We put the neighbouring sugarcane fields to flames, if you know what I mean. He was honest and wanted to bust the drug traffickers in his area of jurisdiction. One day he got a bogus call for a raid and was trapped by the drug mafia. Two of his constables and he were driving a jeep when some unidentified truck came and hit them from behind. They went off the road straight into an oncoming state transport bus . . .'

Jannat is teary eyed. She wonders about the impermanence of life. Chamkaur steers the cab over a rough patch of the road with absolute control.

'That's when I found my purpose. My calling. I decided to become an informer thanks to my boyfriend's connections and started passing any vital information I could collect driving my taxi all around Punjab.'

'He will be proud of you. I believe that's the best way to stay with him, complete the task he was working on.'

'That's too deep for me. Anyway, let's cheer to that with a stiff drink?'

Chamkaur turns the car and parks it on the side of the road, by a small bar. They all need a drink and something to eat. Chamkaur fetches a new deodorant spray and washes herself in it, then showers Jhoomri who sneezes copiously but then jumps out of the car, happy to be in a place where she can eat. Chamkaur sits still, considering whether or not she should take the gun. Jannat pretends to look for something in her bag as she waits to see what she will do.

The place where they have stopped is full of shady characters, faces that can get instantly cast for the

Indian version of *Pirates of the Caribbean.* The only thing that seems to be a little reassuring for Jannat is that Chamkaur seems to know all of them. A few of them raise their glasses of cheap whiskey when they sit down and some others simply drop a hello to the funny-looking trio. Some of the local youth seem to be chasing their drink with a dose of cocaine. Jannat is amused by the menu written on the slate-Dollar Rum, Raspberry, Cash Whiskey, First Choice, Patiala Rose. *I could always do a story on them.*

Jannat is unsure what to do next. The day seems to have been pretty intense up until now. She wouldn't mind going back to the hotel, but in terms of the work done she's where she was at in the morning. Unless Chamkaur . . .

Chamkaur is sitting silently at the side of the table. She looks around, drinking the same cheap whiskey as everybody else. Her eyes fall on Jannat-her shoes, her hair-cut, her clothes, and the iPhone she's looking at. There's plenty of photos of Indian people and Indian families, but only one with Jannat in it.

There's another woman; they are smiling, they seem happy.

'Looks like you. Sister, is she…?'

'No, she is my friend… She is no more. She came to Punjab all the way from London to meet her parents but died in a train accident, she…'

'Oh, are you sure that this was an accident and nothing messier?'

'What?'

'I mean a lot of NRIs die in Punjab when they come for a holiday or to meet their relatives.

It's not always a coincidence. Often it's a murder, a contract killing, or a . . . '

'Nah…why would anybody kill Preet? She got married into a big Indian family settled in the UK. She didn't have any enemies. Preet was . . . '

'Did you say Preet?'

'Preet Randhawa. Train accident . . . '

'It sounds so familiar.'

Chamkaur makes a sign to attract the waiter's attention and then goes out the back door. He follows her a few minutes after. Outside they speak for a few minutes, constantly watching to check if there may be any unwanted visitors. The waiter, a middle aged well built guy, talks confidently. Chamkaur is all ears.

12

Chamkaur goes back inside. She finds Jannat, whose eyes reveal her exhaustion, playing tic-tac-toe with Jhoomri. A month ago Jannat was in Paris doing a story on a street artist and now she is in the heart of the crime belt of Punjab searching for her story. Whoever said you must go out on adventures to find out where you belong? A plate of stale French fries lies on the table. Ah, these Europeans . . . who would order fries here?

Chamkaur places a few rupees on the filthy plastic tablecloth and simply says, 'Let's go!'

'Where to?'

'Preet Randhawa's house . . . '

Jannat is a little overwhelmed by this news. Her feelings are stirred and at once she's fully alert. *Should I go?* I just met this girl. She's good and all but she's also one who didn't have a problem pulling out a gun and shooting a man in the leg. India seems to be populated only by people who have guns.

They get in the car and Chamkaur speeds off as Jannat has now learnt she's used to doing. A few minutes later they find a road sign-Taanda 13 km. Jannat's hands start sweating as they always did when she was nervous.

Chamkaur stops the car a few times to ask for directions. She is in full control of the situation so Jannat doesn't dare ask questions. The rest of their drive proceeds in silence.

For a change Jhoomri looks out of the window in absolute calm.

Preet's parents open their house to Jannat. They have never met her, but Preet often spoke of her. Jannat sits in silence in their modest home, a typical Punjabi house.

They are not rich people. Preet came to England on a scholarship; otherwise they could never have paid for her education. Despite their modest conditions and the small house the atmosphere is warm. An Indian heater keeps the temperature in check. Jannat and Chamkaur are welcomed with steaming cups of tea and the wedding album. She looks at it, tears in her eyes, but with a serene expression on her face, like Preet's. These parents taught her to look at the world's inner beauty. She can tell from their expressions that they suffer, but their pain is muted. Preet's radiant eyes were a gift of this elderly couple. Their large pupils swear that they still haven't lost faith in a supreme power where they expect Preet's soul rests now. There is an infinite distance between them but sometimes they sense that the matrix blurs. They can feel her presence, her purity.

The father sits on a chair by the window; he looks outside at nothing with his deep gaze. Jannat finds a hint of a resolute man. He's now old and frail, but under his thin skin strong bones emerge. Life has bent him but not broken his soul.

It must have been hard for Preet, much harder than Jannat could ever imagine. She came from this rustic town and yet her English was so good, her grades were high and she had a good job in London. She must have been highly impressed when she met Harry, the fairy tale prince with a charming personality. The very Harry Jannat found superfluous, yet he was her passport to escape from this life of evident vacuum. I wonder what she must have felt to come to this again, thinking that her life in England was so opulent-her home in a posh neighbourhood, her high-profile in-laws.

And yet she came to this *pind* to see her ageing parents for whom England was a far away land, somewhere out there, for those who had never even been out of Punjab. Jannat notices a map pinned to the wall. Without a frame to hold them down, the sides and the corners have started to roll over. Russia has nearly disappeared under a huge roll. There are two small flags, like the ones you find on tropical cocktails, one pinned on the village of Taanda and the other one on London. Preet had creatively tried to educate her parents about her new home.

The photos of the wedding-a smiling Preet, an average-looking bride, her outfit, her handsome husband, her colourful wedding-take Jannat back to a past when Preet was still alive.

Her mother tells her how she died: 'She had gone to visit Fatehpur Sikri near Taj Mahal. She was very fond of heritage sites and called us after visiting the tomb of the Sufi saint Salim Chishti. She was sounding poetic, over the moon. That night, on a train from Agra to Urmar Tanda, Preet received a call-the fellow passengers confessed she left the compartment to avoid disturbing the other commuters and then she wasn't there anymore. Someone pushed her out of the train. The police investigated and came to the conclusion that she either committed suicide or fell down in an accident, no one can say for certain.

'Village folk claimed she committed suicide. That she fought with her husband and mother-in-law and abandoned them due to her emotional instability. That's how the village ladies gossip. Maybe somebody poisoned their minds. But I know Preet would never end her own life. She personified life, not death,' declares her mother amidst gentle sobs.

Preet's father is miserable, his face soaked in tears.

Jannat gets up and goes to him, hugging him with all the love Preet would have put in this hug. Only when he touches her face, her nose, her eyelids and her chin, does Jannat realise that he's blind. She feels a lump in her heart, like her heart has stopped pumping blood for a second.

Providence. If he had seen his daughter's smashed face he wouldn't be sitting alive.

'My child, go back. You have no business to be here. I have already lost my daughter. It can't be undone. I don't want to lose my daughter's friend for a futile investigation.'

13

His sobs shake his frail body. His chest vibrates under his heavy breathing. The pain of losing your loving daughter at the age when you are too old to handle emotions can get difficult. But the soul of an honest man, a doting father, a believer in truth, binds it all together. Having lost her own mother at a tender age Jannat knows that if she stays a minute longer she could torment them beyond repair.

As she leaves the house Jannat's eyes look different. Chamkaur notices it and for once is silent. Jannat is in a totally different world, a world where her usual calm and sweet self is turned into a demon. This is not about her writing anymore. This is about the truth, the small justice that she can bring to humanity. She knows only too well that this uprightness will not bring Preet back. Preet's parents know that well and that is also why they haven't gone too far to bring home justice. They live in their modest home, filled with English goods, a British Airways blanket, a gigantic stuffed toy dressed as one of the Queen's guards, a portrait of Preet under the Big Ben and a designer tea set left unused. Their souls have long departed, their bodies are serving the life term that fate has imposed on them.

But Jannat has reached a dead end. She has to accept total defeat. If Preet's parents won't speak chances are nobody else will. She has already had a couple of narrow escapes.

Is it worth it?

She's angry as her mind spins in discord. Her friend's life has been taken cruelly. Preet was not a journalist from England, or a spy. Her only connections to this God-forsaken place were her lonely parents. There was not one good reason to kill her. And after the story of the fall from the train and the planted rumours Jannat knows only too well that Preet has been murdered. She would have never committed suicide. She was unhappy the last time they spoke, but there was no reason at all for her to jump from a train. Not a reason in the world.

Without a word Chamkaur parks the car in front of *Baba Bhole Peer* temple and ties Jhoomri with a chain to the door handle. She rummages in the glove box to find a headscarf. The scarf is not there but she has found a handkerchief and she'll make do. It's her ritual. She believes it keeps her safe on the wild roads of Punjab. As she ties the red kerchief around her head, to cover the hair before walking into the shrine, she turns around. Jannat is not there. Jhoomri sleeps peacefully on the passenger's seat. Lifting her gaze Chamkaur spots Jannat at the street stall. She's buying a headscarf and some flowers for the offering. Chamkaur smiles.

The two proceed to the tombstone of the *peer* and pay their respects. Despite the noise made by the priests and the worshippers the place emanates peace. The air smells of sandalwood. In the centre of the foyer a spiral pool of white smoke ascends towards the clear skies. Jannat uploads a few fantastic pictures on her Instagram.

In a corner a group of singers are rendering Sufi songs; their voices are the most rustic that Jannat has ever heard. They are lost in their self-hypnotic performance. However there is a deep sense of truth in their expression. They are invoking the path of truth. The lyrics are profound and advocate the truth-when your purpose and the purpose of creation align with each other the universe becomes your navigator. Both Jannat and Chamkaur seem to be at peace for the first time on this strange day. A Sufi priest gives them sugar candies and they eat it in silence, each lost in her thoughts. Sufi music trickles to their inner consciousness.

Unable to guess what Chamkaur is thinking Jannat stares blankly in front of her, seeing things but not registering them.

She remembers a day in the London tube station when she was waiting in line to buy her ticket only to discover that she didn't have enough coins. Preet was standing be-hind her and had bought her the ticket home. That's the first time they met. She did it with a smile, but Jannat now understands what it must have meant for Preet. She remembers the noon they went for lunch at Green Park. The morning when she was reading quietly in the tube and raised her head when someone called her name loudly; it was Preet. The day they went for an Indian movie in Leicester Square. The art show they attended at the National Gallery. The first time they went to 'their' cafe, that damn cafe where Preet never turned up and where Jannat decided not to look for her. Jannat blinks twice, as if brought back to reality by something around her. Nothing has changed, only the string of memories has been interrupted. Time is elusive but memory is a soulmate.

Back in the car they drive away without speaking. By the time the old cab pulls over in front of the Amar Hotel it's well into the night. Jannat wraps herself up in her jacket and shakes Jhoomri's small hand.

'Think once again, madam. You are playing with dangerous people.'

'Enough of thinking, Chamkaur! Preet's story will soon be on the front page of *World Weekly* . . . remember the Sufi song . . . it's my anthem from now on,'

Jannat says with pride.

Chamkaur is cautious. 'Discretion is the better part of valour. You are new to this area.'

'I can always return to the UK. I will cover other stories from other parts of the world. I will have a row of trophies on my mantel. But will I be able to sleep peacefully with a conscience that stinks of hypocrisy? The demons of cowardice will haunt me wherever I tread. The blind stare of Preet's father will wake me up in the middle of my dreams. The unbridled pain of Preet's ailing mother will choke me every time I dine on oysters and wine.'

The silence of the night slices through the sentiments of two women.

Jannat pays a sum of money to Chamkaur who doesn't take it straight away.

'Consider this as a token for my friend Jhoomri . . . *Jai Hind.*'

They shake hands. There is more to be said and heard. But not tonight, tonight is for sleeping, for facing one's own monsters and deciding whether to silence them or take them on. Tomorrow the sun will rise again. Will tomorrow be a day of change? Who is to say? But tonight decisions will compete against each other for a winner.

Chamkaur leaves the conversation without another word. Did she want to give part of the money back? Did she want to thank Jannat? Jannat will never know, not tonight anyway. The lady cabbie drives away, her engine roaring on the gravel lane.

14

The early morning sun shines outside the Khanna residence, a white mansion of an old design, not one of those glass buildings they make nowadays. The Khannas have been living here for generations. The sun has for years cast its light on their pride and a shade over their dark deeds.

On the terrace of the second floor the older members of the family are eating break-fast. Puneet Khanna, Rajveer's father, the head of the family, is drinking a glass of milk.In the plate in front of him are some fruits and peeled almonds. But he doesn't eat; he is reading the newspaper. He will only start eating once the reading is over. At his side, Ranjeet, his younger brother, is also reading the paper while dunking a biscuit in a cup of tea.

Rajveer's mother and his aunt are in the kitchen. Their morning ritual is to prepare breakfast for everyone and a tray for Rajveer who consumes the first part of his breakfast, a cup of steaming masala tea, in his room.

Chaman stands quietly by the side of the two women in a spotless uniform, looking carefully at their every movement and calculating the exact time when his service will be required. He seldom fails. As soon as the flower sits tidily by the cup and the linen napkin is folded softly on the silver tray it's time. He lifts the tray, adds the morning mail and carries the tray upstairs where he will wake up the young man by opening the curtains of the room. Rajveer has often shouted him at for doing so, but he takes or-der directly from Puneet Khanna, and if he says his son must be woken every morn-ing at eight that's exactly what will be done.

As the Nepali servant walks into the room he puts the tray on the bedside table and knocks twice before proceeding to open the curtains. Chaman has served in this house for many years but can't really be said to have feelings for any of them. There's something uncanny about the men in the Khanna family; he cannot look them in the eye, because when he does he begins to shiver. It is as though they are encased in a thin layer of steel, or ice.

His mother once told him that sinful people have flames in their eyes. Maybe it's the 'strictly business' attitude of the menfolk. They never discuss work in front of the la-dies, treating them as inferiors. If there are any urgent matters to be discussed the men assemble in the office in the outhouse. The inconspicuous cabin is made of dark wood and glass and erected right across the black stone fountain that hosts thirsty pigeons in the summer.

And it's not without subtle pleasure that Chaman wakes up Rajveer every morning with a knock, making sure to make the most obnoxious sound a couple of knuckles can make when hitting a wooden table.

Rajveer doesn't acknowledge him. He came back late last night and is now sprawled on the bed, hoping to fall asleep again. But the morning light forces his eyes open and he has to get up and go to the bathroom. He turns the hot water on and disappears from the eyes of the servant in a cloud of steam. Above him the vermillion sun on the ceiling smiles efficiently, ordered to be painted by his mother to protect him.

Minutes later Rajveer is on the terrace with the rest of his family. His feet stride confidently on the white marble floor. His father has personally designed the vine etching on the floor and the walls so that the porch merges with the Amaltas trees in the compound. The golden green tree will be ready to blossom in a couple of months. Puneet is feeding biscuits to Tommy, the golden Labrador that has been with the fam-ily for years.

Tommy, old and lazy, wags his tail, happy to have escaped chachiji's eye and enjoying the biscuits.

Rajveer is freshly shaved and in a cheerful mood, ready for a morning conversation. He touches his mother's feet and then his father's.

'God bless, son. Bittu, get me some paratha for Tommy, he seems famished.'

Rajveer greets his uncle Ranjeet with a faint smile. Ranjeet doesn't say anything but pats him on the shoulder. They are all smiling. They are pleased with him, as if he was a hero coming back from the battlefield, which, in a wayhe is.

Just then Bittu, Rajveer's younger cousin and Ranjeet's daughter, comes in with a plate filled with parathas. She serves Puneet first.

'Happy Lohri ji...'

Rajveer puts a hand on her head like an older brother would do and ruffles her hair.

'O rabba, I completely forgot, Happy Lohri...'

He pulls up a chair next to his father, helping himself to a large portion of stuffed parathas.

'The goods have been delivered on schedule, uncle?'

Puneet decides not to participate in the conversation. He continues to chew his almonds, slowly and carefully. He pats Tommy and feeds him a piece of paratha from under the white tablecloth.

Puneet remains as silent as a tomb. His brother nods and follows his example. They do not speak. Rajveer doesn't acknowledge the silence, still trying to fully wake up. He slurps his glass of thick buttermilk. As the silence grows Rajveer notices the atmosphere is heavy, there's something that needs to be discussed and is still not mentioned. He slowly lifts his eyes from the plate and looks at his uncle. Their eyes meet.

Ranjeet takes out a silver cigarette case from the inside pocket of his jacket and casually mixes tobacco in the palm of his hand and rolls a cigarette.

Rajveer takes his time to finish eating, pretending to enjoy every mouthful. Once he is done he cleans his fingers on the immaculate lace napkin by his side. He drinks some water and then looks at his uncle again. This time he nods and fixes his gaze on the newspaper.

Rajveer casually takes the newspaper from the table, as if to kill time until somebody else starts a new conversation, and flips nonchalantly through the pages.

Just then a small group of children appear singing the traditional Lohri songs. For a moment the atmosphere is cheerful, the young children with their sweet force even Puneet to smile.

Sundar Mundariye

Tera kaun vichara ho

Dulla Bhatti walla ho

Dulle ne ti viahiyi ho

Saer Shakar payiho

Kudi de boje payee ho

Shallu kaun samete ho

The children are given money and sugar *chikkis.*

Rajveer stands up right after and prepares to leave.

His aunt runs out of the kitchen. 'Son, come on time today. We need to participate in *the puja.'* 'Yes, *chachiji.* I will be back in timewith a gift for the family.'

'Am I in luck or am I in luck? Rajveer brings home a surprise this evening . . .

God willing. I am excited. *Rab rakkhe*, son.'

They all laugh aloud. Rajveer manages to leave without having to give further explanations. Ranjeet keeps rolling his cigarette. He's ostentatious and he does it with the sole purpose of annoying his brother. And he manages well too. As soon as the children and Rajveer are gone Puneet gives him a disgusted look and leaves. He hasn't noticed that the newspaper is not on the table anymore. Ranjeet smiles to himself. Just then Bittu comes out of the kitchen to clear the table.

'Cigarette smoking is injurious to health, *papaji!*'

'Only smoking them...not rolling them. Now get going!'

'I will! In just a few months I will be in Australia studying . . . Then you guys will know how much you'll miss me!'

Ranjeet hugs her affectionately. In the distance a phone rings.

In Jannat's room the pale light of the morning is filtering through the white curtains.

She keeps her eyes closed. Yesterday was the longest day of her life and there's no reason on earth she would get up before noon today. No reason on earth.

A sound is piercing through her brain. At first she thinks she's making it up. It's the sense of guilt, she thinks, but then she realizes it's her phone. She gets out of bed, not so much to take the call as to make it stop ringing. The duvet has created a warm bubble in which she slept peacefully; now the relatively colder room makes her skin prickle. I swear I'm going to kill whoever is calling at this hour...

The display reads 'Boss from Hell.' *Oh, great... really great start of a glorious day . . .*

'Hi May!'

At the other end she can tell May has just called to make sure she's not dead and is otherwise busy filing her perfect nails or getting a massage in her gigantic personal spa.

'Thank God you're alive! Seventy-two hours go by and not a single call from you.

I was beginning to think the Taliban had had you for breakfast or something . . . '

'Yeah, except that I'm in India, not in Afghanistan . . . '

'Well, whatever . . . Now fill me in. Any progress? Caught any murderers yet?'

Jannat can detect a hint of humour in her tone.

Did she send me all the way here to tease me? On a mock assignment? Am I the afternoon joke that she would share with her boyfriends for high tea? I have been given research material that somebody has randomly collected. Is it all staged as a punishment? But the magazine pays for the travel, the hotel bills and other expenses; it's an expensive punishment . . . But then it's May!

'Not yet, but it's coming along fine.'

'That's not good enough, Gill. Listen, I was wondering, maybe you can do a daily report from Punjab, yeah? We add something to a month that is otherwise so utterly boring for you, okay?'

'Well actually . . . '

'Let me be clear, Gill, I used my nice tone the first time. It's not a request that you can turn down, it's an assignment.'

Jannat is too tired and too cold to argue. She pretends there's not enough network coverage and closes the call by blowing straight into the phone.

'Buzzzzzz. Kkkhhhhhhh . . . Sorry May, network's failing . . . You there? Hello??? kkkkhhhhhh, kkhhhhhh, buzzzz . . . '

Damn you, May! Now I'm so awake . . .

She walks to her laptop, switches it on and begins her research. She's looking for the number of the Jalandhar Police NRI Department. She calls the operator and asks to be put in contact with the number she has found online.

'NRI Department, Jalandhar City.'

'Oh, hi... Good morning, my name is Jannat

Gill. I'm wondering if I could please make an appointment to speak with your senior officer handling the case for Preet Randhawa.

She was killed in a train accident a few months ago. I am her friend from London.'

'Please hold.'

The voice at the other end sounds bored and monotonous. It's clearly someone who answers calls all day long. Jannat fears he'll have her waiting for a bit and then tell her the person is not in the office. She prays to herself to find someone to talk to about Preet.

Suddenly the phone clicks.

'Okay, come at noon. Ask for Officer Kawaljeet Deol. He handled Preet Randhawa's case.'

'That was very nice of you, thank . . . '

But the man has hung up. She smiles, content with how the morning is turning out, and tucks herself back under the blanket. A quick nap before the devil knocks.

15

Across the world, in Toronto, a TV blares in an expensive living room on the twentieth floor of a building. A man is watching it. He's well dressed and has a glass of whisky before him. Considering the number of fingerprints that stain it, it's not the first scotch of the day. In his hand there's a calling card, one of those small cards with a pin number that allows access to an account with a predetermined number of mi-nutes on it.

He scratches the silver layer onto the floor. Someone else will clean the flakes for him. Without ever moving his eyes from the screen he dials the number and almost instantly the nasal voice of the operator, a pre-recorded voice from Eastern Europe, welcomes him in her bland tone.

'Welcome. Please dial the pin number from your calling card followed by the phone number you want to call and press hash.'

The man is forced to lower his gaze from the screen. He punches the number on the keys, quickly and nervously. At the other end a phone rings.

In Jalandhar the office of the local newspaper is full of life. Men look like ants running from one place to another, sipping tea and smoking nervously until the newspaper goes to the press. Then the cycle will break for a couple of hours and start again the next day. The office is covered in paper, news clippings, photos of some of the contributors' families and trophies from some local journalistic prize won by someone a long time ago.

In the Advertising and Classified Department, a small room in the corner, a little quieter but still at the heart of the whirlpool of words, a phone rings. The clerk, over-whelmed by what surrounds him, takes a few minutes before realizing it's his phone that is ringing and then picks it up.

'Hello? Yes, right, correct, got it.' As he is talking he makes a note on a piece of paper.

Once the phone is back where it should be, under a pile of old issues of the paper, he types on the old typewriter that still dominates his office, Jyotish Talwar Bedi.

The next day a delivery boy wakes up before dawn, leaves his home and goes to collect a pile of newspapers to deliver. He has always been his job and hopes itcontinues. As a child he grew up on the streets and lived inside a station, doing odd jobs without ever going to school. Then, thanks to the many newspapers he found abandoned at the end of the busy day inside the station, he learned to read. From that day there has been no stopping him.

Now that he has this job, it's not exciting. He goes from home to home delivering newspapers. But sometimes a cook gives him a cup of *chai*, sometimes a *samosa*; he has his little rituals and for someone like him this is touching the sky.

He delivers to a house where a man wearing a gold ring, with an eagle embossed on it, races through it. His forefinger goes straight to the advertising section. He takes his time to read all the advertisements; he does it carefully, almost as if he tasted each word. Then his forefinger stops where he finds what he was looking for, an astrology advertisement. Generally these adverts have some sort of design, a crystal ball, a third eye, but this one is rather plain, it simply reads, 'Jyotish Talwar Bedi, astrologer, avail-able in Jalandhar.' Next to it there's an international phone number. The man with the eagle ring takes the cap off his red pen and circles it. He then takes the paper and rolls it, filling it with dried tobacco, in the style of a cigarette.

Meanwhile, in Toronto, the phone in the spotless house rings. The TV is off. The man looks more casually dressed. He picks up the phone and a neutral voice starts speaking without sparing a minute for greetings.

'Where can I find the astrologer?'

'Thirteenth January. 9 pm. Hoshiarpur road, Bedi Farms. Give me your fax number,' requests the Indian Canadian man. As he speaks he goes to the fax machine, turns it on and sends a document sitting there, ready to be sent over.

In Jalandhar the man with the eagle ring holds the call. He hears the beep of the fax.

Instinctively he looks in the direction of his own machine and the photo of a man comes through. This is Talwar Bedi.

'Received. Thank you. Send the box of sweets on time,' the man with the eagle ring picks up the photo and leaves. Only when the line goes dead does he realise that the call is over. He looks outside the window and quickly dials another number. This time it's Canadian. He waits impatiently for someone to pick up.

'Tony. Five kilograms of rose *barfi*. Deliver it to Guptaji in Jalandhar.'

Back in India the man with the eagle ring is holding a cigarette in his hands. He creeps to the back of Rajveer's office building. He stands out with his expensive leather jacket and black leather shoes, his protruding belly and gaudy ring. Suddenly from the thick shrubbery a man jumps out. This is the messenger.

'Guptaji, *namaste*,' the messenger greets.

Gupta silently passes on the cigarette and a fax printout to the messenger and walks back to the front entrance of the glass building. He looks around for any trail. There is none.

The messenger runs through the thicket and jumps into a busy lane. He catches a bus and is soon surrounded by the locals. He alights on the highway and enters a tannery oddly located inside a junkyard. But he's at ease; he has come here many times. His only fear is the man waiting upstairs. He stops in his path, looks up at the mezzanine level, musters courage and proceeds.

The place is all that the rest of world doesn't want to see or even know exists-bony men with only loin cloths around their waists stand in small pools filled with coloured water. The heat from the steaming, needed to fix the colours of the raw skins, is un-bearable and the smell of dead flesh enters one's nostrils, strangling from the inside.

The messenger goes up a few flights and meets Moga who is waiting for him at the top of the spiral staircase. The room is sunlit only by cracks in the wall. Moga ogles at him like a hyena. The man has lived and worked in this tannery for so long, the messenger has thought more than once that all the chemicals must have twisted his brain. Moga's cold expression can make the devil piss his pants. The terror that he has bestowed upon others is etched all over his face.

The two don't speak. The messenger hands Moga two cigarettes. One is a little darker than the other. Moga puts one in his mouth and lights it and casually breaks the other one, spilling the tobacco on the floor. He reads what's written on the paper an India Canadian guru, a name and number. He rips the paper and throws it in a puddle of coloured water on the floor. The messenger rolls out a printout to expose a face. Moga looks at it for a few seconds, licks the picture with the look of a cannibal and then burns it with his cigarette. The devilish grin is covered in charred smoke. The messenger chokes on his saliva.

Rajveer's SUV pulled over at a construction site. His uncle and he get off the car and walk around the property, visibly impressed with the progress of work. This is what they do. It's what they have done for generations. In the new India no building should be lower than ten floors, no family should live in a house smaller than a two BHK. And the Khannas are there to provide what new India wants. They enter the office building where they are greeted by the staff. On the walls there are photographs and advertisements of computer-generated facades of hotel projects. Miniature designs of hotel structures under glass cases are scattered around the office for investors to see. Ranjeet is fascinated by the business of running hotels. He has big plans to construct a chain of hotels across Punjab.

After having exchanged greetings Rajveer and his uncle Ranjeet enter a smaller office, the one normally used for private meetings. The room is small and the glass walls glazed to protect the privacy of meetings, solely because the nature of the business is not always transparent.

Inside the office a man, Gupta, is waiting for them. He is not too tall, with a severely receding hairline and a protruding belly. On his forefinger there's the eagle ring.

'*Chai,* Sirji?'

'Not now. We are in a hurry. Let's get to business, its . . . '

'Oh yes. Just received a delivery order from Canada for five kilograms of rose *barfi.*'

Ranjeet looks at Rajveer.

'Cigarette smoked right, Guptaji?'

Uncle and nephew exchange a glance and Ranjeet nods.

Rajveer can take charge of the conversation.

'One kilo rose *barfi.*'

'Sure. Should I withdraw or you want to transfer?'

Rajveer looks at Ranjeet who nods one more time.

'Half needs to be withdrawn, the other half needs to be sent to Melbourne on this address.'

'No problem . . . '

Gupta gives out a hearty laugh and strikes his foot on the floor three times.

He is standing over a foxhole with a perfect mechanism that stocks and transports cash. Clean money. Laundered money.

In no time the process begins. A man waiting for Gupta's signal whistles to somebody else who takes out a stack of banknotes and wraps them in newspaper.

In the back-ground are several men counting and wrapping piles of money.

The money is loaded on a vertical chute that arrives with a short ring near Gupta's desk.

'We always tell everyone that back in the day this place had kitchens and the chute was used to send food up to people in meetings. It works, no one ever asks questions . . . '

Rajveer takes the package of 500 rupee notes and weighs it in his expert hands, 'Yes, half a crore.'

'Fine. Happy Lohri, Guptaji.'

'Happy Lohri to you too, Sirji.'

Guptaji escorts them towards the exit.

On their way out Rajveer asks Ranjeet to halt. '*Chachaji,* this Lohri let me show you our dream project. This will solve the power cut problems of Punjab, we will have a monopoly for this latest technology.'

Ranjeet doesn't look impressed.

Rajveer's assistant is ready with a holographic presentation to be projected with equipment that he has imported specially for his dream project. He gives him a nod.

The animation comes alive with a marvellous hologram of a windmill power project.

The entire office is awestruck. A voiceover describes the process of the fascinating windmill technology that will produce energy to be converted into electric current.

'This is the future at the doorstep of present,' a baritone voice declares.

Ranjeet rushes to the laptop and presses the space bar. 'What a waste of time and resources.'

'*Chachaji,* this our future . . . '

'Raj don't get bigger than your shoes. I am struggling so hard to accumulate the finance required for our forthcoming chain of hotels, can't you see the banners all over this office,' he points at the backlit banners that displays a fancy hotel building.

'Khanna Rooms'.

'Ranjeet Chacha, this is age of energy and A.I.'

'MP Bansal is ready to part-finance this venture. I have to organise our share of the monies and I will spare no efforts to gather the sum.' Ranjeet says with finality.

Rajveer storms out, holding his breath. The staff rushes to their respective desks in pin drop silence.

Ranjeet clenches his fist and whispers in Guptaji's ears. 'Raj is impulsive, keep a check on him.'

16

As it often happens in a diligent duel between destiny and chance, paths in life cross without the main actors even knowing it. As Rajveer races his SUV silently away from his office and stops for a few seconds on the road across the police station, Jannat is getting out of a rickshaw on the other side. Neither expect to see the other here and they simply don't notice each other.

Rajveer waits for a young mother to cross with her toddler in tow. His eyes are fixed on the wide road ahead. '*Chachaji* has an old-fashioned vision, hotels, dead and gone.'

As Rajveer zips away he is no mood to observe. Jannat picks up her white purse that fell off her hand while alighting from the rickshaw. She quickly gathers the items that fell out of her Mulberry hobo bag and enters the police station in anticipation.

At the entrance she gives her name and the name of the officer she's supposed to meet.

She's shown to his office. She notices a flurry of green plants with drops of fresh water gleaming along the stone corridor. The office is small but extremely tidy, unlike the rest of the police station, and there is a distinct smell of a rose-scented air-freshener.

SHO Kawaljeet Deol sits at his large desk with a cup of coffee in front of him and an empty cup ready for her. He is lean and austere. Jannat gets a good impression of him. He may not be an easy guy to talk to, unlike Rajveer, but he seems pretty clean, someone she can trust.

He is glancing through his emails on his desktop and the file concerning Preet is open in front of him. He wanted to be ready for the meeting.Good, trustworthy! There is a picture of the place of the accident and a few pictures of the body covered with rags and black *dupattas*. There are pictures of anything the people who found the body could grab to cover that mutilated corpse. Jannat cannot bring herself to look; this is one thing she doesn't want to see. She wants to remember Preet alive, and possibly in one piece.

Kawaljeet acknowledges her presence and gestures her to sit down. Jannat nods and, without a word of introduction or greeting, says: 'How can you be so sure this was an accident?'

'Evidence. There is enough evidence to suggest she may have either slipped from the door of the bogie or jumped out voluntarily.'

'Or that she was pushed . . . '

'It could be, but we don't have direct evidence of that happening. There were no witnesses, no recordings and no proof of any foul play. Ms Gill . . . circumstantial evidence is not good enough to pursue an investigation forever. I understand how you feel, I speak to many relatives every day who cannot believe their loved ones got on a train and jumped off, or fell off, but these things happen every day. Welcome to India.'

'Thank you, but I guess it was all too rushed. I feel the case needs to be re-opened.'

'Let me get this straight, are you suggesting I am incompetent and unable to do my job?'

The uniformed cop's tone is sharp. She has touched a nerve and must be more careful.

The situation calls for diplomacy, he's the only one who can help her and she doesn't want to burn the bridges before they even start to get to the heart of the matter.

'I'm sorry, I didn't mean to imply that and I apologize if my words may have suggested it. I just feel that there are other elements in this case that need to be investigated. Preet Randhawa was not the type of person who would commit suicide. Whocomes all the way from England to jump off a train in Punjab? I feel there has been some foul play. I think she was murdered.'

Kawaljeet looks at her for a second too long. He's evaluating the situation and this is her chance to make him capitulate and help her.

'I met her parents you know? They are helpless despite knowing in their gut that their daughter was murdered, but they don't have the money or stature to prove it. Everything in this country seems to revolve around money and power . . . '

'Well, Ms Gill, if you haven't noticed, the whole world revolves around money,' he says, pretending to ignore the clear reference to corruption she just made.

He gets up from his chair and extends his hand for a shake, Jannat remains seated, but after a few seconds it is only too clear that he's waiting for her to leave. 'I'm sorry. I wish I could help but I have a busy day ahead. This case has been closed and unless there is more evidence to convince me to re-open the case it will stay that way.'

Kawaljeet picks up a printout that lies in the tray and leaves the room. Jannat looks at the ceiling with an expression of disgust on her face. The ceiling has a missing tile. A young sinister-looking assistant comes in to collect Preet's file. He stands in front of Jannat, smiles at her with his *paan*-stained lips, waiting for her to say or do something.

His right leg shakes with callous delight. Jannat walks away, revolted. She passes a group of cops lost in a world of their own.

As she is leaving the office, frustrated and unable to pick another end of the thread to walk back into Preet's life, her iPhone rings. It is her grandmother enquiring about her stay in India.

'Jalandhar, *bebe*, in Punjab. I am here on an assignment for two weeks.'

'Right, you must be staying with Naseebo?'

'Naseebo . . . Oh yeah, I forgot, she is your first cousin?'

'So you are not with her?'

'Sorry, bebe. I am staying at a hotel.'

'Are you nuts? Go to Naseebo Kapoor, Model Town, check out of your hotel. Ask any goddamn soul in Jalandhar about the late SP Karan Veer Saini. Naseebo is his wife.'

'OK! Relax, *bebe*. I will go there. Love you, speak to you soon.'

A couple of hours later Jannat is getting off a rickshaw in front of a *kothi*. The red brick façadesurrounded by lush pasturesfeels warm and inviting. The golden-coloured creepers on the arches linger like scintillating memories of a bygone era.

Jannat pulls out her purple suitcase and a few shopping bags labelled with Punjabi designer stores. The rickshaw is small but she seems to have been able to fit half of Punjab in it. She pays the fare, walks to the door and rings the bell.

An old woman, dressed in a modest *salwar kameez,* comes to open the door. In the unusually strong sunlight she takes a few seconds to make out Jannat's features. As she does she cries out and her eyes fill with tears of joy.

'Come dear, I recognised you when I heard your voice, very similar to your mother. This is your own house, make yourself comfortable and . . . '

I bend down to touch her feet.

'Shut up and give me a hug, stupid girl!' Naseebo jibes.

A servant comes silently to take Jannat's suitcase and bags. Another maid walks into the hall with a tray of tea and water. She stands silently watching the two women hug.

'What will you eat, sweetheart . . . Can I get you some . . .'

'Sometime later please. First I need to try these warrior uniforms. I mean Punjabi *salwar* suits.'

At sunset the Khanna residence is finally ready to welcome guests. The lights have been lit in the garden and decorations in the lawns give a cheerful look to an otherwise austere white mansion. Rose petals laced on the entrance carpet tell the story of times to follow. Rajveer's mother, Simran, and his aunt, Divya, are glowing in their new *salwar* suits with full *bagh* embroidery, shiny footwear and *kundan* jewellery. Eve-ryone who attends their Lohri party tonight must know, must understand from the way they look that the Khannas are the Khannas. They are a dynasty, always have been and always will be. Rajveer's mother has worked really hard and endured every possible pain inflicted by her mother-in-law to finally become the matriarch of the family. The rightful wife of the oldest son and. All this wealth and all the envy from her guests finally belongs to her. Her Lohri party will be discussed in Jalandhar papers. Who amongst the friends of her youth can say the same?

It's true; it was hard to get here. Being from a lower caste didn't play in her favour and her in-laws reminded her every day where she came from. She had to turn a blind eye to obscure family businesses in which she was not meant to interfere, but in the end the old in-laws died and the obscure family business generated a fat profit. Money is money, no matter where it comes from. And for Simran Khanna, all that wealth, ministers and their wives hanging out in her garden and a seemingly sheepish husband were all she needed. She had wanted to emerge from the dirt of her poor neighbour-hood more than anything in the world and she had always played her cards very well. She proved to be a modest, devoted and trustworthy wife with no inconvenient friends and a loving mother. What more could they want?

Tonight is her night. She walks tall. The party is ready. Waiters walk around the house and the garden with silver trays filled with the most fashionable selection of western and Indian finger food, the kitchen has prepared a sumptuous dinner under her personal supervision and the music is playing softly in the background, ready to be ignited once the guests start to dance. Simran looks at Puneet, that insignificant man who seems not to care about this. 'Dear, why do you worry so much? I love you, you love me, who cares what people think?' he told her once.

She remembers , as she looks down at her *polki* diamond necklace, how irritated she had been when she had heard those words. How could he not understand that the only thing that mattered was what people thought? Was he so much of a spoilt brat so as not to notice what people said or was he just too stupid to care?

That day, so many years ago, she had decided that her run towards success had to continue without him. Of course, at one point, she had been charmed by his sweet character and by all the poetry books he had read, but that night she understood their roads had parted a long time ago. He wanted what she ran away from anonymity.

And she wasn't going to give up all she had fought for since she was a little girl. Simran had come a long way and grown beyond being just an object of customary beauty.

Tonight, with MP Bansal on his way and a handful of other dignitaries sipping champagne in the garden, she is finally fulfilled. Now all she needs is a good marriage for Rajveer and her revenge against the world will finally be complete. She smiles as she observes the women glancing at her intensely. They are rookie players in this game of prestige and hospitality. She picks up a crystal glass of wine for something to hold in her hand.

She never liked the taste but she couldn't possibly drink coke or *chai* at a party like this.

Some of the guests form small groups by the braziers on the terrace, in the veranda and in the house; they talk and munch on appetizers. But the person Rajveer's mother is really looking forward to meeting, her very own guest of honour, is the lady Rajveer has hinted he'll bring. Rajveer usually never singles out a lady guest for a family affair.

Could she be the right one? My dear son is in his thirties, handsome and rich. But what if he's forced to accept a woman who doesn't deserve him only because she is a seductress? This one seems all right. Indian blood, British breeding, a good combination . . . But is she too smart?

As the duo makes their appearance within a nimbus of warmth Simran and Divya *Chachi* are on them in no time. Simran looks at Jannat like a predator looks at its prey. Jannat is striking in her pink chiffon suitand white sandals.

Yes, she's perfect. Isn't she?

'Mamma, this is Jannat from London.'

Rajveer looks a perfect match in his azure blue velvet *sherwani* with a raised *jamawar* collar. These are two individuals who radiate their own persona. And when the chemi-stry between them is explosive... Sparks chequered with envy and admiration fly across the floor as they walk with casual impudence. One of the serving staff freezes when he sees his master, Rajveer, with a matching beauty. His hands shake; the tray with the white wine glasses almost falls out of balance. Thankfully no one notices as everyone's eyes are still locked on the dazzling duo, the talk of the town.

There is a momentary silence between the three of them-Jannat, Rajveer and his mother. A contagious silence that speaks volumes yet says nothing. Nothing at all.

Puneet is on the other side of the room talking to some business associates of the past, but soon he sees Jannat, so candid, so proud and modest. He is pleased. Eagerly he joins the couple in the limelight, chatting with his wife and Divya. Bittu, dressed in a pastel-coloured *lehenga,* butts in from nowhere.

'*Wow, bhaiya*. You've lucked out. The princess bride is here.'

Jannat, holding a drink, spills some on her dress. Her cheeks turn red as she flushes.

Feeling mortified, clumsy and unsure what to do, she's taken aback when Simran bends down to clean her *kameez* with her satin handkerchief.

Twenty years ago her mum used to wait for her to come home from kindergarten with a glass of milk. Jannat would be so eager to drink the glass that she'd end up spilling it every day. Her mum would clean her uniform and scold her with a smile. Her dad, during one of his infrequent appearances, had even shot a short video of it.

Needless to say, as soon as she relives this scene in a totally different environment, with an outsider re-enacting the role of her mother, her eyes fill with tears. Simran pats on her shoulder, 'You must be missing your mother, child.'

'Yes, she died when I was six,' answers Jannat, wiping away her tears from her pink cheeks.

'Child, never shed tears for the departed. They are meant to go and marry their fate, wish them well and let them be in peace, wherever they are.'

Simran has done everything right and yet Jannat can't help feel suspicious. Somewhere deep down she feels she will have to watch her back. It all seems to appear like a fairy-tale. And life is the exact the opposite, she corrects herself.

'Love and death are our best soul mates. They are the only real things in this unreal world,' Simran caresses Jannat before turning to the other guests.

Rajveer greets all the guests while Jannat is introduced to a few by Bittu and Divya.

Most of the guests move to the bonfire outside, the heart of the Lohri celebration. A few connoisseurs of scotch are pinned to the barstools.

Jannat is dragged to the centre with all eyes glaring at her. Rajveer follows his dazzling guest of honour. The family sings; Jannat doesn't know the song.

'Sundar Mundariye . . .

Tera kaun vichara . . . Ho

Dulla Bhatti walla . . . Ho

Dulle ne ti viahiyi . . . Ho

Saer Shakar payi . . . Ho

Kudi de boje payee . . . Ho

Shallu kaun samete . . . Ho

Chacha galee dese . . . Ho

Chache choori kutee . . . Ho

Zamindaran lutee . . . Ho

Zamindara sidaye . . . Ho

Gin-gin pole layee . . . Ho

Ik pola reh gaya . . . Ho

Sipahi farh ke lei gaya . . . Ho

Aakho mundao taana . . .

Mukai da dana . . .'

Everyone throws something in the fire-peanuts, grains and rice. The fire destroys and purifies and it's auspicious to throw something in. Jannat and Rajveer do it too, exchanging a glance in the romantic glow of the fire.

Without anyone noticing Gupta walks into the room. He goes straight to Rajveer as he seems to know no one else and sticks close to him for a while. After the bonfire ritual everyone moves back in and Rajveer goes from one group to another to make all the guests comfortable, some of whom include important local politicians. MP Bansal approaches him.

'MP *sahib,* Happy Lohri. Welcome. Please, *tussi bhi shagun paa do.'*

As Rajveer talks to his business associates Jannat decides to wander around. The house is beautiful, an eclectic mix of contemporary design and heritage structures. The people invited to the party are diverse and demand reverence. Some overdressed women touch each other's silk fabrics and comment on the quality and price. A group of teenagers, throbbing in tumescence, go for the beer cans and a race to see who finishes faster. Their eyes are, however, glued on the young girls moving around in their finery with budding flair. Jannat wonders if there is a designed connection amongst her Punjabi origins, her British education, her affinity towards

Indian men and her professional assignment on NRI contract killing. It's time to walk through the room for investigation and inroads. But before she can hit the nail on an inspiring group she's trapped by Bittu and her college friends who want to know all about England and have eyes only for her beautiful Punjabi dress. They click a few pictures to update their social status. The girls try to teach her a few steps of an ethnic dance. Her feet are out of sync but her stunning good looks and her graceful movements attract everyone's attention. No one wants to stare but everyone has turned their eyes to her, including the MP's assistants.

Rajveer is uncomfortable thinking of the less than virtuous intentions of everyone ogling. Add to that the abundant alcohol. The men, especially the older ones, are shameless; they look at her like hungry dogs. The generous swigs of scotch or perhaps the latent lust makes them perspire in the over-pleasant surroundings. Rajveer tries to get into their line of vision but they keep moving to catch the smallest glimpse of her. His assistant follows him in tow with a drink in his hand.

Rajveer tries to catch Jannat's attention. She moves back indoors to dance with the other girls.

'What happened to your brother's Canadian visa?' he tries to change the topic of the conversation and to catch his interlocutor's attention. 'Did I tell you that Bansalji's son-in-law from Canada is visiting Jalandhar . . . Bansaljihas promised me that he will organise the visa through him . . . Bansalji's brother-in-law is a big shot in Canada . . . Talwar Bedi, from Toronto . . . You must have definitely heard his name . . .'

Hearing the name, the messenger, Rajveer's assistant, shivers. He looks for Ranjeet, but he's busy entertaining guests, so he leans forward and whispers something into Rajveer's ears. Rajveer is troubled too and walks away, followed by Gupta, out of the room for some time alone to think about what to do next. Puneet moves to intercept him.

'Son, what's the rush? Eat something.'

He ignores his father and walks out, followed by Gupta and Ranjeet. Right then Jannat walks around the foyer, clearly looking for him, but Rajveer is already out. She follows him with her gaze and walks past Mrs Bansal and her odd-looking daughter, Diljeet. They give her a spiteful look as she wanders around, visibly jealous.

17

Rajveer has rushed out of the *kothi* followed by his uncle and Gupta, the messenger. Beads of sweat flower on their foreheads despite the cold and their eyes keep looking around as if waiting for something. They enter the adjoining den and start whispering. Rajveer is the most concerned; he is young and still has to prove his value in the business.

Thirty minutes to nine.

The atmosphere is dense. The steam coming out of their mouths condenses in the centre of the small circle they form and the cold humidity drenches them to the bone.

Their hands are sweaty, their foreheads are wet

as a water fountain, the same sweat drips down the collar of their shirts and dies on their hairy chests, pinning the shirts to their shivering bodies.

Jannat walks out. She's looking for the charming host who has invited her, enticed her and then disappeared. She finds a waiter going back to the room with a tray full of glasses. He offers her one and she refuses it.

'Have you seen Rajveer, sir?'

The waiter indicates the neighbouring den with a movement of his head, or his chin rather. Jannat thanks him with a smile. She has a strange feeling. Almost like a foreshadowing, but there's nothing to worry about tonight, it's a splendid party full of interesting people and she's having fun. Rajveer has an illustrious family.

Not being able to define her uneasiness Jannat blames it on the piercing cold. The Indian dress is beautiful but how do women here stand the cold? The chiffon is so thin that she can feel her goosebumps. *Am I feeling a strong pull towards Rajveer? Is that why I am seeking him out?* She looks at the den for Rajveer, but as soon as she adjusts her neckline gently with her hands, Mrs Bansal and her daughter block her way.

'Did you notice, Diljeet, these NRI girls are too quick. They can go to any lengths for a prominent catch?' Both of them wait for Jannat to react furiously.

They are both guests of the Khannas; it wouldn't be appropriate to start a fight. Jannat is looking for Rajveer, her interest in Mrs Bansal and Diljeet has been very limited so far and right now is dangerously close to none at all. Jannat rolls her eyes and pretends not to have heard them. But then she thinks. *She wants to see Rajveer but there's no reason why she shouldn't talk back to this wicked witch.*

'You're right. Maybe we are not so decorous as you politicians but the day we decide to exhibit our dignity you politicians will have no place to hide, I promise.'

Mrs Bansal's eyes keep widening as Jannat speaks and she can hardly keep a straight face as she sees the arrogant middle-aged woman turn purple. The woman didn't expect such a prompt and witty response from the restrained NRI girl. Diljeet is also speechless. She keeps opening and closing her mouth like a fish, gasping for air and for something to say. But then her shallow IQ cowers under her hollow audacity. The scene is funny enough as it is. Jannat is a professional, a journalist from London. She's not one of those people who pick fights at parties. Mrs Bansal probably is and so be it. But Jannat is calling herself out of the game.

She walks on and heads for the den. As she approaches it she sees Rajveer gesticulating in anger and the short and chubby assistant with his head down. She gets closer on the tips of her toes to try and hear what they say but before she's close enough the three of them storm out. Rajveer and the short, chubby man get into Rajveer's SUV, and drive away. The smell of burnt rubber leaves Jannat wheezing.

Jannat is puzzled. This is not what she expected from a Lohri celebration with the family, but in Rajveer's defence she saw him deeply troubled and reckons there must be something wrong at work. They have a construction company and in India they work day and night and accidents happen all the time. The only thing Jannat can think of is that the stout man came and told Rajveer about an accident and he went to check it out. It's strange that his father or uncle didn't join him, but it's also true that someone had to stay and entertain the guests, that might as well be the head of the family. Rajveer's father is anyway too old to handle business affairs.

The girls she danced with before are all by the door and call her. She turns around smiling and shakes all bad thoughts out of her head as she runs back in for one more dance. Look at these young girls wearing their innocent dreams on their gleaming smiles and I have all the negativity to bog me down.

Rajveer drives like a lunatic, blurred with fear, lifting a cloud of fog behind the wheels of his car. Twenty minutes to nine.

In a small village on the outskirts of Jalandhar a large ancestral kothi is brightly lit. A man on the terrace is talking on the phone, laughing heartily every now and then. A woman gets close to him, kisses him on the neck and then hands him a baby to kiss goodnight. The man does so and gestures to his wife that he'll be with her soon, just as soon as he ends this conversation. The woman walks back inside. She's thinking that if the baby falls asleep while her husband, Talwar, is on the phone, then they can have a night to themselves for a change.

Meanwhile, in the murky tannery, among the carcasses of dead animals that wait to bleed out for the night before being skinned the next morning, Moga is getting ready to leave. His look is unusual. He wears dark, western clothes, a leather jacket and black gloves. Hanging from his neck is a pendant-a bull's head with red eyes made of small fragments of rubies.

He makes sure the bull's head is inside the jacket before zipping it up to his neck, a thick and dark neck. He exits the tannery, exchanges a few polite but not friendly words with his colleagues hanging around and gets in his small van. He drives away.

Rajveer is speeding through the night. Gupta, sitting next to him twitches like an eel, panic stricken. Talwar Bedi is still carelessly talking on the phone and enjoying the view from the balcony in the cold night. Rajveer looks at his talisman, the stone ring for some luck as his car zips across a flyover.

Moga parks the van carefully behind some trees, making sure that the bright light of the moon doesn't shine on him. He takes a double-barrel gun out of a rough black bag, checks if everything is in order and takes a comfortable position to take aim. He only has one shot before the victim's wife hears the blast and runs out to check what has happened, which is when, if everything goes well, she'll find him dead. He must kill or he'll have to kill her too, and that's against the rule. No additional casualties. Only the target victim. That's his rule. He kills only the ones he is paid for. If she re-cognizes the van she will turn into a witness. And then he will have to kill a whole bunch of people for free. The woman, her child, her lawyer, even the agents who have given him this job before they can turn their guns on him. Moga is a scavenger first and then a gun for hire. He is a lunatic who would shoot his own leg if it decided to betray him.

Talwar is talking but he's trying to cut the conversation short to go join his wife inside.

He paces up and down the terrace, too fast for Moga to adjust his aim.

When he finally manages to mark the target a black thing moves in front of him with a swish. *Damn owls!*

But it's not an owl. It's Gupta's hand stopping him. One more second and Talwar Bedi would have been dead. Moga didn't hear Rajveer's car approaching despite the noise it must have made judging from the cloud of dust that is still lingering in the air. Moga sniggers in disgust.

Back in the den Rajveer nervouslypaces up and down in heavy silence. They saved the man, but by a split second. Moga doesn't make mistakes, he takes a little more time than others but once he has pulled the trigger the bullet never misses its mark. A target has only a few seconds left to live.

How could this happen?

Rajveer is lost in his thoughts, lost in that fraction of a second where Talwar, an influential man, might have died.

Ranjeet walks in merrily. He has had a few drinks and is far more relaxed. The fact that Rajveer is back in the den can only mean that everything went well and therefore there's no reason to stress.

'Oye, where the hell did you disappear to for so long? Your bright girl's looking for you!'

Rajveer looks at him with fury in his eyes, he can't answer because his voice would tremble with rage. He paces the room again and runs his fingers through his hair so often and so hard that he nearly pulls it off.

'Raj, are you still stuck on your power project? Trash it.'

Rajveer finally does speak, his voice shuddering as he feared, '*Chachaji,* Moga was on his way to assassinate MP Bansal's brother-in-law, Talwar Bedi. Do you understand the repercussions?'

Ranjeet stares at Rajveer. Their eyes meet and hold. Ranjeet doesn't know how to re-spond, as if the situation is only now sinking in. He walks over to the nearest chair and sits, his forehead covered in small and shiny beads of sweat. He breathes deeply.

'Thank God . . . I reached there on time...or else we would be in so much shit right now . . . ' Rajveer's voice reaches him in bursts.

Puneet has entered the room but waits to hear more before making his appearance. The room reeks of anger and accusation. Overwhelmed by the heavy silence that seems never-ending he speaks, 'Brother, I have warned you umpteen times. Dump this syndicate. One small mistake and we are all finished forever!'

Ranjeet looks at Puneet. Then he points at Rajveer.

'Exactly . . . Someone tell this Alexander of Punjab that none of us has ever been present at the scene of execution. For three generations we have lived by this commandment . . . this is our secret, this is our strength, our forefathers have slaughtered traitors and executed men from their inner circle just to safeguard the privacy of our family trade. And you, Raj, you broke the most vital rule. Your presence at the scene of crime, one single eyewitness and it could have got us doomed . . . disgusting. Why did . . . '

'What nonsense! If I hadn't intercepted Moga the police would be hunting for us. MP Bansal is a wretched man. He wouldn't have spared anybody in order to track the assassins of his brother-in-law. Remember he is the only politician who knows about our cover and our operations, he . . . '

'But how was I supposed to know that Talwar Bedi is so well-connected, Mr Juvenile?' Ranjeet is equally furious.

Puneet thumps the glass table with his bare hands. It cracks into two.

'Oye, enough. Before I lose my mind the two of you shut up or else . . . '

Just then Jannat enters the den accompanied

by Rajveer's mother. The three men Gupta went away with Moga, in the woods, just after they saved Talwar's life-look at the women, dumbfounded. They don't even seem to remember that in the next room there's a party with several dozens of people.

'Child, please have your dinner!' snaps Puneet at Jannat to take charge of the pande-monium.

'*Ji,* Uncleji,' answers Jannat, her voice trembling like that of a schoolgirl. She has no clue of what she has interrupted but the expression on the faces of the three men is frightening.

Rajveer gives her a second glance, but his face, his gaze, the very creases on his skin are not those she's used to. She doesn't dare speak one more word. Rajveer's mother takes her by the elbow and sees her out with an encouraging smile. Jannat notices Simran give a nasty look to her husband that relaxes her a little; it means the matter is not that serious. Or is it?

Once the women are gone, Ranjeet, who is still sitting on his chair, takes a deep breath and exhales. He turns to Puneet. He's calm but uses the tone he would use when speaking to a child. 'Brother, this is strictly our business matter. Don't get me wrong but it's been a decade since you retired. In this game we need to follow the rules and be vigilant. Today Raj broke a big rule and this can destroy the whole game.'

Puneet is visibly hurt. Rajveer doesn't lower his stare from his uncle's face. He tries to avoid meeting his eyes but keeps his own just high enough not be taken for a coward. Puneet leaves the den with a few last words, 'Beware, you fools. Someday this game can get so bloody that it could spatter the walls of our own house!'

The sounds of celebration filter into the room for a second before the thick wooden door shuts with a thud.

Ranjeet puts his hand on Rajveer's shoulder as if to give him a pep talk. 'Son, keep in mind that for the rest of your life this is your profession. We have to live by it. We have to die by it. It is not only our business . . . it's our ritual. It's been handed down to us. Like this ancestral mansion, the gold, the artefacts, the valour. It's who we are.'

Rajveer ponders, he is confused but understands what his uncle means. He detects a series of photographs of his ancestors framed on the wall. They smile with pride with no sign of fear in their eyes. He nods at Ranjeet with reconciliation. Ranjeet exhales, relieved, and pats his nephew on his back. He gets up to leave the room. Rajveer tries to regain control of his racing breath. He shuffles from one end to the other with a fuzzy vision. The grey walls of the room still appear to be upside down. He looks at his cell phone that has three missed calls from Jannat. He tries to call her back but the call goes straight to her voicemail.

Hope she didn't hear anything. How could she, she was with Mamma. Thank god!

He heaves a sigh and unlocks the wooden chest. He stares at the cutting of the astrology advert with Talwar Bedi's name encircled on it. He nods his stiff neck in exasperation.

18

In the unfriendly cold night Jannat is driven home by the Khannas' chauffeur. The roads are deserted. The darkness is too eerie for comfort. The chauffeur with his grey hat is almost non-existent. She can barely see him breathe. There is a feeling of emp-tiness around beside her own reflection in the tinted glass of the luxury sedan that glides like a ghoul. She hasn't seen Rajveer again, after their eyes met briefly in the den; he disappeared and the party wasn't as fun anymore. When they had walked in she was pleasantly embarrassed with all the attention and when she had left nobody had cared, not even Rajveer. I simply didn't exist for him. She has evidently interrupted something and she expected him to come to her and tell her that everything was all right. He didn't. Everything wasn't all right.

On the other hand how exactly was I supposed to know that there was trouble? He invited me to a party, to show me the real Punjab, the real Lohri, he was evidently flirting...and then he disappeared. What was I supposed to think?

But then . . . Life is not about what you desire but what happens to you?

The driver has taken proper instructions for the address and without a word he drops her off in front of Naseebo's *kothi*. As soon as she has gotten off he speeds away without waiting for her to get in, strange for the driver of such a high-class family. Jannat looks at the chic Honda driving away with a roar, a sound Rajveer's car doesn't make.

The number plate reads CHOWDHURY PUNEET KHANNA. Jannat shakes her head and walks in smiling at the thought of these old families' egos. Who writes their name on the number plate? *I guess all he is seeking is love and appreciation!*

Jannat finds Naseebo warming her hands by the fire. She is falling asleep with her chin on her chest and her eyes are still half closed when Jannat walks in, but as soon as she sees her all dressed up like an Indian Cinderella she gets up and greets her.

'You are back my child! How was the Lohri party? Doubtless there were big people, big talk, big show . . . Punjab then and Punjab now are two different worlds,' Naseebo sighs.

As Jannat takes a chair and sits down by the fire, unsure what to tell Naseebo about the party and the strange turn it took, Naseebo takes a frame hidden on a shelf on top of the chimney. The glass is all greasy and darkened by the smoke but the shape of two uniformed men in their forties is still clearly distinguishable.

'This is your grandfather, my late cousin, Senior Superintendent Karan Veer Saini. And this is his best friend, DSP Paramjeet Deol.'

She strokes the photograph and begins to giggle uncontrollably, her whole body shakes and Jannat is left a little embarrassed not knowing what to do. After a few minutes though she realizes that the giggles have unexplainably turned into sighs, louder and louder. Naseebo is crying and Jannat hugs her, frustrated with her inability to say anything.

'Both died on duty. This was the late eighties. Punjab was rampant with terrorism. Two terrorists from the Khalistan Liberation Force barged in and shot them at close range. The two best friends were on duty and were sharing their lunch at the Patiala police station. Bastards didn't even let them finish their lunch,' she smiles in irony. 'And where is the rest of the family? I am the only family left behind. I have a son who migrated to California for higher studies, got a job, got married to an American girl and never looked back. Doesn't visit, rarely calls. He hates India. As long as he is happy it's all good. Every son is not like Kawaljeet, what a . . . '

'Kawaljeet?'

'Son of Paramjeet Deol, who died on duty. Following his father's footsteps.

He is currently serving as Senior Inspector, Punjab Police.'

'Kawaljeet Deol? NRI Department?' Jannat is incredulous.

'Haan, wahi.'

Jannat keeps staring at the photograph; now that she's been told of the relationship, she does see the resemblance between Kawaljeet and his father. He was so unpleasant during their last meeting that she honestly would have never expected to find out something so personal about him. How different can he be from his father? She stays in the chair even afterthe fire is nearly dead and only the ashes burn with a red glow in the dark room.

In the dead of the night there is another individual who is awake and looking for something. While Jannat is looking for answers, Moga is looking for blood. He is brooding over a cancelled assignment. A pack of wolves inside his bloodstream are howling in pain. The spatter of human flesh, the sprinkle of warm blood, the release of the last breath, all of this is fodder for the devils that multiply within every cell of his body. His demonic mind feeds on blood and gore. Buried deep in the jungle, he sits on a *machan,* smoking pot. His eyes sparkle in the night to the likes of a fierce predator, next to him, quiet as a loyal dog, is his gun, which he caresses. The gun that he bought somewhere in the state of Uttar Pradesh, country-made, but can give the sophisticated brands a run for their money. He smooches the muzzle with intense passion. Neither has worked tonight, neither has hunted, neither has spilt blood and the tension hasn't been released. It won't be until they kill together.

A sound in the woods makes Moga hope for the best, he sharpens his ears and focuses his sight: a deer. Then a fast movement, leaves, a lighter, softer, more delicate set of steps: a cheetah.

This could be a good night after all. The deer runs but its fast and yet heavy body makes a sound that can be heard throughout the forest, there is no escape.

Moga swallows his saliva, his mouth is getting dry, and all his senses are focused on finding the deer. It's too dark to see. He will have to feel, hear, smelland get into the mind of the deer-feel the adrenaline cloud its brain, try and shake off that impending doom, find a way to save its life.

But Moga is a killer. The only reason he wants to get into the mind of the deer is not to save it but to be the first one to kill it. And he is a spotless killing machine. Every cell of his body burns incessantly with the instincts of a butcher.

Suddenly the sounds come closer and with a jump the deer heads for the machan. On the opposite side the cheetah heads for the deer, jumping above Moga's head and onto the neck of the animal. But the hunter won't let an animal steal his prey. He closes his eyes and shoots the perfect shot that pierces through the deer's neck and leaves the cheetah with nothing more than a piece of dead flesh between his paws. The big cat, evidently expecting some struggle to kill its prey, looks astonished. Its lush green eyes shine in the night, they are the only light Moga can see. With a single shot Moga hits it in the brain. The animal doesn't have time to suffer. In a second everything goes black and with a sigh it dies.

With the skill that only long-term survivors could possibly have, Moga lights a fire, skins both prey and predator and leaves the deer to be eaten by other animals while he roasts the spotted cat. He doesn't even know what the meat tastes like, some might even say it's too gamey, but what Moga was looking for tonight is the taste of death. Not just death but of death by his hand. And looking at what he got he can say he's fairly satisfied. Men or animals don't make a difference to him. He loves the sound of blood pouring from an artery, the choking sound of breath tripping between one's clenched teeth, the smell of fear mixed with adrenaline and urine being released by a dying body. He got all this tonight. Twice. It's a party.

Next morning Rajveer slips into his running gear and leaves the house for his morning jog. He is fit and the sun on the bare skin of his arms warms him. Flashbacks of the previous night keep coming back to him. He runs, looks around, enjoying the lush green, but his mind is with Jannat. What in the heart of nature generally enchants him today keeps breaking his thought. He thinks of her and a bird flies low, he tries to re-member her suit and how perfectly it fell on her curves and he finds himself on top of his favourite cliff. The breeze reminds him of her fragrance. Was it Burberry or her natural body that was so scintillating? The world is too loud for him today, too many things, troubling things, have happened in the last twenty-four hours and all these co-lours, the sound of nature, the very essence of running surrounded by beauty feels too demanding. He decides not to finish his routine and runs back.

The farther he looks the more he sees her.

Once home he throws the sweaty clothes in the laundry basket, looks at his body in the mirror-this job, being a grown up, is taking a severe toll on his body-and takes out the clothes for the day before jumping in the shower. Rajveer pulls a drawer open and inspects a wide range of wristwatches, his guilty pleasure. He doesn't care about clothes too much. He's not one of those designer freaks, of course he likes nice design, but he's not fussy.

What he really loves and collects are wristwatches. These add to his self-esteem. Without a fancy watch he feels incomplete. He quickly checks the clothes on the bed-white shirt and blue trousers. Blue watch. Dark blue of the metal? Dark blue with a silver quadrant?

Once this little ritual is accomplished, and while he waits for the water in the shower to be extra hot the way he likes it, he takes his phone and types.

Jannat opens her eyes to the beeping of her phone. She stretches an arm out on the warm bed to and finds a message from Rajveer.

Sorry about last night. Something urgent that I had to attend to it came up. Would like to make up for it today. With complete dedication. Promise.

Yeah sure, this is a good excuse, particularly original too. Nobody ever used that before!

But then again, what if it's true? Who am I to judge urgent business? They are evidently an affluent family. Only God knows what happened. In the end he took me to the party and the whole family has been incredibly nice to me. It doesn't seem like a lie. Or if it is it's extremely well staged . . .

But before she can respond a call from May comes through. *God this woman . . .*

I bet she stays in the office late just to enjoy waking me up at dawn!

Jannat picks it up, but instead she puts on the voice of an automated operator and speaks in Punjabi, '*Dial kita hoya* number is *vele band ha. Kripya thodi der baad* dial *kare.* The number you are trying is switched off, please try again later.'

Across the world May is fuming but is unsure if she's entitled to be angry. The voice-mail sounds exactly like Jannat Gill but she could have recorded the message herself. God knows what those funny words meant and who knows how the phone system works in India. It's amazing that they manage to have one at all . . .

As Jannat's editor she is still furious with her reporter for having disappeared on an assignment. *She better be bloody kidnapped or working undercover or as soon as she comes back I'll rip her contract to pieces!*

Jannat throws the phone aside and gets up to go take a shower. Just then the phone rings. She looks at the display to make sure it's not May again.

'Hello stranger!'

'I know, I know . . . Shoot me. I am . . . '

'I'm an ardent fan of Buddhism remember? Total believer in non-violence.

But that doesn't mean you won't be punished. I can . . . '

'Of course . . . I am the sinner . . . I surrender with . . . '

The silence between the two is as rich as the Dead Sea.

'Life can be magic when you turn the worst moment of your life to the best. I call it the magic opportunity,' Rajveer speaks in a deep tone of voice.

At the *hawala* office Ranjeet is waving at Rajveer, gesturing him to follow him inside.

He responds with a movement of his hand that he'll join in five minutes. If he wants to have a second chance with this splendid lady he must be more careful about how he plays his cards, and he's motivated to play them well. Outside he can hear the sounds of people working and talking, but inside his air-conditioned car Rajveer can hear Jannat's voice as if they were standing at the fort on an ice-cold night.

'Listen there's something I'd like you to experience. Something I'm truly passionate about . . . '

She doesn't say anything but he can hear her breath inside his ear; he can almost feel the warmth of it

'I'll pick you up at 3pm, be . . . '

'I'm busy today. I'm sorry.'

Usually he can tell when she's smiling, she's not this time. She means it.

He remains quiet, waiting.

'Fine . . . You win. Pick me up at 4.'

'3.30.'

'Demanding . . . Okay done!'

Ranjeet gets in the car as soon as Rajveer ends the call with Jannat. From his expression Rajveer can tell the business for today is done. Instinctively his gaze falls on his large leather sports bag, loaded with money. Ranjeet hands it over to Rajveer to count. Rajveer knows his uncle doesn't like dealing with this business alone, 'The family is family at home and you need to focus when it's time for business!' this is what his uncle used to tell him when he was young.

Ranjeet drives away in silence.

'We need to deliver the cash to some important people. They are waiting at the Vajra Golf club.'

Rajveer is hunting for an excuse to slip out later. There's nothing he can think to sooth his uncle's mood. His fingers start flickering the notes with a bank cashier's precision.

19

Jannat's fingers move in rhythm on her laptop, as if she were pressing the keys on a piano. She concludes her blog with the lines-'Out to conquer the world, let me be gin with myself. Conquer yourself, conquer death, conquer eternity,'she signs off Jannat, the sage with a hangover.'

She closes her laptop and tidies her hair; she has to look presentable for her upcoming battle with the police officer. Now that she knows about his father she has a slight advantage compared to the first time they met. SHO Kawaljeet didn't seem friendly last time and there's really no reason why he should be friendlier today unless it's his birthday. She stops for a few minutes before stepping out of the door. A quick five-minute meditation calms her anxiety. Punjab has been quite a roller coaster ride so far.

She gets into a cab and minutes later is knocking at the policeman's door. Before he can respond or invite her in she storms in and sits down. First rule of war: choose your ground. If she appears decisive it's going to be a lot harder for him to kick her out.

'Preet Randhawa was murdered. I have the testimony from her parents and enough evidence to suggest that her husband conspired in her murder,' she states this in the calmest and coldest tone. What she doesn't want is for him to find a reason to refuse to reopen the case. She must sound sure and determined.

Only then does Kawaljeet raise his eyes to meet hers. There's the hint of a smile on his face, nearly undetectable, but it's there. Jannat can't quite understand if he's happy to see her or if he's simply scoffing at her drive. With a wave of his hand he sends his assistant, Balwant Kundra, out; it doesn't take many men to handle a lunatic.

'Oh, come on, madam, not again. Are you on some substance, I can charge . . . '

Jannat is out of patience already. She went in with all the best intentions and this man has the power to get on her nerves. 'Money! Is that what you're after? Like all other cops in the police departments of this country? What disappointment to see the country of Mahatma Gandhi go to the dogs because of people like you, who would do, or not do, anything for money . . .'

'Excuse me? Watch what you say. Don't make me arrest you for insulting an honest inspector. This is my . . .'

'Yeah. Some honesty. A decent woman gets thrown off the train, case closed... This is what you call honesty? Because if it is you are like any of them . . .' she gestures to the main door to imply that all the other policemen are corrupt.

Kawaljeet's slight smile fades from his face, he looks away. He thumps his foot on the footrest under the table. Jannat keeps touching the button of corruption and this is something he cannot stand. He is not one of *them.* His men are not them. Sure there are corrupt policemen in India, but isn't this the case in almost every country?

He answers with a touch of irritation. 'You want to hear the truth? I am honest, but I need to survive. This is not a business that I own. I follow orders. I am all for live and let live, Jannat Gill.'

This sounds like a final statement, but this time she's not prepared to just go with the flow and let him make her leave. She'll leave only when ordered to. Besides she has one more card to play.

Kawaljeet has stood up and gone to the window. He's turned his back to her, probably hoping that by ignoring the conversation she'll eventually grow tired of the silence and leave. Jannat rummages in her bag and when the noises stop Kawaljeet goes back to breathing normally. She's found what she was looking for and now she'll go.

Instead she straightens out on the table the photo of Kawaljeet's father and Naseebo's husband.

Jannat casually puts it in on the table and lets out a sigh, 'What a shame that with a father like yours you are unable to be braver . . . you succumbed to . . . '

Kawaljeet turns around in a split second. His eyes have turned red and he's ready to shout that she knows nothing about him or his father; that she should leave before ending up straight in jail. But he sees the photo on the table and his heart skips a beat. Jannat looks at him, pretending to be casual, as she sees his sweaty face and red eyes. 'Naseebo *dadi* gave it to me . . . I hope you make your father proud someday. He deserves it.'

With this she walks out.

Kawaljeet is left speechless. He can't take his eyes off the old photograph.

Jannat has left, almost sure that the last sentence will twist events. It's her last chance.

If this doesn't work she can cross out the police for help. She waits twenty seconds outside the room, behind the closed door, pretending to look for something in her bag; then she walks out slowly. He still hasn't come out.

She walks down the stairs, one by one. *Nothing.* Jannat walks out in the bright light and in the noises of the city. *Nothing.* She looks straight at the sun. She is blinded for a minute.

Overwhelmed by the sense of failure and by the smells, noises and sounds all around, she hails a rickshaw that comes promptly and stops by the side of the road where she's standing. She turns around one more time to check if someone's coming and she sees somebody running.

Kawaljeet's assistant, Balwant, tries to get to her before she sits down, his breath short and face red, 'Ma'am, can you come back in? Two minutes?'

Jannat smiles. She thinks Kawaljeet sent for her and lets the rickshaw driver go. She's obviously surprised when Balwant pulls her gently away from the entrance of the police station.

'Madam, actually . . . I could be of some help . . . But . . . '

Balwant scratches his head. Jannat remains quiet, not knowing what he means. 'But what?'

Now Balwant rubs his fingertips together. 'Money'. Jannat understands and opens her wallet to hand him a few hundred rupees. Balwant smiles as he makes them disappear in his pocket.

'Follow me, madam.'

She does. He takes her to a filthy place, a narrow gully where small businesses are flowering. Jannat has to cover her nose and ward off flies as they land on her face every now and then.

Finally they arrive at a small shop selling mobile phone cards. Maanka Seth, a man of dubious appearance, looks at Balwant with his fair-skinned girl and smiles vulgarly. His skin is very dark and so are his eyes, like a demon of the night, he looks around suspiciously and Jannat can only see the whites of his eyes and his teeth. She's a little intimidated by this black man with his long limbs and devilish face.

'Balwant sir . . . good to see you!'

'Listen, madam needs some important information. Give it to her. You handle her, I have to return to my duty.'

Balwant leaves Jannat with the man. She looks at him go, her eyes imploring him to stay, but he has to go back to work and smiles apologetically. When she turns around she finds Maanka looking at her and lighting his cigarette.

'Now you can ask for what you want,' he blows a puff into the air in slow motion.

Jannat looks around and finds that there is a crowd gathered around them, checking her out. It's what she rationally knows to be a harmless crowd of unemployed youth and beggar children, but she's uncomfortable. She would prefer more privacy.

'Can we go somewhere else and talk?'

Maanka looks around, pondering. He then scribbles something on a piece of paper and hands it to her. 'I can't leave my shop right away, but I can meet you tonight at eleven thirty. This is the address. Be there. You will get whatever information you want, official or unofficial,' he winks.

She takes a quick look at the paper and then her watch. It's two in the afternoon.

A couple of hours later Jannat is sitting in a blue Jeep Cherokee next to Rajveer, the sound of a revving engine whirlpooling in her brain. Jannat notices a smart watch on Rajveer's wrist that he sets to the race. The dial of the Giuliano Mazuoli watch, de-signed like a speedometer, appears to be waiting to blaze. They are in the outskirts of Jalandhar. The sun is radiating its presence. Rajveer's hands are glued on the steering wheel, his tattoo of the sun more visible than ever. There are at least three other jeeps a few metres from them. It's a race in the middle of nowhere. Jannat feels the intensity in Rajveer's body language.

'You seem to be a man of many dreams.'

'One life, one world. Is just one dream good enough?'

'Depends on the intention behind the dreams.'

Rajveer looks at Jannat intently. He taps Jannat on her hand, a touch of warm blood.

'So you don't believe in my dreams?'

'I do. People who don't believe in the dreams of others can never fulfill their own.

Dreams are great, but at the cost of your . . . '

'Jannat, my father taught me a beautiful thing early on. First, find meaning, then find a mistress.'

'Really?'

'I have found meaning. Help me find a mistress,' Rajveer smirks.

The two of them knock fists together. Rajveer notices a certain discomfort in her eyes. *Why?*

'I hope you are not afraid. I have been racing since I was in my teens.'

'As long as the car is being driven by rationale and not blind emotions I am good.'

'Is that coming from a lady?' his eyebrows rise.

'Men are more into emotions than women, they just don't know it,' she smirks.

'Death is just a neighbour.'

'All I know is that right now I am sitting next to you.'

'To make love to life you must first seduce death.'

Jannat smiles, 'Finally.'

All of a sudden an SUV pulls up next to them. A spoilt brat from a rich farmer's family of the district sits in the car and grins. Plonked next to him is Diljeet Bansal. Her eyes are shimmering at Rajveer's presence. She grins because she's finally found someone richer than Rajveer who takes her out. What she doesn't know is that the guy only wanted a woman to race with him: it's the tradition, you never race without a woman at your side, it's bad luck. It could have been Diljeet or anybody else; she said yes first and he was short on time. But after the race, before going to drink and celebrate, he'll drop her off. He doesn't want to be seen with this husband-hunting hound.

Jannat and Rajveer ignore them, which makes them even angrier.

'So you like to live dangerously . . . '

'Where's the feeling of power if one doesn't live dangerously?'

Jannat laughs nervously. She could easily do with a little less sense of power.

I'm one of those bloody people who won't cross the street without the red light and where do I find myself? At a private car race, in the wilderness!

'Power is very profound, Rajveer. Power comes from within.'

'This is not the UK, princess. To survive in India you have to broadcast your power. Fate keeps screwing things up for people.'

'Sometimes fate is kind enough to make you realise that the power within you is greater than all the power in the world . . . '

Their eyes meet for a split second. There is combustion of thoughts.

The race is about to begin.

The guy in the car next to them lowers the window and screams.

'Nice. Flavour of the month, Raj?'

Diljeet says to him, loud enough to be heard by them too, 'She's typical *firangi* type . . . The weekend special . . . '

Rajveer is fuming.

'Relax, Rajveer. You know they are losers, probably just trying to get you distracted.

You not racing is the only chance they have to at least finish the race . . .'

Rajveer sees the guy accompanying Diljeet blow a kiss at Jannat. Rajveer is furious with his drool. He fists his palm.

Jannat puts her hand on his fist, 'Stay cool in extreme situations and you can carry the cosmos in your palms like a dewdrop.'

The final whistle blows and all the jeeps take off at the same time.

'Fine. Let's enjoy the game. The final victory is just an illusion.'

Rajveer is on course. He rams his speed pedal and drives like an eagle onhunt, like a cheetah chasing down his prey. Jannat holds onto her seat belt, enjoying the thrill of speed. Rajveer steers the car through the winding roads with élan. There is no tar, this is a dirt track. A couple of stones get hit at the edge and they fly in the air like a bullet. Had it hit any bird in its flight it would have torn it into shreds. A couple of cars neck with Rajveer's Jeep. A slight error of judgement by any one racer and all three cars would turn into bloody scrap. Rajveer slows down all of a sudden when he sees the dirt road narrow down. But the two racing cars on both sides of him are not in the mood to take it easy. The narrow path has place for only one car. Jannat wonders if it'll be the red one or the yellow. But before she can say 'London Bridge' the metal bodies of the two cars brush against each other. One of the drivers swerves to his right and throws the other car completely off the road. It goes ramming into the shrubbery. Jannat notices a dent in the mustard fields in the distance. Black smoke casts a dark shadow on the sunlit landscape. Two terrified humans jump out of the car that they expect to burst into flames. A Sikh and his girlfriend. Jannat is spellbound by the accuracy of Rajveer's navigation. Rajveer's eyes are locked on the road. This is not an amateur driving, she thinks.

Jannat breaks the monotony of the sounds of revving engines. 'Rajveer, all good.'

'Never been more in control, lady.'

In an exciting race the cars rush towards the finish line. Grit takes over. Bodies are frozen. Eyes are getting bigger. Breaths shorter. Minds are numbed. Lines blur be-tween life and death. A part of the intellect is lost in prayer. Another part is lost in passion. Unexpectedly Diljeet and her pal are close by, but Rajveer quickly takes the opportunity to get close to their car.

When the time is right he swerves and pushes them off the track into a muddy ditch.

'Good riddance to bad rubbish,' he swears.

'That's probably where they belong,' Jannat adds.

Rajveer thumps on his breaks. They have hit the finish line. A group of people is waiting on the side of the road as Rajveer's car screeches to a halt a few metres ahead of the marked finish. A few spectators are decked on the roof of their vans, busy filming the near death race. The whistle blows on them, flags come down, hands go up and cheers fill the air. Rajveer and Jannat give each other a high five.

Their car eventually lands on an open space and whirls around. Rajveer lets go off the steering wheel and enjoys the edgy, stimulating experience of his revolving, un-touched, unguided, free-spirited car. Rajveer, like most men who win a car race, is high on the rush. Jannat is entangled in the oozing energy. She inhales the aroma of octane that engulfs Rajveer. There is a sparkling bout of attraction. Her body is dying to get wrapped in the comfort of a man's muscles. She can feel the pull. It's magnetic. It's more than just magnetic. It's as good as atomic. The cells in her body are dying to explode. The hormones seem to shoot up faster than the speed of light. Rajveer looks at Jannat. She looks back in gay abandon. Finally they can indulge in looking at each other. Rajveer's car twirls 360 degrees. Within a couple of those twirls Jannat has a re-verie of sorts. Is she impressed by

Rajveer or is she psyched into the adrenalin rush that has altered the chemicals in the brains? She experiences random images of Rajveer and herself on a mountain-climbing adventure with mist kissing their faces. She finds herself with Rajveer on a vintage military motorbike navigating the thicket of a dense forest and then all of a sudden the bike skids into a gorge. The duo slides down to reach an amphitheatre settled in ruins, right in the middle of nothing. The dirt of the forest hills envelops the two as they roll down the scanty hill and reach the rich earthy terrain.

The cloud of dust dramatically metamorphoses into present times, back to reality where the tyres of Rajveer's SUV scrape against the dirt track and splash the red soil across the emptiness.

20

The sound of revving engines permeates Jannat's brain; every crease, every fold is filled with the noise and the stench of burnt petrol. Slowly the sound becomes more metallic, as if millions of iron wheels were scratching and clinging on a rail.

The light is dim, swinging first to one side and then to the other as the train moves swiftly yet irregularly. The light bulb, framed in a small iron cage, casts a sinister light on the walls of the compartments. Shadows outgrow their owners and melt into each other in a morbid carnival.

Jannat suddenly feels a cold chill, as if someone had opened the door of the train. Why would anyone open the door of the train in the middle of the night?

But before she can answer the question the soft touch of a dark scarf strokes her cheek. At first she doesn't recognize the feeling, but when she turns around, recognizing a scent, a black void swallows her. The black and cold hole screams her name. Jannat! And it's to her name that Jannat wakes up. That voice, it was Preet . . .

Her forehead is covered in small pearls of sweat and her pyjamas are drenched. She looks at the clock by the side of her table, 11.10 pm. She rolls over a couple of times but she cannot sleep. Each time she closes her eyes Preet's voice explodes in her head.

Minutes later Jannat is walking the street to Maanka's place. The road is dirty and at night a million times more frightening than during the day. On its sides, instead of the clean and neat sidewalks, as in London, Jannat sees soft parcels moving as if eaten by worms. These are people sleeping on the pavements. Burnt wood emits the last few strands of smoke. The stench doesn't vanish in the evening coolness. When she finally reaches the warehouse, Maanka's frightening eyes, of which she can only see the whites, and his pig like laughter are nearly reassuring.

'Tell me about the nexus between the NRI murders and the contract killing syndicate.'

Maanka laughs and doesn't lower his eyes. He keeps looking at her to make sure he remembers every detail, as if he is mentally undressing her and keeping the memory for later.

'Fine. I will part with the secrets of the trade, but you will have to fulfil your end of the bargain.'

His filthy look makes her very uncomfortable and she takes a roll of banknotes she had prepared previously in her pocket and hands it to him. Meanwhile she takes her iPhone out of a pocket and puts it on record, placing it very close to his mouth so he doesn't get closer.

He gets closer anyway and she shivers but decides to let it go.

'Talk. Who are the people behind the NRI killings?'

'Let me come closer for the machine to catch my voice.'

'No need. You can speak from where you are. It's got a powerful microphone.'

Maanka closes his eyes as if remembering something. When his eyes are closed he disappears in the darkness, but like any good predator he can't be seen but sees very well. He snaps his eyes open and she's more uncomfortable than ever next to him. He slides his hand and places it on top of hers.

This is too much for her to take. *But is it?* My friend Preet is dead. Women in India get beaten and raped every day. One more wouldn't change the statistics, whether it happened or not. And then a ray of light enlightens her. He's prepared to go any length. This is not a scoop anymore. It's something personal. She has done what a journalist should never do combine the personal with the professional. Now deciding when to step back is difficult.

But Maanka makes it easy. It's clear he wants her. Jannat can tell from his heavy breathing, from his smell that is still lewd but is now charged with hormones . . . It's time to go and do it pretty fast!

She slips the iPhone back in her pocket and gets up. He forces her down to the seat again. He fondles her. She screams. He tries to gag her with his hand but she manages to bite him. He retracts in pain, holding one hand with the other and showing the whites of his eyes as his pupils dilate in pain. She dashes out of the room. He tries to follow her, but in the darkness he hits a few pieces of furniture that fall. She mentally calculates how much time she has. Jannat runs down the dark steps, two at a time. But he is not far behind. Like a hyena he chases her with lustful eyes. Jannat darts like a spear. But her foot strikes a fallen trashcan and she stumbles. Maanka's shadow gets bigger in the background. Jannat panics.

She's on the street and can hear a car coming. She waves it down as the lights blind her.

The worst-case scenario is that it's another rapist. *Maanka would have raped me, so I'm in the exact same position, but there's also a good chance that he's a good person . . .*

The car stops and Jannat finds Balwant at the wheel. As soon as she realizes that he has no intention of taking her back to Maanka she gives him the evil eye first and then a proper talking to.

'What were you thinking, you idiot? That I would not tell your boss?

I'm a British citizen, our embassy doesn't like these things, you know?'

When she's finished talking she notices SHO Kawaljeet is sitting in the back and that the car has stopped. For a moment Jannat holds her breath. *Is it a set up? Are they waiting for him? Was I used as frigging bait? What is it now, rape or death?*

They are waiting for him indeed, not because they want to trap her but because they want to catch him. And now they h ave the perfect pretext.

As soon as Maanka appears in the slice of light Balwant is on him. He handcuffs him and throws him into the back of the car where he keeps hissing and making strange noises.

Back at the police station Balwant is suspended for a week as punishment for having put Jannat in danger even though Jannat is not too sure if Kawaljeet really was unaware of what was going on. 'Okay, come on. I'll drop you home . . . '

"There's no need. You've helped me enough today thanks. I'll get an auto . . . '

Kawaljeet looks at his watch and sighs. 'You are truly stubborn. It's 1.30 am. All of Jalandhar is asleep. Come on, I'll take you home. You don't need to make me coffee.

I am on a coffee detox, I swear.'

Jannat finally manages to smile faintly.

In her room she struggles to get the right flow of thoughts. Her fingers type with discomfort: 'A life filled with epiphanies, big and small, is a life filled with experience and discovery.' What am I thinking, this is a battlefield, I need to investigate. There has be a *modus operandi,* a network of diverse professionals.But India has a population of more than one billion. It's difficult to keep a tab on every crime. However, one strong lead and the whole chain can get exposed. I don't think that is going to happen, I am an alien in this state, I can't trust anybody. Even Kawaljeet could be one of them. Perhaps Rajveer could be of some help, but he is a big mouth and still bathing in his flamboyance.

Her phone rings but she chooses to ignore it, it's either May, whom she doesn't want to update, or Rajveer, who is going to ask her to do something glitzy when she really needs to work. She has had her share of thrills. She has deadlines. May, the scorpion, is waiting to sting. No further distractions.

She gets up and paces in the room, drinks water, switches on iTunes on her phone.

'Someone like you' by Adele is her first choice. Finally she goes back to her laptop and types something, then re-reads it and deletes it all one more time. She takes out her iPhone and opens the 'victims' folder. Names that once referred to a person in the flesh start pouring out of the device: Hardeep Mann, Lucky Singh, Sanu Gupta, Preet Randhawa. She stares at the screen helplessly. She has a broken jigsaw puzzle in her hands. All these people are so different from one another. They led different lives, had different friends and came from or lived in different towns. The only thing that they have in common is that they died in accidents that took place in mysterious cir-cumstances. There were no clues, no evidence. This is the devil at his best.

Jannat sighs with frustration and shuts her laptop. Her phone rings again and is ignored one more time. Then the doorbell rings.

Overwhelmed by all these questions that seem to infest her mind she goes to open it. As she does she's surprised to find Kawaljeet holding Maanka by the handcuffs. 'Good morning. I've decided that it's time I lived up to my dad's legacy . . . '

The first news of the day! Jannat's smile cuts her face from one ear to the other.

She gets two chairs for them to sit on. Maanka, handcuffed and out of his sinister cave, doesn't look as threatening as he had the night before.

Jannat sits in front of him with the iPhone pointing at him to record his confession.

Kawaljeet intermittently hits Maanka when he stops talking.

Maanka talks about a girl being shot dead on her way to a party, in a parking lot; of a man shot on his own doorstep before the very eyes of his wife; of a couple found dead in a hotel on their wedding night. Kawaljeet and Jannat can hardly believe what he's saying.

'Maanka, are you sure these are premeditated murders, contract killings?' the cop asks.

'Kawaljeet *saab,* the people who have a relative who has died of murder know only too well who is the suspect and why. If they call the police more family members will die.

These are assignments with a lot of money or family pride involved. But I am just a small supplier of illegal guns. I've heard a guy named Moga monopolizes the contracts in Jalandhar. I don't know who he is. It may not even be his real name. He is invisible, a ghost. No one knows who he deals with, who commissions the killings and who protects him. If Moga was to speak half of Jalandhar would collapse like a house of cards!'

'I have heard this story before,' Kawaljeet looks at Jannat with an apologetic smile on his serious face. Jannat gives him a stern look.

'What the f___'

'I was playing safe, no confessions, no leads, I need . . . '

'Yeah, right.'

Jannat follows the two to the police station where, in the basement, she finds several piles of dusty folders that Kawaljeet and she will spend the day double-checking. They start with copies of death certificates. They check the list of cases withdrawn for alleged murder. They scrutinize the file that compiles the reports of missing citizens. Then Kawaljeet drives Jannat to Preet's house. His gaze is fixed on the road. The two avoid eye contact. Together they interview Preet's relatives who are stunned at this sudden interest from the police in their daughter's murder. This time they have no option but to speak. Kawaljeet's background helps him win their confidence. Preet's father's tears continue to flow mutely. They are now part of his destiny. Kawaljeet, with Jannat in tow, probes the entire neighbourhood. They take notes. Jannat archives vital information on her laptop while Kawaljeet relishes some tea and *samosa* at a local *dhaba*.

'It's a day's work.'

Jannat fights the dust that turned her into a sneeze machine but her impatience erupts.

'You mean you never got to investigate a contract killing?'

It's always been a dead end, lack of eyewitnesses, evidence destroyed, pressure from higher authorities, case withdrawn. Don't make me repeat myself, it's tough . . . '

'Care to explain the details . . . '

'The dead bodies are disposed off in a private funeral or are missing forever, buried in the fields, burnt in the woods, thrown into a valley. Death certificates are easy to forge or extract by bribing lower-rung officials. Families of the victims feign ignorance. Eyewitnesses turn hostile. Life goes on. It's all a very hush-hush affair.' Kawaljeet leaves his tea midway and gets into his jeep with a mutter, 'I am giving my best, lady.'

Back at the police station Jannat transfers files from her pen drive to Kawaljeet's and vice versa so that they both have all the information. She uses a pen drive in the shape of a bullet that also doubles up for a steel pendant so that she can slip it around her neck without raising suspicion. But a pair of eyes and ears have followed them, seen and heard them at the *dhaba* and will report the day's progress to those who should be the last ones to know.

Tonight several phones ring covertly throughout Punjab. These phones are made within a plush villa, a phoney SIM card shop, a *hawala* agent hideout, a rundown in-dustrial area, a deserted farmhouse, an inconspicuous police station, a shady hotel room, government quarters and a swanky office building. The news of how much Jannat has discovered reaches as far as a ritzy apartment in London.

Preet's mother-in-law, Kim, picks up the phone. She is sporting a very classy Indian outfit with a touch of western style-a pair of beige straight-cut pants paired with a long tunic top. She wears her hair in a neat bun and the deep black becomes nearly blue when reflecting the light of the crystal lamp. Kim is also wearing a pair of diamond earrings and a string of pearls around her neck and an expensive Pashmina shawl over her shoulders.

She panics as she listens, her hands shivers as she tries to put the phone down and she begins fidgeting. Harry looks at her with a severe look that is even darker tonight. They exchange very concerned looks. The silence is charged with suspense until Harry pulls out his phone and dials a number. 'Classified section? Make note . . . Jyotish Janna . . . '

He begins rattling off the astrology advert request but his mother intercepts and takes the phone away from him.

'There's no other way mum. We have to get rid of her.'

'Preet was a terrible mistake, a misfit, a shame to our stature, a nosy babble mouth not worthy to bear your kids, so we got rid of her. Now we have to be extra careful.'

'Mum, this time we will have no comebacks.'

'Not like this. God only knows what and how much she's managed to dig up. You need to go and handle this yourself, Harry! This is how these things are done!'

'What? Go all the way to Punjab? You've got to be joking!'

'Your life may be a joke but mine isn't. You're getting on the next flight to India. And make sure you find out everything she has before you get her blown up!' says Kim dryly before leaving the room, as if this was a regular after-dinner chat. She enters her study, picks up a butter knife and plunges it into the apple kept in the fruit bowl. Her slender hands stop trembling as she grips the silver knife.

Moga cuts an apple with surgical precision. He relishes every slice. He wonders why he didn't get any assignments this night, or even before, and he spent the week in breathless anticipation, running places every now and then to see if any news or messages arrived yet. It feels like being bloodless. His handlers are keeping low for much longer than normal in order to be safe. *Bloody mice.* The cops in Jalandhar have been alarmed for a while to find out how one died, and when and who killed. The *Jalandhar Times* has articles on the deaths every day. *Fun.*

It's about ten in the night when a car pulls in, curving around so that he could swing out easily. He eases up through the stairs, knocks on the door and stands still, taking off his shoes. *Why is the door spinning?* He feels nauseous. He hardly knows what he was going to say to her. Maybe he likes her, but his way of life especially work doesn't al-low such commitments. She smells like butter.

The door opens an inch or two. Then it opens all the way and she stands gaping at him.

'Yes?' she says coldly. She is dressed in sleeping shorts and a shirt and her no make-up face is drawn with sleep. But none of that matters. She yawns openly and says, 'Yes?'

Moga doesn't speak. Guess he wants to stare open-mouthed like a teenage boy.

'Oh it's you!' she laughs suddenly. 'Come on in. I don't usually sleep this early in the night but . . . '

Moga rushes in and locks the door again, 'I'm sorry, but we are going to have a long night.'

'It's all right. But I'll have to have some drink first. You slide into the bed.'

He passes through the little hall to the bedroom, listening to her pour some alcohol.

He acts like a chump. The room has a fragrance of air freshener-rose. He takes in a breath and sneezes. Here is a pretty girl who he wanted, to hell with work. The top dresser drawer is open a little, and the mirror tilted slightly. Ladies are one thing and ladies undercover are something else. He takes a piece of paper out of the drawer just as she comes in with the drinks tray. Her eyes flash and she slams the tray down on a table.

'What,' she snaps, 'are you doing with that?'

'What were you going to do with it?'

She doesn't say anything. She just takes her purse off the dresser, opens it and pulls out a Swiss knife. Moga gives her a goofy smile but doesn't step back. His hunch about her had been dead right. Now he is set for something else, not just the break-up. He slaps her so hard that her ears ring, first on one side then the other. She swings and keeps swinging. The knife falls. Moga stoops to pick it up and she slams her knee under his chin. He stumbles backward on his heels and sits down on the floor.

'Gosh, Moga. I didn't mean to… I…'

'Sure,' Moga grins. His vision is clearing and he finds his voice again.

'I know how it is. Give me a hand, will you, sweety?'

'You…you won't hurt me?'

'Me? Aww, no, love.'

'I know you won't,' she walks over to him slowly and gives him her hands and whispers, 'promise I will make you taste heaven'.

He pulls himself up. He holds her wrists with one hand and swings. It almost stuns her.

Moga doesn't want her completely stunned. He wants her to understand what is happening to her. 'No, love,' his lips draw back from his teeth. 'I am not going to hurt you. I am just going to beat the ass plumb off of you.' He jerks her top up over her face and ties the end in a knot. He throws her down on the bed, pulls off her shorts and ties her feet together with them. He takes off his belt and raises it over his head.

After he gets back to his senses he realizes his arm aches like hell and her body has one big bruise. He frees her feet and hands and pulls the shirt off her head. He pours the drink between her lips and licks it. And all the time while he is licking he pulls the knife off the side table and slits her neck. At last her eyelids flutter and open. He brushes his lips against hers one last time. 'Don't back stab me honey,' he says. 'I am just an ordinary guy'.

Her body, lying perfectly still on the bed, is draped in cloth now. He washes his hands quietly in the sink, wondering how long he has, and gently touches the body. Young skin is his favourite, soft and plump, with the texture of a mustard flower.

He moves his lips around the body, arm to leg, leg to arm, arm to torso, torso to neck, until the whole thing is covered in blood, spit, and alcohol. The room smells like death, whiskey and a rose garden.

'There's a big difference between a murderer and a contract killer.'

He remembers that pretty face. 'So you are not a murderer,' she had once said.

'Contract killer. What's the difference between both, Moga? I don't see a difference.'

21

An anonymous black sedan picks Harry up from the airport. Hell, no one must remember seeing a posh car or a limo picking up a wealthy businessman from London.

If anyone ever asked, but no one will, he'll just say he did go to Punjab on a family visit.

He hasn't been back since Preet died, so it's more than reasonable that he wanted to pay a visit. He may also throw in that he went to visit her parents for good measure. The two old derelicts are poor and sick to the bone. They may not remember seeing him but Harry's sure he could help them remember with ten or fifteen thousand rupees . . .

He gets in the car and reads out the address to

the driver. He manipulates the tone of his voice to blend with the Punjabi dialect. The stench of smoke is strong and Harry's face is grim. He tries to hold his breath for a while but then succumbs and opens the window. The cold air of Punjab whirls in but the smell it carries is the scent of home, of fennel seeds and curry, or fried food and basmati rice. In England the air smells like muffins and pancakes; it's always a synthetic smell of something sweet that someone assembled but never entirely cooked.

It's the smell that Preet loved more than anything in the world. For her, it was the perfume of a new life, where she could be rich and buy British Airways teddy bears for her parents who had never been on a plane. For Harry it was just the stench of a life he was forced to live because it had been stitched onto him. Although he loved the golf and weekend hunting trips with friends, deep down he hated England. He had never really lived in India and yet he knew he belonged here a lot more than he did while studying at St Andrews or at the unending Sunday lunches where you keep eating those soggy roasts drowned in gravy because the weather outside is so miserable you really have nothing else to do.

Lost in the memory of an India he has only dreamed of and high on the myriad of smells that have invaded the car he gets to the Khannas' residence. He stops at the outhouse. Harry knows the protocol for these kinds of dealings. As he gets a glimpse of the inconspicuous façade he finds Ranjeet in the oval porch, rolling cigarettes with care, as if each one was a piece of art. Harry clears his throat to make sure the man knows he's here and gets the feeling the man has noticed him but is plain uninterested in making conversation. Harry just crossed half the world for this bloody conversation and the middle-aged man better stop rolling cigarettes and greet him.

To be fair Ranjeet has seen a plain-looking man enter through the main door and has no clue who Harry is, not that if he did he'd grant him a much warmer welcome. Therefore he greets him but then goes back to his work. He assumes the stranger is a visitor, some medical professional for his elder brother looking for a way into the mansion.

'*Namaste ji.* Sorry, do I know you?'

'Harwinder Randhawa, from London . . . Preet Randhawa . . . Does it ring a bell?'

'*Nahi ji* . . . No club . . . Maybe you are at the wrong address, try next lane?'

'Impossible. How dare you? I paid you half a million pounds for this job. It is not done, Mr Khanna,' Harry finally has Ranjeet's attention.

The sound of the words-half a million pounds-is so familiar, a killing from which he had profited.

The man blinks a couple of times, just to be sure he is where he thinks he is and the good looking man in front of him is who he says he is. He looks around. There isn't anybody else.

Yes, Harry Randhawa, Ranjeet remembers him. It was a woman . . . One of those stupid killings a few months ago that Ranjeet despises despite the large sums of money paid.

The Khannas are assassins, not cheap murderers, but nowadays the market calls for this sort of crap. The wife came from England and, if Ranjeet remembers it correctly, a staged train accident, the papers talked of it as 'the English princess who came to kill herself at home'.

Of course the job was done! What is this fool talking about?

Meanwhile, on the scenic Himachal roads, Rajveer is taking Jannat on a motorbike ride.

The milestone reads 'Palampur 90 km'. The wind is whipping her hair into her face and the feeling of freedom is beautiful. As they go up the winding road the world is covered with soft, thin white tulle; the clouds are below them. As he accelerates the black 500cc bike Jannat feels her hands, tightly gripped on his shoulders, nearly fly away, and the more unstable she feels the deeper she digs her nails into his leather jacket. The Bullet by Royal Enfield is what Rajveer grew up on since his high school days. After umpteen falls he now rides like a warrior on his steed.

'Slow down please, I'm not insured!' she screams, afraid the wind will carry her words away.

But Rajveer hears her all right. He slows down, lets go of the handlebar with one hand, takes Jannat's hand and puts it on his chest. She does the same with the other hand: now that she has a surer grip she smiles to herself.

'Now you are,' he says, nearly reading her mind.

'Where are you taking me anyway?'

'You'll see. Just trust me, okay?'

'I'll try,' she responds flirtatiously.

The motorbike gains speed under Rajveer's strong hands for the last part of the climb.

Everything on this mountain is quiet and peaceful; it's almost a shame to ride a bike in this lush green. As they propel the motorbike up the hill Rajveer's phone rings. He sees that the call is from Uncle Ranjeet, but right now he couldn't answer even if he wanted to, and with Jannat's hand tightly gripped to his chest the last thing he wants to do is speak with his uncle, his partner in crime.

On the other side Ranjeet is furious.

Rajveer on his side of the magical world, high on the fresh and brisk air, sings along with the ringtone of his phone, a tune by the legendary RD Burman.

Ranjeet keeps calling but Rajveer is simply enjoying the music, oblivious to the fact that it's a ringtone.

After the tenth attempt Ranjeet looks at Harry, empty-hearted.

'You have my word. You need not worry. Your job will be done.'

Harry pulls out Jannat's photos and scribbles 'KILL GILL' behind it with his red pen: he then hands the photos to Ranjeet.

'Take this, hand delivered, finish her, immediately.'

He looks at the photo again and adds enigmatically, 'Look . . . It has been difficult to trace you guys. I have used all my clandestine contacts to get here. There's no room for error now, or else . . . ' and on the unfinished sentence he leaves the room.

Rajveer's motorbike pulls up in front of a beautiful farmhouse nestled in the midst of pine trees; the style is almost like that of a Swiss chalet. For a moment Jannat is unsure of where she is. She can smell fresh jasmine from the extensive gardens on one side of the fence. Rajveer pulls out his arm to reach for her hand, she follows him.

Everything is so beautiful, and it almost seems impossible that only a couple of hours away the real India is bursting with its markets, its traffic, its beggars. Here is a slice of paradise. Here the climate is peaceful and clean. Everything smells of the foliage that surrounds the place; it's not that full scent one can smell and get intoxicated by when the summer begins in this part of the globe but the delicate and beautiful aroma that hits the heart like a wave.

'Jannat. A girl who breathes in silence and one silence gasps for.'

Ranjeet, stationed in his dark outhouse office, is struck by the determined face staring up at him from the photograph, the same pretty face he saw at the Lohri celebration with Raj a few nights ago. What a chameleon! Finally a girl with guts.

Steely-eyed, he gets into the car and drives to the construction site.

Gupta is surprised but greets him; Ranjeet is the boss and can come and go as he pleases. 'Need a little refill, boss?'

'No. We do have a safe computer, one that cannot trace back to us? Gupta, listen to me carefully, do we have a web connection that is absolutely safe?'

'Yes sir, downstairs; the basement doesn't exist so everything there is safe, but . . . '

'We need to run a check on a person, but this search cannot be traced back to us, understand?'

'Yes, Sir. We are equipped for that. Come with me.'

They take the narrow staircase that is supposed to be closed, since the basement was 'locked up for good'. The stairsare dirty enough to lead any negligent cop to think that no one has used it in years, but if someone were to look more closely they would see that the remains of food and drink are recent. This is dangerous. Ranjeet points it out to Gupta.

I'll see to it, Sir.'

Gupta turns on the computer hidden behind the tattered curtains. He types the name jotted on a piece of paper-Jannat Gill. A few Jannat Gills crop up. Ranjeet is perplexed. Is Harry playing a game? Is he for real?

And then Gupta punches on page two of the search engine website.

Immediately Jannat's face appears on the screen as the cover photo of her blog. This is the same girl who came to the house with Rajveer. The two men read what she has been posting lately. The most recent posts are updates on her research on missing NRI's and NRI accidental deaths. She has also invited bloggers and readers for any useful leads. Gupta prints all he can find while Ranjeet paces around the room, fuming and swearing against his inconsiderate nephew.

'Young fool. There has to be a slip. Is it worth the price that she will pay now?'

They shouldn't be killing women for any reason as far as possible. Preet was an exception to the rule as it happens in all businesses, because the money was huge. And now they have another girl to eliminate who happens to swim into their net . . . This has to be done, but it's really unfair. If only she hadn't stuck her prying English nose into their business she could keep her inadequate, worthless, reporter's life. But then business is business.

Jannat and Rajveer, unaware of what awaits the two of them when they get back, sit on the veranda of the villa, on the comfortable armchairs with their legs on the wooden railing, facing the sunset that embosses the tree plantations. Their faces have turned orange from the warm light of the sun going down. They engage in small talk even though they both know, or at least suspect, what will come after.

'And you? Any siblings?'

'Nah. Only child. My parents decided to split

when I was three. But I lost mum to breast cancer a few years ago; it was detected very late. As for my dad . . . well I never had much of a relationship with him, he walked out and remarried and that was it. A few cards at Christmas, he came to my graduation, but nothing more. He lives in Scotland, where he's a professor at Edinburgh University. He had two kids with his new wife. For years I wondered why someone should leave the family he has to go and build another one. I wondered if he loved his children more than he had ever loved me. What was he hungry for? Sex? Companionship? Status? Or was he running away from the ghosts of the past? Then I stopped worrying. He is just an acquaintance to whom I can refer to if I'm in need but who is unable to offer his love spontaneously. Maybe he is too clinical. Some people are simply made that way. They live life with surgical precision,' she scoffs, 'I grew up mostly with bebe, my doting grandmother, and of course my mother. They were my real family and that was enough. I'm still alive as you can see!'

'God can't be everywhere so he made mothers... And grandmothers too!' adds Rajveer.

'You're right; my *bebe* is the most important part of my life now. But I still miss my mom . . . '

A golden yellow feather blows right in front of them. Rajveer catches it and takes Jannat's hand. It looks as though it belongs to a *bulbul.* He holds her palm still in his strong and dark hand and strokes her thin fingers with the small feather before placing the feather onto her palm. 'Now blow it away.'

She obliges, never lowering her eyes, which she keeps fixed onto his, lost in his dreams that are becoming, against her will, hers too.

'The trick is to let go.'

She watches the feather fly away. They smile at each other. Rajveer rests his hand on hers with familiarity and fortitude. 'Thanks for pampering me like this . . . ' 'Anytime, darling. How about some chai… a steaming cup of ginger tea?' Jannat probably expected, or wished for some more romance, but Rajveer saw in her eyes what he had never seen beforelove.

Yes he'd had many women; he slept with them, he flirted with them, taken them out to dinner and charmed them with his countryside rendezvous, but never once was he in love. Those sweet sensations that throb inside your heart and make the earth look like a drunken paradise. He was too familiar with machinations to fathom the depth of an art that belongs to the soul of mankind-love. Right now, in the orange shades of sunset, his eyes met Jannat's and for the first time he felt love and was afraid. This was a revelation for him. He comes from a family of assassins, getting killed is part of the game, and yet he had never been as afraid as he is today. To kill is easy, it only takes a moment, but to fall in love is to yearn for a lifetime. If he was addicted to love it could prove detrimental to his choice of life. In Jannat's eyes he saw a fresh start, a different life, children playing in the higher altitude weather and the struggle to pay the bills at the end of the month. He never had that. He comes from a wealthy family, more wealth coming in every day, and there will always be crime, hushed and paying. His parents were together because they were meant to be, not by destiny but by the decisions of their parents, and his turn would come sooner or later.

She's different. She is girl who wears her destiny on her heels. Her fears are the trea-sure that she is out to seek. This is a woman who packs a suitcase and goes to India for work. She is educated, she has travelled, she seems to be aware of the world around her. And even though she lived with little money and her parents parted when she was a child, there's that inner happiness in her that he envies and would like to learn to build for himself. Where does she get it?

Is it her fair, clean feet? Or is it her serene grey eyes?

Is it the strength in her heart or is it the thickness of her hair?

She expected romance, yes, but if I gave her

romance now, in a kiss, in a tear, in a word, in a glance, in a touch, I would be trapped. And as much as I want her and her vigour, I am afraid of such a sudden change. Why do I fear?

'Fear is death, a serpent camouflaged in a flowering face.'

And the future might not be as fresh as the dewdrop on the grass outside in this present. Rajveer tightens his chest. His mind starts toying with its own soldiers. The battle gets gentle and fierce. 'We don't romance with someone for who they are but instead to fathom who we are.'

22

Jannat is walking around the living room. The fire lit in the black fire place bathes the room in a golden light that makes everything look as if it came out of a distant and sweet dream.

'The more we are different, the more are we the same.'

If this were a house in England she would have said it belonged to a grandmother with traditional tastes. The walls are covered with photos of Rajveer, his brother and other members of their family. It is a little intimidating to walk past so many generations all at once. She ventures into the dark corridor to the left of the living room. The space is dark, only dimly lit by the reflection of the fire, and cold. There are many doors on both sides of the corridor, all of which are locked. Jannat feels a chill run down her spine; she has been taught not to snoop around and yet she can't help her-self. With every step the curiosity grows.

Under her unsure fingers all doors seem locked, until she turns a knob that lets her into a small, dusty, sub-world of that big world that's the house where Rajveer took her. At first she hesitates, her breath quickens and her palms grow moist, but it's only a second; she can't resist and opens it anyway. She walks into the room, feeling the wall next to her for a light switch, which is nowhere to be found. She takes the iPhone from her pocket and turns its light on. The sterile white screen is not bright enough to light a room and the space around Jannat looks mildly grey and a lot colder than it is. In the white light that shines onto the room she can distinguish a small cupboard, a single bed and stickers on the wall. This is a boy's room.

Sports trophies line the shelves on the wall along with pictures of Rajveer in his teens, wearing a hockey kit, holding up a trophy cup. Jannat is mesmerized. This world doesn't match with the image Rajveer tries to portray of himself-so powerful, so fearless, he looks like he had never been a child. She walks around the room feeling the bedspread, picking up a toy train and putting it back on its model track on the wooden table. Then her eyes fall on a collage of Polaroid pictures; she used to have one of these boards in her room too. These are photographs of Rajveer. In each one of them he is with a different girl. Under each photo there's a name and date; the last one is only six months old.

Suddenly the light is turned on and all the objects in the room lose their halo of mystery and regain their role as memorabilia in a child's room. All of a sudden Jannat is almost disappointed with what she sees, as if the switching on of a light bulb stole her secret and made it visible to anyone. Rajveer appears in the doorway.

'I . . . I . . . am, I mean . . . '

'I was wondering where you disappeared . . . ' he says nonchalantly.

'I'm so sorry . . . I . . . I just . . . '

'It's okay. This house tends to have this effect on people.'

His gaze falls on the collage at which she was evidently looking. She lowers her eyes, as if by doing so she can convince him that she didn't notice a three-foot tall card-board with pictures of his former girlfriends on it.

'Come, your chai's getting cold.'

Jannat leaves first. Rajveer looks around the room. He smiles as he walks to the card-board collage and puts it in the cupboard, where it used to be kept. He had taken it out a few days ago, he cannot say why.

Jannat sits on the floor, on the white woollen rug in front of the bonfire, sipping her ginger chai. Rajveer joins her with his blue mug, his face half-hidden behind a cloud of steam. Jannat shivers at the sight of those deep black eyes that seem to pierce right through her.

'So you are into Polaroids. Serial stuff or just plain kinky?'

'What is that supposed to mean?'

'A real hero is always at war with his unconscious, death being the prime villain, and you . . . '

'This is who I am.'

'Yeah, yeah. Whatever. I saw all those escapade victims . . . No servants... no caretaker . . . So this place is your little weekend getaway where . . . ' she jokes. The joke, however, can't hide a sort of retrospective jealousy. This is typical . . . there has been nothing be-tween him and me, what right do I have to be jealous? Or even to want anything from him? But all those girls . . .

'Look, a man has got to have his adventures, right?' he interrupts her train of thought.

'Protected adventures I hope, Raj!'

Rajveer pinches his throat in oath.

'Always.'

They both laugh out loud.

'And what about you?'

'Me? I'm a good girl . . . '

'Oh, come on . . . No flings, no boyfriends? Someone as gorgeous as you . . . it's rather hard to believe!'

Suddenly Jannat becomes sombre. 'Andy, my ex-boyfriend, used to think I was boring:

too focused on my career, too adventurous and a bra-burning feminist, who . . . '

'No way . . . I wouldn't have suspected that . . . But I also haven't seen you burning a bra yet, please do it, it would be a very sexy . . . '

'Yeah whatever, I'm not sure you understand what the symbolism of burning a bra is and let's just keep it that way . . . We broke up last month. He proposed; had it all figured out. We would get married, I would leave my job and stay at home cook meals, grow plants, make jam and have lots of well-behaved children so other parents could envy us . . . But despite the horror plan he had for me, he was great in bed . . . '

'Too much information, girl! Can you see through that window there?' he suddenly asks.

'There's a . . . big field . . . '

'Well, yeah, it's a field now. But hopefully in a few years' time there will be a solar power plant. It's my vision, my dream if you like. I do things for my family's business that I am not very happy about. Very often I feel that my life should go elsewhere. In a different direction. And after much thinking I think that this is where it should go . . . with plenty of air and sunlight in this region. It's a viable project,' Rajveer slides across a black trolley with a miniature model enclosed in a glass cabinet. He lifts the satin cover to reveal a white plastic mock-up of a solar power plant with all the works. The spherical tower beside the solar receiver is strikingly tall and the small pieces of mir-rors used as reflectors add to the glamorous design.

'I'm sure it takes a lot of money; how are you going to . . . '

'Yeah, Miss Dream Wrecker! But this could change the lives of people in this district and Punjab, you know what I mean? Besides I know some people who might just get interested in funding!'

'I believe if God wants to make you miserable then he would fulfil all your dreams. It's a sure shot recipe for disaster! But this one is a brilliant plan, I pray it happens.'

'Yes it is, and that's why I am so passionate about it. Passion changes all the rules of the game.'

Jannat, impressed, smiles at him: she would have never guessed that someone like Rajveer could dream of something so beneficial. A desire to influence events is usual, but generating power in the true sense is noble.

Rajveer stares at her, fishing for muted compliments. 'So . . . '

'So what?' she grins. She shrugs at him, trying to make sense of her complicated life. Where does she fit, in the curve of so many dreams, so many roles and so many lives?

They look at each other, and as the gaze becomes more intense Rajveer moves closer and puts his arm around her. She looks up at him, incredulous.

'So am I your January escapade, Power Man?' she whispers in his ear. It tickles him wet.

'I don't think so . . .' he replies in his deep, husky voice. He wants to taste the texture of her skin.

'Yeah? What is it then?'

Their faces are really close; they can feel the warmth of each other's breath on their skin and the potent smell of ginger embraces them. Jannat looks into his eyes. Her almond eyes of a luscious green piercing through his like those of a panther in the night. He has no escape, nowhere to run, nowhere to hide. And he succumbs. While her clothes slideoff her soft tanned skin he can't resist the urge to caress her shoul-ders, follow the curve of her collarbones onto her ribs, her breasts and her stomach. Jannat's skin vibrates from the cold and under Rajveer's touch, but it's as if her mind was somewhere else. All around her, inside her, the feeling of having found a home, at long last, is overwhelming.

This is her home. This man, his arms, his grip, his eyelashes, his eyes, the black hair of his forearms and the soft hair on his stomach. He incarnates the home, the protective shield and the fireplace to which she'll always return. He rests in her his masculinity, his attitude, his verve, she feels secure. She feels ro-bust. There is heat. There is harmony. In the precincts of their flaming muscles occurs a subliminal outburst. A gush of mint-cool freshness.

And then there is the thirst for more.

His body is a map, like hers for him, and they both discover main roads and shortcuts into each other's lives. Sometimes they stop and tell each other the story of a scar and then go back. Love. They both have had lovers before, boyfriends, girlfriends, but lovemaking, they discover now, had always been mechanical, carried out for its own sake, more of an outlet for buried emotions. It was something that made them feel good, but it had always been, before tonight, an independent matter. They had said 'I love you' a million times, but never before tonight had they really meant it. Not be-cause they lied but simply because they never knew what it really meant.

Every time they lock lips they learn something more about themselves and about each other; every time their hands run over each other's skin a rare feeling is stirred, new emotions are exposed, fresh spots of joy are explored.

The night is swallowed by the pink dawn without their noticing. The air has a scent that each has never experienced before.

As the fire dies in the hearth and they lie down, exhausted and entirely happy, Rajveer's lucky charm, the gemstone ring, is caught in the rug fibre and he lets it roll off his finger to avoid breaking the spell of the beautiful moment. It rolls on the marble floor and eventually ends inside Jannat's handbag. The two are so tired and yet eager to have more of one another that the thought of the ring quickly slips from Rajveer's mind.

He lies next to Jannat on the black blanket they had put on the floor and falls asleep holding her in his arms. Two bodies entangled in each other like lush vines.

It's a while before Rajveer gets up and from the pocket of his trousers extracts a silver cigarette case. He lights one and then hands the case to Jannat. She holds it in her hand, unsure what to do next.

'I didn't know you smoked . . . '

His shirt is glued onto her naked body, leaving nothing to the imagination. And yet it's not sexual, there's something more about her that forces him to get closer every minute:he's drawn to her and there's absolutely nothing he can do to fight back. Secretly, unable to confess it even to himself, he hoped that making love to her would be an emotionless experience, as it had always been, to wipe her out of his head, but it wasn't. It was amazing, it was powerful and soft, the way she held his head in her hands, the way she sat on him, the way she kissed him, the way she numbed him . . . it was out of this world. Now she's there, almost talking to herself and not realizing what a powerful spell she has cast on him.

'I gave it up after college, but you know how one never really stops . . . I was a bit over-loaded with work and then the Andy thing happened. Wish I hadn't started again.'

'I don't smoke unless I'm over the moon about something.'

Jannat furrows her eyebrows and looks at him quizzically.

'Meaning?'

'Meaning... I have to be extremely happy, feel free . . . that's when I smoke . . . Weird, huh?'

'I'll say, half the world smokes because they are too damn sad and I meet the only one guy who smokes to celebrate his happiness!'

Jannat lights her cigarette and takes a long drag. They look at each other as if they were still living in their dream, as if their bodies were resting but their restless spirits were making love to each other. Unperturbed.

'You know there's something I need to tell you . . . '

'Yeah?'

'I haven't been upfront with you about something. I actually have come to . . . '

But she's interrupted by a power cut.

'Oh shit . . . I just hope there's enough oil in the generator!' he hisses as he gets up and quickly wears his trousers.

'Hold that thought. I'll be right back . . . ' and he gets out of the door, his skin still moist with their sweat and the cold air from outside pouring in.

A few minutes later Jannat hears a generator start in the background; its loud whacking noise is followed by instant light filling the room again. Rajveer comes in; his skin is covered in goose bumps. Jannat smiles at him. And at once they know what's going to happen. The room is filled with soft noise. This time it's far more seductive, but the sensuous banter continues.

'Love can shake you up.'

'Love can give you stability, strong as steel.'

'Yeaaah!'

In the Khannas' residence, at the back office, Ranjeet takes Jannat's photograph, the one Harry gave him earlier, and sticks it under a pile of astrology advertisements, then shuts the chest close. He locks it with a brass key and on it rests a tray with glasses and a jug.

Where is Rajveer? Is he in danger? Is he with her?

He sits on a wooden chair and phones to arrange with Gupta to hire Moga for tonight.

23

Jannat's room is dark as hell in the middle of the night; shadows as black as Darjeeling tea melt on the chest of drawers and the thin rays of the moon that manage to filter through the window are chased away by the night. Outside, in the distance, a faint light can be seen, maybe a car, maybe a street lamp. Dawn is still far away.

Jannat sleeps, cuddled by the warm blanket and with the sound of the sharp wind shut out of her door.She's not worried, she's in love; the man she fell for loves her back. She sleeps with a smile on her face, without having to fear anything in this cozy room, with the fond memory of his body wrapped around hers.

What Jannat doesn't know is that among the shadows of the night moves another shadow, thicker, heavier, not just a shadow. A person. This person smells of cigarettes and is dressed in black. People like him are not afraid of the night; they slither along with dark spirits and disappear as the first golden rays of the sun wash over the country.

Moga wears his black leather gloves, his black leather jacket and moves like a hungry wolf. The eerie rhythm of his footsteps is silent and smooth. His dark shoes slide like the paws of a deadly beast excluding the claws. He looks at Jannat sleeping; she frowns, but only for a second, and as soon as he's sure she won't wake up he bends over her. He does it ceremoniously like a prince would in a fairy tale. His vicious face glides above her alluring body. With his thick neck bent and his hairy chest letting out the sparkling sight of the red-eyed bull's head, he smells her like a wolf would smell its dying prey.

Hell descends in a flash inside this fateful room.

He kisses her on the forehead, later he wouldn't be able to explain why he did it, but he kisses her crudely, as if to apologize, to express for once a love that he is not en-titled to. As soon as his lips part from her head, he pulls out a gun and places it where his wet lips left a mark, she moves, rolls in her bed as if just faintly disturbed by a fly, then opens her eyes to check the time and sees him. He darts the most evil ray of crude energy.

She would have wanted to scream, have time to be heard, have time to fight back, have time... But there was nothing she could do. As soon as her fingers tighten their grip and her nails sink in the blanket, as soon as she drew a breath, the trigger was pulled, and a rivulet of blood started flowing from the centre of her forehead, washing away Moga's kiss. Forever.

Ranjeet's eyes open at once, his pupils shrinking as soon as the light hits them. It was all a dream, nothing has happened, yet. But it has to. This is a foreshadowing. This is meant to happen, the sooner the better.

He gets up from the old armchair in his office where he likes to doze on the hot summer days and, apparently, also in the cold winter nights, and goes to his desk. The table is covered in cigarette papers and tobacco; a few pens are scattered on the side. He takes one, a black one with a very fine nib and scribbles Jannat's name and a phone number on a rolling paper, then he rolls a cigarette, slowly, carefully, making sure that the creases of the paper keep his secret until it's in safe.

At the farmhouse the sun is knocking at the windows, warming Jannat's cheek and waking her up gently. She hears music while her eyes still linger in the last minutes of sleep; it comes from somewhere close. It's not recorded, someone is playing and he's in the room.

She opens her eyes and sees Rajveer, sitting bare-chested next to her, playing the mouth organ. His chest moves softly under the breaths that he draws with every note.

'You surprise me.'

'Oh, I can do stuff you can imagine and the stuff you can't imagine'

'I could never imagine music out of you Raj: ever heard of melody from an exploding star?'

'Everyone is born a poet, Jannat, they just need to fall in love.'

'Love is an art, a little bit of science, but at the core . . . infinite obsession.'

'It's your energy, Jannat, blazing with love, and I am getting sunburn.'

He stops playing and stares at his tattoo, a sun's outline imprinted on the back of his palm, suddenly the room is silent, like a ghost just passed by. The tension grows imperceptibly as Jannat realizes that she is in his house, in the middle of nowhere and she's not sure if last night was just a one-night stand or the beginning of a relationship.

What the hell. Okay, Jannat, calm down. He's

here sitting next to you, he watched you sleep.If he thought it was a mistake why would he stay and not wait for me outside? No, he stayed because he wanted to. And I want him to be here too. And now he played this wonderful tune.

'Thank you for that, it was a striking way to wake up . . . '

'Each present moment is like a fire helmet, it will protect you from the infernos of the past and the future.'

She is getting pulled into the vortex. Flawless charm. His words spell power. He is in command. He hands her the instrument without saying a word.

Oh yeah, he's dropping the bomb, be prepared, Jannat, its coming! Fetch your bra and shirt before it gets really awkward . . .

'For you. Take it, you can . . . ' Jannat is taken aback.

'But I can't play . . . I mean . . . '

'Keep it. It's to remind you of this morning, this . . . '

And why, where are you going she would like to ask, but she can't. She knows it's coming to an end. She has been through this in high school. He smiles and asks her if she wants breakfast. His eyes are a giveaway. There could be more! This is way past high school romance!

'Breakfast? I can make French toast from scratch, cooking is . . . '

'You really are full of surprises!'

Half an hour later, as Rajveer's motorbike rolls down the hill on the winding roads that seem so soft and warm now, Jannat hugs him from the back and thinks of this first time that she's utterly in love. Not like Andy love, not a planned, efficient love where two people with similar backgrounds and expectations put together their hearts to build a house, a cage in Jannat's case, around it. Rajveer is everything she didn't know she wanted and also didn't know existed. It's just him, all about him. They drive past the graveyard she saw at the end of her first day of 'real Punjab' but she doesn't even notice it.

She's on a different page now, everything has to be re-written.

'Do you believe in an ideal woman, Raj?'

'There is nothing like an ideal woman and there is nothing like a perfect man; there is only an ideal moment where the perfect romance is born.'

He presses on the accelerator with the sound of victory. Jannat for once is thought-less, like a little girl stepping into a valley of flowers.

As Rajveer drops her off in front of Naseebo's *kothi* he kisses her goodbye, a long moist kiss that attracts the attention of the children playing around. For the first time Jannat doesn't care, the whole world can look at her if they want. She feels whole for the first time.

Rajveer's bike pulls over at his city home a few minutes later. He waits for a servant to open the gate and drives through. As soon as Ranjeet hears the powerful engine he walks down to greet his nephew. He's anxious and disturbed, the night has been long and only he can understand what a moment too long can mean. If that spark has lit the fire it is too late, the job is going to be painful and Rajveer will be out of the game, for a while at least. Ranjeet himself fell in love once, with the woman he was meant to kill; she smiled and made plans with him, unaware that her innocence made it even harder to stay away from her. But she had betrayed her husband; she had stolen mon-ey for another man, possibly her lover. Ranjeet discovered that he wasn't her lover; her lover double-crossed her, ran away with her money and deserted her the way she deserted her husband. The money was gone and her husband was sure she was the culprit, absconding. He hired the Khannas to kill her and get vindicated. At that time Ranjeet was a young bachelor, his father powerful, and all his protests weren't enough to stop the job. Ranjeet did the job himself; he wanted her last minutes in this life to be happy. He didn't want some dirty scum to scare her to death before butchering her. He drove her to a log cabin in the hills. Ranjeet made love to her, and as she fell asleep he kissed her on the forehead and shot her in the head. He burnt the body to ashes in the deep pinewood jungles. That was the only murder anybody had ever committed in the entire Khanna family. Nobody else has been privy to this dirty secret that was buried with his father when he died of a heart attack. His father was deeply disturbed by the guilt of his own son becoming an assassin even if it was for business.

From then Ranjeet became a cold machine, unable to love, unable to feel emotions. The only things that mattered were business and family, in this order. He had seen people kill and get killed for very little. A family only stays together as long as all the components that make it stable stay. Wives in their family were spoilt; would they stick around if suddenly the Khanna men lost all their money? He didn't think so. Children would have to leave to get jobs elsewhere. So yeah, in Ranjeet's view of the world business comes first. It's what allows him to have a nice house filled with a loving family. Business first.

'Harry Randhawa was here!'

'Who Harry Randhawa?'

Ranjeet reaches for his silver cigarette case.

'First tell me, who is Jannat? Who is she really?'

'Wait . . . What? What are you getting at, *chachaji?*'

Just then Puneet and Rajveer's mother enter the room. Ranjeet quickly puts his cigarette case back into his pocket as Rajveer bends down to touch their feet.

'Bless you. Come get ready, we need to attend the Kapoor wedding.'

'Papaji, take the driver.'

'Son, Kapoor Uncle will feel bad. He insisted I get you. Maybe he wants youfor his daughter?'

Rajveer tries to protests but to no avail. His mother gives him a stern look and waits for him to go and change, Ranjeet, a strained and frustrated look on his face, stands there in silence.

Rajveer walks to his wardrobe and pulls out a *sherwani,* nicely ironed and starched. He takes another chrome watch from his watch closet.

Puneet notices the frustrated expression on Ranjeet's face and stares at him suspiciously. 'What's with you?'

'Nothing,' answers his brother, waving him away.

Puneet leaves the room, shrugging.

Ranjeet takes out the silver cigarette case again and walks over to Rajveer with a menacing face. He takes out a cigarette; to any person looking at them they'd look like a distressed uncle who is smoking while engaging in a fight with his young nephew. What they wouldn't know is that the cigarette holds a name. *Her name.* Rajveer looks at it. He knows there's a name, but not knowing which name makes him careless, as if an anonymous life was worth so much lesser than a known one. But in the end, isn't it so?

'Deliver it today . . . It's urgent . . . The job has to be done smoothly.'

'Harry Randhawa, you mentioned that name, what was . . . ?'

Rajveer takes the cigarette and places it on his bedside table.

Puneet and his wife enter the room again. 'Let's leave son!'

'Yes mom . . . one minute!'

His mother exits while Puneet lingers and waits for Rajveer to finish dressing. Rajveer checks himself out in the mirror, sprays some cologne and joins his father while leaving the room. Ranjeet interrupts, first by clearing his throat and then by speaking out loud, 'Aren't you forgetting something, Rajveer?'

Puneet leaves as his cell phone rings. Rajveer looks back and sees the cigarette waiting to be taken from his bedside table. He looks at his uncle with a puzzled expression, as if to say, 'So, am I supposed to go to a party with a gun and stop for a job as others would for a cup of coffee?'

But Ranjeet's expression leaves very little to be interpreted.

Rajveer quickly runs back to the bedside table and picks up the cigarette and places it in his own silver cigarette case. He sees his parents waiting at the entrance and smiles warmly.

24

As the day ends, Harry, in a mix of excitement of being home and weariness from all these recent and undecipherable events, walks into the bar of a luxury hotel. Having been brought up in a wealthy Indian family in England he brings with him the very essence of Indian expats; he loves the vibe of India but also can't stand the lack of modern services and leisure. Therefore for his sundowners he doesn't pick just any bar but the most expensive one in the city, where he is sure to find highclass people and not some prying idiots who would make him the talk of the town the next day.

In fact, the moment he walks into the bar, he knows he picked the right place; the waiters are silent and clean, their uniforms immaculate and they only bow their heads to show they have understood the order without wasting time in stupid conversations. The room is nice, dimly lit and warm with a wonderful view over the magnificent city. He orders a gin and tonic and sits there in a corner that makes him seem like a busi-nessman from a faraway metropolis who has no personal connections in Jalandhar. As the gin and tonics keep flowing Harry gets more relaxed; he stares at the Punjabi lady receptionist until his phone rings.

'Oh, hello there! Mama?' he says in his perfect English accent.

At the other end Harry can hear the sounds of a party. He knows these parties, knows exactly what the high Indian society in London likes to wear, what they smell like, what they talk about, what they read. He knows what he's missing out on and for once he's happy to be exactly where he is. He remembered being attracted to Preet initially only due to her strong rooted connections with her family in Punjab.

Kim is on the phone, irritated because she can't hear Harry speaking, and from the broken pieces of the conversation she realizes he can't hear her either. She wears an expensive silk *salwaar kameez* with solitaire earrings and a string of pearls around her neck. Her hair is neatly wrapped in a bun and her makeup is simple and elegant. Unlike many rich Indian women she dislikes the outrageous display of wealth when they are at one of these events. This one is the NRI Women's Rights Charity Ball to fund raise against domestic violence.

'*Beta*, burn her alive if you have to.'

Sounds come from the other end but before she can repeat herself someone appears behind her making her start with a fright.

'Madam, your speech is next.'

Kim smiles at the lady and when she's sure she's not being overheard she repeats, 'Kill the bitch but make sure you get all the information from her first . . . You need to attend to this personally. You don't screw up on that!' and hangs up. A second later she's walking gracefully to the podium where she is handed the microphone and everyone bursts into applause.

Lights dim and Kim begins her speech-the most gracious and powerful tone that can give any American politician a run for their money.

'Domestic Violence against our NRI girls . . . There's so much to say about it, but I want to make sure my message sticks with you tonight. I don't want you to wake up tomorrow and say "Oh God that speech was so long" . . . '

The audience laughs.

'Ladies and Gentlemen, I urge you to take a pledge with me today. I want you to scream the words until they penetrate in your very soul and you deeply understand and feel their meaning. Please repeat after me-zero tolerance for domestic violence!'

'Zero tolerance for domestic violence!'

Everyone erupts in cheers, and as they clap their hands for her Kim looks at them with her malicious eyes and beaming face. She whispers to herself, 'Bunch of filthy rich assholes.'

After this any accusation targeting her or her family, if there ever were one, is bound to disappear. She smiles a victory. Her thoughts rush back to Harry.

What Harry, like most Indian men, doesn't understand is that action in itself is never enough. We don't live in a world of uneducated people anymore: people talk, watch TV, speak to those useless feminists from NGOs, have access to the Internet. Solving problems must be approached from many different angles. People must like you if you want their support. This works in politics, in business and also in social relations. The British people forgave Lady D for running away from her husband and children because they loved her; she made sure every person liked her, in her kingdom and as far as Kolkata, before wearing skimpy swimming costumes in the company of her bodyguards. I can't say she wasn't smart . . .

At the other end Harry hangs up, confused by the gin and by the orders he seems to be receiving rather than giving. If there is one person he values more than his own self it's his mother. He calls for the driver and a few minutes later he's in the car, not knowing where to head but certainly knowing whom to call first.

Ranjeet's phone rings as he stands on the terrace watching his elder brother's family leave, the other branch of the Khanna family tree. He always wanted a son like Rajveer. Rajveer is in the car and looks like a child being taken away from a playground.

'Hello?'

'Khanna *sahib* . . . Don't kill her . . . Just get her kidnapped, I need to ask her a few things first...'

'But... how can that be possible now . . . Sorry, too late, Sirji.'

'You can't screw up the second time around. Think twice . . . If you don't oblige this could turn to be absolutely fatal for you . . . '

'Are you threatening me?'

'Threat? Don't forget that I am a wealthy and influential British citizen. One phone call and all the evidence against you will be given to the right authorities. I can get as much information on you as I wish with my connections. And as far as I am con-cerned by then I will be enjoying a nice lamb roast with mashed potatoes and peas on my flight to London. Now get that bitch alive before I bury her . . . '

And just as suddenly Harry feels relieved. He has given orders. He has been assertive and imposed his will, just as his mother has always taught him. Now his night can go on. Sometimes it's good for him to take a break from his London life: he may even try and set up a sort of business connecting the 'demand' in London and the 'suppliers' here. It could be his little window of freedom every now and then. This way he's free, can enjoy life without having to rush home for meals, doesn't have to bear with his mother's never ending phone calls and can have some man fun away from the prying eyes of London.

Not bad, not bad at all.

As soon as the conversation ends Ranjeet uses his phone to call Rajveer, but the phone rings and rings, melting in the air the sweet notes to which Rajveer and Jannat danced the night before. Ranjeet thinks he can almost hear it, in fact he does, but he's just so sure that Rajveer has his phone with him that he himself thinks he's day dreaming. The truth is that Rajveer left his phone on the bed and now Ranjeet can hear it ringing from the terrace.

Ranjeet panics: Rajveer must do nothing before he receives new instructions, but how does one reach him?

Rajveer stops the car outside the office. 'I'm sorry. I need to stop one second by the office . . . '

'Raj . . . '

'I'm sorry, Mama, it's urgent business . . . '

Rajveer knows that in their line of business they can't leave any traces behind, which is why all orders are hand delivered. This practice has always kept the family safe, and thus they follow it blindly. Sometimes no change is the best innovation. The cigarette that carries the name of the target victim is burnt into ashes. No digital footprints, no paper trail, no clues, no evidence of anything that is handed over to anybody. The messenger, who is always anonymous, meets Rajveer at the back entrance of the of-fice, which leads into the shrubbery of an unused disputed land. The messenger dis-appears into darkness as usual as if he never existed. Rajveer still doesn't know what terrible secret the cigarette he handed out to his messenger holds. Rajveer hasn't had time for a shower, and Jannat's perfume, the scent of her skin, of her mouth, of her love is still on him. And it might last longer than her actual life if this message makes it to the right hands.

He drives away, leaving behind him only a cloud of dust; the business was fast, the cigarette has changed hands without anyone noticing. Even his mum didn't complain about the time taken, that's how fast he has been.

Uncle Ranjeet will be happy, at last . . .

Ranjeet lifts Rajveer's unattended phone from his bed. His forehead is now shining with perspiration. Harry is one of those clients you can't displease, even if you don't like what he wants. You have to bow down to his might because he is right, wealth and power combined with a pinch of London professionalism can wipe the Khannas off the face of the earth. After all they are illegal operators in a small city like Jalandhar with their tentacles spread as far as the borders of Punjab. Ranjeet knows Puneet doesn't carry a cell phone and calling up Simran for an urgent business matter when she is at a social gathering is inviting trouble.

Panic-stricken he runs down the stairs and jumps onto his BMW motorbike. He hasn't used his beauty in so long and for a split second is happy to hear the roar of her engine again. It's like the voice of an old lover who over the years got a little hoarse but holds the same old charm as she whispers every night.

25

As they arrive at the venue for Mr. Kapoor's son's wedding they see a vast number of people crowding the lawns.

'I told you we were late. Now we'll have to queue with everyone else to greet the parents . . . how shameful . . .'

Puneet smiles at his wife's constant quest for primacy. They are an old family, used to being rich and respected. She comes from a different family, a different caste: for her appearances are still very important. Over many years she has never understood that those who really have power have nothing to prove.

After they have greeted the parents of the

groom and the bride they enter the second room, each of them looking for their own friends.

Rajveer's mother joins the other mothers to talk about the fine clothes and jewellery they see at the wedding. Puneet joins a group of businessmen talking about the stock market; he doesn't love it, but this is what society requires. He stares into a corner where some old ladies flaunt their diamonds.

Meanwhile Rajveer joins a party of other young men the majority of whom are already married and enjoy teasing the others, a slender minority, for not having settled down yet. Behind every joke there's a hint of jealousy. All of Jalandhar knows of Rajveer's whereabouts and of his new flame. Not everyone in the group was lucky enough to choose if and whom to marry. Rajveer knows that and he takes the jokes with a pinch of salt he knows he is envied but also knows where this envy comes from, and he smiles at those hinting at his trips in the night and the fair-skinned lady he took to his family's Lohri party.

No amount of mockery can take away the magic of the moments that you spend with someone in absolute intimacy.

Ranjeet finally makes it to the party, greets everyone absentmindedly, saying something about the wedding and how beautiful the decorations are, but is really trying to spot his nephew.

He sees him in the crowd, in a small group of young men like him, drinking whisky and soda and grinning at someone's jokes. He rushes to Rajveer, pushing people aside.

'Where, where is it?'

'Where is what, uncle?' asks Rajveer, puzzled to see his uncle at the party and unsure what he's referring to.

'The message! Give it back to me.'

'I can't.'

Ranjeet's face turns pale. His nephew has read the message and wants to protect her. This is going to be so much worse than he had expected . . . How do we handle this sit-uation in the midst of a celebrity wedding?

'Wh . . . why?'

'Because you told me it was urgent and I dropped it off at the office. Mama wasn't happy about the detour but you told me . . . '

Ranjeet freezes.

'*Chachaji,* you know the messenger is not supposed to carry any phones or have any address, there is no way I can stop . . . '

Rajveer can't even finish his sentence because Ranjeet is gone at once. He runs through the crowd and swears, this is only his fault; the boy is not to blame, he would like to blame someone but Rajveer did as he was told . . . And the communication system is so well protected, or else we wouldn't have survived. This crazy Harry, he should be the one getting a lesson!

Ranjeet's black motorbike devours the asphalt road and roars at every change of gear. He travels a few miles away from the city. The bike rides through a series of mud roads that only someone who'd lived a lifetime in Jalandhar would know. The bike ultimately arrives outside a warehouse that is shielded with panic grass. The place smells of chemical dyes and has a flat structure made of bricks and mud. There are huge rectangular vats with toxic water in the frontage that smell of filth.

Inside the main tannery, where all the dark transactions take place, a hand is unrolling the cigarette and straightening the paper: Jannat Gill and a link to a webpage. The wretched man wriggles his bull's eye pendant. Moga reads her name and licks the pa-per as if it was dyed with her blood. The messenger enters the room with a laptop. He quickly types the link on the computer and Jannat's photo appears. He takes a print out. Then the cigarette paper is torn into minuscule pieces and dropped into a glass of water to wash the ink off it. Then it will be dried and burnt.

The messenger looks at the photograph: he is a little disturbed by the image of Jannat. It's a photo taken from her blog, nothing fancy, but in its simplicity it displays Jannat's personality to the fullest-a no-frills modern girl. The messenger always admired strong women, and for a moment, only a moment, he is disturbed by the idea of wiping one off the face of the earth. But the most distracting part of the photo is that she seems very familiar to him. She isn't a local. Where have I seen her before?

Ranjeet's bike pulls over and her lioness roar stops at once. He struggles to run up the stairs. The darkness and the humid dampness of the place make each step slippery. Moreover he has put on quite a bit of weight and the rotten wooden banister seems to crumble under his grabbing hands. But he runs because every second matters.

He breaks into the room and Moga instinctively pulls out his gun and points it at him, lowering it only when the messenger orders him to do so.

'Khanna *sahib?* This is Mr Khanna, Rajveeer's uncle. What brings you here?'

'I gave you the wrong note... You don't have to kill her.'

'What do you mean?'

'Just kidnap her.'

The messenger and Moga look at each other. They are clearly perplexed and would like to enquire further. However Ranjeet is struggling for breath and the hiss fighting its way out of his mouth convinces them that the time for questions will come later.

The next day the world seems new to Jannat. She walks from her house to the nearest ATM; she hadn't heard from Rajveer all of yesterday when she suddenly got a text just before falling asleep, 'You are becoming a little too important to me, Miss Gill.' It was cute. No one can talk about love after only a few days, but Rajveer is indeed some-what different. When you stumble upon something so new-fangled, don't all the rules change? Could this really be love?

She hails an auto and one pulls up immediately. *This is my lucky day!*

'Please take me to the *gurudwara* near BMC chowk.'

The driver nods in silence and drives away. Jannat inhales and then takes her iPhone out of her hobo bag to write a witty response to Rajveer's text message. She is not worried about where the driver is taking her, so she does not look out at the road. It's funny how many people in India ride the auto-rickshaws every day, several times a day, and never really look at the driver. If Jannat had looked closely she would have noticed that this one was a peculiar driver he didn't turn on the metre and didn't even attempt at bargaining a price. She thinks he's going to ask for a crazy price when they arrive at the destination but she doesn't feel like bringing it up now. Otherwise they'll fight, she might have to get off and threaten to not pay an excessively high fare. If he tries to screw her it's for less than a pound, does it really matter?

Jannat doesn't seem to come up with a good response to Rajveer. She wants to be wit-ty but also imply that she feels the same way. At the same time she doesn't want to be too melodramatic or sound excessively romantic.

She notices suddenly that the road the driver has taken is not the one she knows. Her sense of discomfort increases while she remains silent, but then decides to stop him.

'Excuse me, are you going in the right direction?'

The driver doesn't respond.He just speeds up as he ascends a broad flyover. They are getting out of the town and heading towards the outskirts. She realises something is amiss, but she can't figure out who this guy is or what he wants. Hopefully he'll just take her far away citing a miscommunication and ask for money to take her back to town, but what if that is not the case? She would like to scream but feels stupid, would anyone ever care?

She tries talking to the guy again. 'Can't you hear me? Are you drunk or doped?'

Just then the auto suddenly screeches to a halt in front of a dodgy looking van. As soon as Jannat notices three people, thugs, getting out of the undistinguished van, she knows this won't just be fixed with money. It's more complicated and possibly more dangerous. She is forced out of the auto and into the van. She kicks and screams but is gagged with her entire face covered in black cloth. The van speeds off, veering onto a dirt road. The auto driver heads back to the city with no concerns. Nobody was there to see anything.

In the darkness she tries to think of ways to get out of it but all she can think of right now is rape and murder.

The reason why she was kidnapped is not clear to her. She hasn't done anything to stir suspicion and all her research has not helped her discover anything that lethal. All she has done is to confirm what she already knew. *No scoops.No loud mouthing.* So it's unre-lated to her job, possibly, but . . . India? This is the first time she has come back in decades; she doesn't even know anybody here except for Rajveer. Is it about him? His family wants to keep them apart?

At the *gurudwara* Rajveer is waiting for her, leaning against his car. She should have been here half an hour ago and her phone is off. She probably overslept . . . He is slightly worried, but it's an irrational fear in the back of his mind. He decides to leave and send a message on her phone. While he's typing he throws his head back on the soft seat and in a second feels again all the powerful sensations of the earlier night-annat's soft and smooth skin, her bones gently pulling out, the sweet smell of her breath, her fingers through his body, her featherlike lips caressing his chest. With his eyes closed, shut in the silence and coolness of his car, all he can think of is the crazy things he would do if only Jannat was here now. He indulges in a daydream about a future that, he hopes, may not be that far away-Jannat and a little boy running to-wards him through a mustard field. A wooden house stands next to a windmill and a stable that is filled with dark horses. The pungent smell of mustard attacking his no-strils and the deep feeling of happiness as he watches mother and son running to hug him without a care in the world.

Jannat has fainted on the way. She's still unconscious as they drag her out of the wagon and tie her to a chair in a dimly lit room. She can hear noises in the background but she has hit her head (or have they hit her?). As soon as she opens her eyes the dark world around her swirls, so she prefers to keep them closed. She's tied in a sitting position, so no one is planning to rape her, not in the near future anyway. They prob-ably mistook her for somebody else. As soon as she explains who she is they'll know she's not who they were looking for. She will be let out with a threat.

In the next room Harry is speaking excitedly. Moga listens, faking attention (he has done this a million times, he does not need an English idiot to teach him his job) and the messenger lies against the wall, playing with his phone and listening absentmindedly.

'You didn't have to give her such a large dose of chloroform! Hell knows when she'll wake up!'

'Listen . . . we are experts. She will regain her senses very soon. Then you can do whatever you want with her.'

Jannat opens her eyes very slowly. She tries to work out where she is. There's a distinct smell of hay, of cows, it could be a farm, but the sounds of the city can still be heard. She can't be too far from Jalandhar, definitely not in a very remote area. The sound of a TV is very close though. It covers other sounds too much. It's a cricket match and people are talking over it.

In the adjoining room Harry is sitting on the couch. Moga and the messenger watch the match and chew on tobacco. They are betting on the players. Harry is losing his patience and just before he's about to erupt he speaks in the calmest tone possible, 'You said ten minutes. Go check if the bitch has woken up.'

Moga and the messenger exchange a meaningful look. They turn the TV off. Moga licks the tobacco off his hands and then the two of them walk into the next room.

26

The messenger enters the dimly lit room. Jannat's body is crumpled in a corner, on a wooden chair. He inspects her face with a small torch he keeps on his keyring but her eyes are still only half opened. The chemical ether they gave her was strong and she, not being used to it, had a stronger reaction than they expected. She's evidently un-conscious. Questioning her now would be a colossal waste of time and the match is still going on. He wonders what kind of a contract Rajveer has given him this time. It requires so much patience. All the previous assignments have been quite smooth. Rajveer gives him a name rolled on the cigarette with a link to the photo of the victim. He hands it over to Moga. He takes a printout of the photograph for Moga to have one look at and set it up in his memory. Then all he needs to do is burn the cigarette and the photo. His part of the job is finished. In a couple of days Moga does the needful and all is forgotten. But this bloody firangi girl is a liability. Just then he recalls. He has met her. He has seen her at the Lohri party with Rajveer. In fact she was being spoken about as Rajveer Sir's special friend.

He walks back into the room, shakes his head and says to Harry, 'Still dozing.'

Moga sits on the stained couch, turning the sound of the TV back on. He gestures to the messenger to get him a beer. The messenger hands him a can and sits next to him. Harry is frustrated, but if the bitch is taking her sweet time to wake up its no one's fault. The good thing is that because she doesn't know anybody here no one will look for her for a while. The adrenaline is finally flowing in his veins, his face is lit with a strange madness but he is a little over excited about the situation. The messenger and Moga exchange a glance.

At this point, with Harry so agitated, it's pretty clear that things are not exactly going too smoothly. Jannat is not a normal Indian woman, scared to death and prepared to agrcc to their every request; she has family in the UK that will, sooner or later, look for her. They could pull it off, probably, with a regular car accident, but no drugs must be found in her blood stream (which means they have to wait a day before killing her) and this increases the risk of her escaping or, worse, somebody searching for her. On top of that Moga and the messenger know only too well that Harry can't do the questioning. He's evidently new to this and he will most certainly end up hurting her. When she dies she must have no sign of beating or torture, or they are screwed. This particular killing is a delicate job. It has to look like an accident.

The messenger is lost in confusion. But why did Rajveer Sir take her home to his family if she had to be killed? *Strange*. He mentally calculates all the risks they are running for this idiot's fault and thinks it's necessary, at this point, to bring in the boss to try and see how the situation can be solved with the least possible risk of getting caught. He excuses himself for a minute. He uses the tannery workshop phone and quickly dials Rajveer's number. When he hears Rajveer's voice the messenger spits out what he needs to say all in a single breath. This is not going to be easy and it better be done quickly.

'Sir . . . Sir, sorry, it's an emergency or else I wouldn't have called you. Sir, your friend Jannat is lying unconscious; she is on Moga's list . . . I was wondering if you knew that . . . '

In the room next doors Jannat quickly opens her eyes. She managed to breathe in only half of the chemicals they sprayed on her face, thank you yoga lessons and breath balance, and she's fully awake. Pretending to be still unconscious gave her a few more minutes, precious minutes, considering that she's planning on using them to save her own life.

She unlocks the parachord survival bracelet tied to her left wrist. The black band that Andy gifted her has a rope and a concealed blade. *Thanks Andy, this may be the biggest reason why you came into my life*. She remembers the day-a few weeks ago-when she and Andy went camping to Snowdania national park. As soon as she got into Andy's car he asked her to wear it around her wrist. She liked the look of it, never imagined it would be handy or help her to escape goons. *MacGyver* rocks. She cuts the rope with precision. She quickly finishes untying her hands and then frees her ankles.

She rises on her feet to move a few steps and searches for something to use in order to reach the window. She can hear the TV next door so the door is not an option. There's a small hole in the ground that's big enough for a baby sheep or goat; she would get stuck. The only viable option is the ventilation window. But it's high.

On the other side of the room, she finds a wooden box, not too sturdy but almost certainly steady enough for her to step on and pull herself up on the window.

Jannat crosses the room with short, soft steps to avoid attracting attention. She picks up the box and brings it to the window. She plants the chair on top of it and climbs on it. The box can collapse any second. She's hanging with her bust between the scorching hot sun and the rather cold interior of the stable when Moga gets back in the room. He looks for her in the corner where he had left her but she's not there; only as he sees a shadow kicking its long legs out of the window does he scream to at-tract the attention of the other two. Too late. Jannat runs like there's no tomorrow. By now it's clear that whatever the intentions they would kill her eventually. Even if she wasn't the one they were looking for, she saw their faces, not much of them to be fair, but they don't know that. They will kill her.

And with this thought in mind she runs across the cows sitting in the sun. The stench of cow dung and rotten flesh is revolting. She's in a tannery and the streams of blood coming from the main building suggest that animals are skinned there. A chill runs down her spine. Her vision is still blurred by the drugs she inhaled but she strives to run as fast as possible, zigzagging among the cows that sit there idly, unaware of their destiny.

Moga lets his eyes grow accustomed to the darkness. She can't have run away, there's no opening except that window up there. Too high. But then there is the wooden box to hide the weapon in case there is a raid.

'Just go, check for her again. I will just shoot her. She is taking too much of my time!' he screams in anger and disbelief.

At once Harry is in the room, followed by the messenger. As soon as he realizes that the room is empty he bursts out in anger.

'Moga! Bastard. That bitch has disappeared!'

'Jannat, just come out from wherever you are hiding! You bitch . . . You'll never walk out alive from here,' spits out Harry.

Jannat keeps running, oblivious of what's around her. She runs, she doesn't know in what direction, but her side hurts. She hasn't run in a while and her body is rebelling against all this exercise, but she knows she can't stop now.

Suddenly, she finds herself cornered. Behind her is the tannery and in front of her a pond, a big, still, muddy reservoir. If she turns back she'll end up right where they are waiting for her, if she goes on she'll have to swim in this mud. She doesn't know how deep it is and what liquid it contains. It certainly means swimming through sewage. On the other hand, it's her life on the line here . . .

In the background the voices of Moga and Harry get closer by the second. One of the voices has a strong British accent and sounds familiar but right now all she can think about is how to get out of this situation. Jannat still doesn't know Harry is here.

'Where can she go? Slut!'

'It's all you fault, you dimwits!'

'My fault . . . okay . . . now do us a favour, find her and kill her yourself. She is now your problem, you English buffoon!' *They are fighting. I can gain a few minutes from that.*

Without thinking twice she dives in. The three men stop for a second. They didn't expect her to disappear in thin air, that too in their town where they can map every nook and corner of this vicinity.

She swims until her muscles can't stretch anymore and lifts her head out of the water only when her lungs are about to give up. She had considered the cleanliness of the water, or rather the lack of. But she realized what she really should have thought about is the temperature. Her arms are close to falling off, but by the time her head emerges from the dark water the voices are far away and faint. They are still audible, but now, for the first time since she was abducted, Jannat really thinks she has a chance.

She gets out of the water, breathless. She can collapse. She has swallowed toxic waste. She lies face down in surrender, but she imagines a strange image in the moss filled reservoir-a pair of blind eyes gape at her-Preet's father's face reflects in the eerie water. She pinches her ear, almost tearing it apart. It's a chimera. She gets up rolling her neck backwards. The impact of the temperature outside the pond is even worse. She shivers and clenches her teeth but knows the run will warm her up. The downside is that she has no clue where she could possibly be, one wrong direction and she could be as good as dead. She pulls out her iPhone and tries to turn it on but the wa-ter dripping from it tell her this is not going to work. She has to take her chances.

She races but has to hide under a tree almost instantly. A car engine is roaring in the distance, approaching her. Unsure who it might be Jannat considers it safer to hide. Thirty seconds later she sees a black SUV devouring the road. Through the window, she recognizes Rajveer. She's relieved and about to jump out but her shirt is tangled in the thorns and she's delayed by about ten seconds, enough to see the car pull over in front of the tannery.

He found me. It is true love. I didn't show up and he must have gone to Naseebo's house, asked her where

I was and then enquired around the ATM place. Someone must have seen me getting into that damn rickshaw . . . Come on Raj, take out that gun before they kill . . .

But she can't finish her thought because her eyes see something she needs all her energy and mental strength to believe. The three men who held her captive gather in front of the SUV and greet Rajveer with a sort of respect, the kind you'd use when talking to a boss. Only one seems to be less respectful, but the other two stare into Rajveer's eyes to detect any sign he may make to shut the guy up.

She cannot believe what she sees. Rajveer was in it all along, he is the one who com-missioned her kidnapping, he used her, he gained her confidence first, with all those poetic words about love, and then . . .

Jannat is distraught. She can hardly breathe and her hands are turning blue because of the cold. She needs to get out of here if she wants to live.

Meanwhile Rajveer and the three men have gone inside the tannery. Jannat stands fro-zen, one small error of judgement and she can lose her life. What Jannat doesn't know is that Rajveer is in the killing business, always has been and possibly always will be, but because his uncle knew about his relationship with Jannat he made sure

Rajveer didn't find out until the job was done. The messenger didn't know about this detail and that is why he called Rajveer, his first link to the family, the person he always calls whens there's a problem.

Rajveer is enraged. He is a strong man and Harry is somewhat more of an English businessman than a street fighter, so Rajveer takes less than a minute to pin him to the wall, his gun planted into Harry's mouth so deep he can hardly breathe. There's tension in the room. The messenger realizes what a huge mistake he has made and knows this is not something he'll get away with easily. Moga doesn't want a dead Englishman in his workshop; a woman is different, she was a contract, but a man . . . wealthy, English and powerful, and not part of the deal, no, not a chance. However, both Moga and the messenger know that Rajveer only needs to hear a fly buzzing too loud to shoot, so everything they say, every movement must be extremely slow. If they all want to live then Harry must live. There's no doubt about that.

'You son of a bitch, where is she, I will . . . ?' roars Rajveer in a voice so deep that makes the messenger shiver.

'Khanna *sahib*, relax, she ran away, I will . . . ' implores Moga.

Rajveer turns and gives Moga a threatening look. 'If you hurt her I swear I'll hunt you down and kill you. Wherever you are in the world, I'll find you!'

He drops Harry to the floor where he kneels down, coughing, trying to find his breath where he had lost it.

As soon as the fear is gone and his heart has regained its regular beat Harry is taken by insane fury. In a minute he had gone from being the one who ran the show to being the buffoon. He won't take it. With the remaining breath his lungs can exhale he hisses, 'No one frigging tells me, Harry Randhawa, what to do. I pay, and how . . . that whore . . . ' But he can't finish the sentence because he just gave Rajveer what he needed to explode, a reason.

Rajveer is on him, punching and kicking. Harry slowly falls back onto the floor and neither the messenger nor Moga manage to stop him.

Under the last, hardest, punch Harry faints, his face mashed in a pool of blood. The whites of Rajveer's eyes are injected with blood too and his shirt is sprayed with the Englishman's deep red blood. He cleans his face with the water running from a bro-ken tap in the wall and walks away without a word, the engine of his SUV roaring as he leaves. Moga and the messenger move closer to Harry to check if he is still breathing.

He is. They take a cloth and start cleaning his face and assess what the damage is. Despite all the beating Harry's face, once cleaned of the blood, doesn't look too bad. He certainly won't be going to party any time soon but with a few dressings everything will be solved.

Rajveer, in the car, dials Jannat's number, hoping with all his heart, his brain and his soul that she hasn't lost the phone in the rickshaw or the van or the tannery. He just wants to hold her and reassure her, tell her that everything will be all right. That he is still around.

27

Jannat runs, her energy being drained from her body with every minute. But she knows she has to run. She reaches a small village near the tannery. The awful building can still be seen in the distance, but the smell of wastewater and stale blood is in the air, and as long as the smell of rotting meat follows her she's not safe. Her clothes are still wet but the run has indeed warmed her up, she's sweating in the freezing wind. This is what her grandma would have called 'a recipe for a good flu', but she can't stop now. Trampling over a rickety footbridge she dives into the narrow alleys of the village. The brown and dark red walls ogle at her. Every building looks like the pre-vious one and the next one. She will eventually get lost, she knows that already, but she has the advantage of time. She got here before them so she'll get out of it before them. Unless they are waiting for her at the other end. Jannat shakes the thought out of her head. Fear cripples her judgement. The lines between reality and illusion begin to blur. Is this for real? What am I running from?

The village life flows wild and clumsy—messy girl smiling at the sky, women carrying bundles of straw on their heads, gardeners plucking flowers on the estate, children running, old men sitting by a *chaiwallah,* sipping *chai* and telling each other stories of the old days. Everything seems to flow until Jannat crosses the path and breaks their routine. At once they are aware of her presence, of her smell and her wet clothes. The masons, the green grocer, the ironsmith all get distracted by this pretty foreigner. The roadside barber, about to slide his blade on his customer, stops midway to catch a glimpse of the wet Cinderella. In a minute Jannat knows she can't go unnoticed, that if anyone came and asked about her all these people will know exactly who they were talking about. If she had time to explain she could convince people to cover for her, say she never was here, but the three men, possibly even Rajveer, are after her. All she can do is run and confuse people on her whereabouts.

Rajveer's SUV stops at the gates of the village. Moga and the messenger, who have followed him after having attended to the bleeding Harry, are right behind him but he takes no notice. There's only one thing he has to do now, find her and reassure her. Village people, especially younger boys, gather around the shiny car. Rajveer asks them if they have seen a beautiful woman running through the village.

The boys would not disappoint the man with the dazzling car for anything in the world. If he wants the girl the girl he shall have! And maybe after he has found her he could reward them with a ride. Where to? It doesn't matter; they just want to be in the car.

They give him directions and before they are done talking Rajveer jumps out and sprints across the narrow alleys. There are darker patches of moisture on the red clay; this is where she stopped to catch her breath, and he's on the track.

Meanwhile Jannat has slowed down, she's so tired and so cold that her legs are almost about to let go. But before she can stop running she hears a woman's voice say, 'Look, that firangi is on the run, sirji.' She gave her away. He's behind her. Not far, the voice was faint but audible, and he's near, too near for her to stop now.

Suddenly Jannat notices a possible way out-a set of one-storey homes with roof ter-races. If she gets onto one of those her trails will be lost and she might save herself. She runs up the stairs and kneels down behind the low wall that protects the terrace. She can see Rajveer and the two men behind him. So, this is him, the real Raj, a sugar-coated bullet.

Rajveer's heart pounds. She can get into deep trouble. He tries to call her but her phone is switched off. He is desperate to save her. They reach the small square where the facades of the low houses open but she's nowhere to be seen. With no people around they have finally lost her trail. She breathes a sigh of relief as she sits, leaning against the wall, and closes her eyes. Just then a beautiful kite that she had noticed be-fore, colourful and skillfully moved by the hands of an invisible child, falls down due to a sudden gust of wind and hits her. If she had kept her eyes open she wouldn't have been startled, but because her eyes are closed she screams when the kite strikes her hard. She lifts her head above the wall and sees that the men have heard the scream and spotted her.

Jannat untangles herself from the long kite cord. She calms her dashing breath and surges for the next house. She slides down a pole, then a drain and jumps over a fence to enter another courtyard. An old lady who is drying pickled carrots gives her a be wildered look. This time she slides straight through the courtyard like a cat, past the adjoining dairy farm, jumps over the tube well tub and climbs a ladder onto the roof of another home.

Her sleeve gets stuck in the fence of the terrace. She rips it apart. A big piece of cloth flutters on the terrace fence. Rajveer keeps trying to call her but her phone is dead. While running from them she could seriously hurt herself and all he wants to do is talk and explain things.

Jannat sees the grain fields, a long stretch of green. *Safety.* She walks across the terrace roof and stands on the edge. Can I make it to the ground, it's about twenty metres? She notices a haystack. In a flash she is reminded of her ballet lessons, her feet are dexterous. She lands safely, deep into the bundle of hay. She takes just enough time to draw a deep breath. The smell of hay gives an allergy. She sneezes a few times. Her lungs echo with pain. Then she jumps off the hay bale, dusts off the straw and begins running across the fields. Her foot lands on something sharp. The soles of her shoes are pulsing due to too much running and jumping. The thin streak of blood spilling from her foot forces her to stop. She falls to the ground like a wet cloth and takes a deep breath. In a moment she's brought back to her childhood when, practicing her routine in ballet class, her feet would hurt and her teacher, Mrs Bouquet, would tell her that only the toughest made it to the rank of etoiles. A voice rings inside her ears. It's her own thought reverberating loudly, 'It's your mind that is limiting you, ignore.' She stands up, quite as if she was doing it for Mrs

Bouquet herself, and looks at the small gang. In the distance she thinks she has made out Rajveer. This is the last straw. She will run for her life and against him.

Rajveer can finally see her. She's really far away, a figure in the distance, but at least he knows which direction to take. There's a road over there and a truck is approaching.

She needs me. I have to rescue her.

He sees it in the distance and mentally calculates how long it will take her to reach it. She shouldn't be able to make it, considering how tired and cold she must be.

But he hasn't considered Jannat's will to live. As soon as she spots the truck she takes one last jump and is in front of the truck. The driver brakes just inches away from her standstill body. The air is filled with the smell of burnt rubber. He curses her, but be-fore he can say anything she's on the passenger's seat. She gives him a sharp look. The veteran gets the message; he presses the accelerator with gusto. She is out of breath but, hopefully, finally safe. Her foot keeps bleeding, she's in pain, but every pain is numbed by the adrenaline which, she knows only too well, will fade soon, leaving her with a deep sense of emptiness and drowsiness.

This turn of events was unexpected for Rajveer.

He curses the truck driver and runs towards his car so that he can follow the damn truck.

Jannat breathes freely for the first time since this morning. Her escape was reckless, but so far it has worked out. The cabin of the truck is warm, that steamy warmth that comes from a body closed in a small space for many hours. There's a pleasant smell of chai and she feels, for the first time, safe enough to close her eyes.

The *sardar* is an old trucker, not one of these young boys who want to make a lot of money and leave a girlfriend in every city they visit. *Sardarji* has a wife and two daughters, going by the photograph of three smiling women on the dashboard. The cabin is invaded with an uncomfortable silence. This girl is wet and afraid. Yes, she stinks of cow dung, and the *sardar* cannot pretend not to notice or suppress the grimace of disgust. But at the same time it's clear she needs help, which is what she'll get from him. The expression on her face says she has a million questions, but her eyes give away hurt.

The *sardar* is a devout fan of Kabir's poetry. Without much ado he spits out some cryptic words that ring a bell with her soul. Jannat becomes aware.

'Chalti chakki dekh kar diya kabira roye . . . Do patan ke beech mein, sabit bacha na koye . . .'

He explains the meaning of the couplet to a foxed Jannat.

Life is full of duality, like the good and evil, like the heaven and earth, but the one who rises above these dualities to discover the single most truth, that mortal rescue's the self from the grind of duality and death.

It takes a while for Jannat to absorb it. The timing is correct or maybe it's perfect. But then as soon as a flash of lights hits her from an oncoming truck, she has a stark moment of self-realization sparked by the profound words that she heard a few minutes ago. 'We are living in an era of evil, total darkness, but then there will be daybreak.'

He looks at Jannat again and shakes his head. He reaches for the back seat and brings forth a shawl that he throws on her as she's falling asleep. With her last strength she grabs it and covers herself from the tip of her toes up to her neck.

'Where would you like to get off? I need to reach Delhi early in the morning.'

Jannat wakes up with a start. She takes her phone from her pocket and tries to turn it on with little success.

'What happened?'

'My phone isn't working; I need to go to Jalandhar. I wish I could call him.'

Behind the truck Rajveer's SUV is devouring the long overpass to catch up, overtak-ing cars and other trucks with the agility of a motorbike and the recklessness of someone who is fighting for the one and only thing he has ever cared about in life. Rajveer is alerted by an oncoming train that storms onto the adjoining railway bridge. The siren from the monster engine gives him a chill. *Why am I soaked in fear?*

Inside the truck the driver has rolled up the windows to keep Jannat warm; she blows into her cupped hands to warm them and neither she nor the *sardar* see the SUV approaching.

'NRI police station, SHO Kawaljeet Deol.'

'Right, I have heard of him. I know where the NRI police station is.'

In a final attempt to catch up with the truck Rajveer accelerates and tries to overtake the last three cars that separate him from Jannat. But a bus full of people, overloaded equally with suitcases and boxes is driving on the opposite direction. The brakes are lazy and by the time the SUV is faced with the bus there's nothing else to do but for Rajveer to throw himself on the dirt road by the side of the road to prevent it from crushing him. His car spins to a standstill. The bus and its passengers stop and scream at the reckless driver and then move on to avoid clogging the traffic.

Jannat is falling asleep and the *sardar* is determined not to stop until he delivers her where she can be safe . . . right in the hands of Kawaljeet Deol.

Rajveer sees the truck drive away and tries to restart the car, but the ignition doesn't seem to work. He'll never catch up with them, he will never know where she's going. He curses the car and the two idiots who didn't consult him before engaging in this madness. Then he pulls out his phone and dials a number.

The sardar finds the police station without difficulty, he asks for SHO Deol and waits until he comes out. Then he explains the situation and only when he sees understanding on the policeman's face does he decide that Jannat will be safe with him. She is woken up by the strong and callous hands of the driver, which are also unexpectedly delicate. He waves out to her, 'Rab Rakkha.'

Jannat is still in a daze. She jumps up in distress but Kawaljeet's slightly monotonous voice reassures her. He tells her she will sleep at his house tonight while they set up a guard in front of Naseebo's in case someone has the brilliant idea to go look for her there.

Jannat is not delighted with the arrangement but she cannot think of anything better. She needs to take a hot shower and change her clothes, eat something and finally sleep. She's so tired she can't even think anymore.

When she gets to Kawaljeet's house she's tired and confused. She jumps in the shower and when she gets out, wearing one of the old tracksuits he has taken out for her, she sips the soup he gives her in a bowl and goes to sleep.

'You have to relax. There's no way we can know what Rajveer was doing there. I promise we'll find out everything tomorrow. Okay?'

Jannat smiles.

As he walks out of the door, turning the lights off, he simply adds, 'Call out if you need me . . . I'm in the next room, alright?'

She smiles again. She's grateful for what he is doing and for what *sardarji,* the generous truck driver, had done, but she can't shake the sight of Rajveer at the tannery out of her head.

What was he doing there? How does he know these thugs? How involved is he with them?

She's so tired she can barely keep her eyes open but all these thoughts prevent her from sleeping. How can she possibly sleep knowing that the man who made love to her so gracefully, so softly, so lovingly, is involved in her kidnapping? Why her? Why does he always carry a gun? Is he one of them? The syndicate? The contract killing club?

She can hear Kawaljeet brushing his teeth and getting into bed, and then the house is silent and dark, but only for a moment because as soon as he falls asleep the rooms are filled with his loud snoring.

It is now impossible for her to fall asleep. She quickly leaps out of bed, snatches her wallet and makes sure that there is her thick pen inside. She pulls out a slim torch from her bag, checks its intensity and sneaks out the main door.

The cold air of the night is a punch in her face. It freezes her but also wakes her up. She walks in search of an auto-rickshaw. She trips on an uneven slab. Her knee is hurt but there is no apparent wound. She limps for a few steps but then braces her will. I have to conquer, I have never been surer of something until now. I need to get to the root of the matter. *I have to get there. It's risky, but then, no guts no glory.*

28

The gate to the Khanna residence opens without a sound. The night watchman is out touring the perimeter. It is not hard for Jannat to open the wooden entrance and break into the house. She's in the spider's web. By walking in without protection she's basically signing her death warrant, but she needs to know why Rajveer made love to her the way he did, as if he didn't know.

Could he have not known about her kidnappers? Why was he there? Is he just friends with them? If he's genuine, he'll help her escape, if he's not . . . Well she'll figure out a plan as she goes. But he is definitely connected to them.

Jannat's memory of the premises is limited but she remembers only too well how on the night of the Lohri party Rajveer locked himself up there with those people, one of whom, she recalls, was one of her kidnappers. All she is afraid of now is the dog. She walks carefully and tries not to make a noise, even while breathing. She's in the out house, in Rajveer's den. She is careful not to make any noise and not to turn the light on. The rays of the full moon and the slim Maglite torch she has with her will do.

She's scavenging the desk but all she finds are documents any construction company keeps bank statements, investor brochures, blueprints and layouts, nothing covert. She keeps rummaging through the small office until she finds something worth her attention. In this room there's no vault, no safe, nothing that is locked. Everything exists in the cheerful Indian disorder: a locked chest with a tray of glasses and water jug on it is really out of place.

Jannat shifts the tray and pulls the lid really hard. She has looked everywhere and found no key. This means someone in the house, possibly Rajveer himself, is the one holding the precious key. She pulls harder and harder as she sees the lock loosening until the whole chest falls. Jannat falls on her back and the strongbox falls on the floor with a loud noise. She stops to make sure no one is coming, the noise could have aroused suspicious,but after five minutes no one seems to approach, not even the watchman. The dogs seem to be drugged or maybe they are used to such noises coming from the office at all times. She decides to leave. As she tries to rush out her foot slips on a Kashmir rug. She notices a slight bump in the oval shaped rug. There is a hidden pocket with a key inside. She pulls out a key like it is a sword.

After she has made sure no one will pay her a visit Jannat inspects the contents of the secret chest. She's startled to find only a bunch of faded newspaper clippings of advertisements for astrologers. *Astrologers?* This is crazy. Who would ever think of keeping astrology adverts locked up when there are agreements worth thousands of rupees lying around the room?

She looks at it carefully and it all starts to make sense. The names of the astrologers ring a bell, but she has to go through them twice before noticing something rather chilling. She sees the name of Preet Randhawa and the picture begins to clear up. All the names looked familiar because they are the same names she had saved in her iPhone. These are the names of the victims whose families she visited.

Poonam Bawa, Simi Mehra, Preet Randhawa, Hardeep Mann, Kuljeet Kaur, Sonam Gupta and finally, Talwar Bedi. There are tick marks in red on the side. But there are no photo-graphs. This can set them scot-free.

So this is how they do it, which is why there's never a phone record, no email trail that nails them . . . Bastards!

She also finds an old leather diary with names of people who have paid them huge sums. These include a lot of NRIs. UK, Canada, USA, Australia, Switzerland, Singapore are the prime countries from where they have received contracts. Likewise there are a couple of private bank documents where apparently they have illegal accounts. There is also a list with names of some top ranking government officials including po-lice sub-inspectors with a corresponding entry of monies paid to them. There is date mentioned next to each entry for record. MP Bansal's name is on top of the list with a handsome sum delivered to him. Thorough professionals, this is how nobody can speak against them. And to keep it all in a trunk in plain sight! Smart.

Among the bundle of paper clipping and post-its a photo falls on the floor. She picks it up and looks at it by the window. As soon as she recognizes the face on it she lets it fall again. As the picture turns she reads the red scribbled writing Kill Gill. Underneath there is an underlined name-'Harry Randhawa Urgent'.

She can see the sweet taste of her fond memories

turn to ashes. Her heart feels as if it's been shredded into a million pieces. The blood that runs in her veins turns cold, she could freeze a glass of water if she held it. She remembers her own words to Andy-passion is what transforms you first and then the rest of the world. She removes her thick black pen, which is nothing but a concealed digital camera with a memory card. She has used the HD mini-cam with an LED flash for many of her interviews.

She shoots the lists that the pages of the leather diary are filled with. She also films her photo and the writing on the back of it. She's filming the secret bank account details when her hands hits an ancestral painting hung on the wall. It comes crashing. Luckily it falls on the rug so the sound is partially muffled. She spots a brick shaped tile behind it. She quickly removes the tile. She could be discovered any minute. She finds a couple of pistols and a few rounds of bullets all wrapped in a jute bag. The firearms are definitely illegal. This will prove to be a case big on evidence. She films it and puts it back in a jiffy. She hangs the painting back on the wall. Fortunately it didn't have a glass case. She shoots the entire room in one shot with enough evidence that it belongs to the Khannas. She places the diary and other documents the way they were, locks the chest, fits the key inside the rug and places the rug on the wooden floor with geometric accuracy. 'Thank you BrainHQ.com,' she finally smiles.

Her thoughts are interrupted by the sound of footsteps climbing up the staircase. She is speechless. She tucks the surveillance pen camera inside her wallet and slides it inside her bra. She needs a moment to catch her breath before jumping out from the window. How high is it? If she was doubtful before she is certain now; what on earth made her come here alone? She should have listened to Kawaljeet, who is now snoring in his bed because he knows she's safely tucked in the bed next door. What did she do? She has peeped into the snake hole. There's no escape, unless . . .

But as she turns around to reach for the window and then sprint until there's no air left in her lungs, the light is turned on with a click. As soon as her eyes grow used to the sudden brightness she sees Puneet pointing a handgun at her. He is at the far end of the room: she can still try to leap out

Rajveer's father always appeared to be a changed man, retired from business and trying to redeem himself. He was born rich and he seemed to want to enjoy his wealth and his old age, breeding his dogs, reading his books and not have a care in the world. Rajveer's mother was, in Jannat's eyes, of a totally different breed-firm, fortified, shielding. She expected Mrs Simran Khanna to have a gun pointed at her, not her husband. Actually Simran would have shot straightaway, not pointed a gun. But now Puneet's eyes swear of the same consequence.

This is it. The room is not that vast, Puneet is less than ten metres away from her, his gun must be loaded and he can't miss. He couldn't miss if he was blind. She takes a deep breath and looks at him right into his eyes. In the black pupils, surrounded by the hazelnut skin of his ageing eyelids, she sees a good man, one who has been trapped into something for many years and could now enjoy being free from it. But the deep brown eyes also show a crudeness she didn't expect from the lovely old man. Puneet is knows how to fire a gun and would have no regrets or fear of doing so. She shivers, not knowing what to expect but knowing only too well that right now her life is entirely in Puneet's hands.

The sudden roar of Rajveer's car entering the gate interrupts her story. He drives up to the house but then, possibly because he noticed the dim light on in his office, turns the car around. As the engine stops and the door of the car shuts with a thud, the sleeping dog goes to greet him; he indulges them for a few seconds.

It is in those few seconds that Puneet lowers the gun and, with a movement of his head, shows Jannat out. She thanks him with a nod of her head and slides out of the window with a small jump without making a sound. The best things in life happen in silence.

After having patted the dog and played with it

for a while he takes him inside to feed him some biscuits. Rajveer absentmindedly walks into the kitchen. He's too tired and too worried to walk up to the office to switch off a bulb. Puneet tiptoes to his room. He feels redeemed yet anxious. *How dangerous can Jannat get, she is just a girl, immature, she also likes Raj, I think she is perfect for him.* As the Khanna residence becomes silent once again Jannat walks out of the gate unnoticed. The darkness of the night for once pro-tects her. Or is it the resolve in her eyes?

Minutes later Rajveer walks up to his uncle's room. Ranjeet is lying in the darkness, hoping to find solace in a good night's sleep, but he hears a knock on his door. At first it's just a feeble scratch, then it becomes louder. Ranjeet can do nothing but get up. He knows only too well who this might be and he dreads the conversation that will follow this nighttime visit.

'Chachaji!'

Ranjeet's wife rushes to the door and opens it. Rajveer barges in. Ranjeet sits up on the bed.

'What happened? Why do you look like hell?'

Rajveer's and Ranjeet's eyes meet.

Ranjeet knows it has to do with Jannat's death warrant. His nephew has never challenged him before and he recognizes the flame in his eyes.

Ranjeet looks at his wife and nods. She understands that despite it being the middle of the night she has to leave the room. Puneet enters with his wife as she is leaving but as he sees Ranjeet's wife leaving he suggests the two women go and make some tea to smooth over this small incident. The women leave, pretending to gossip, as if they weren't asked to leave their husbands alone in the heart of the night, plucking them from their own beds.

Rajveer stands with his arms folded looking at Ranjeet, fuming.

'What is the issue?'

'Why Jannat? What harm has she done to you, she is my . . . ?'

Ranjeet cuts him off, leaping from the bed in anger.

'Jannat is a bloody spy, she is not some ordinary journalist... She was here to investigate Preet's murder. Thank God we figured it out before she would have got us hanged, she . . . '

'What crap. Have you gone crazy, are you in . . . ?'

'Rajveer . . . mind your tongue, your dear friend has collected evidence on Preet's murder and God knows what else. Harry Randhawa, who happens to be Preet's husband, found out about

Jannat's probing and he came down here to erase everything. Just assume Jannat Gill was another name rolled on the cigarette paper . . . a routine death warrant . . . we are done with her, Kill Gill...'

Rajveer looks unimpressed. 'This is impossible. This is a big misunderstanding, I can . . . '

Ranjeet walks over to a brown chest. He opens the cover, pulls out an A4 size paper and hands it to Rajveer.

'See it for yourself. This is the same Jannat you know, except not as innocent as she led you to believe. You have been . . . '

The paper Rajveer is holding has Jannat's face printed on one side, the name of her blog in the centre and, just beneath it, the title of her latest post *Contract killing in Punjab: is it for real?*

As sparks blind his tired eyes Rajveer sees on the page a myriad of small, passport size photographs. He knows those faces because he has seen most of them when they were still alive. He is shocked, but he knows his uncle is trying to break his nerve with this article, to push him over to the other side of the barricade. Rajveer knows that if he wants answers he can't let Moga, the messenger and, least of all, his uncle ask the questions.

This is between the two of them, Jannat and Rajveer. This is a war aimed at uncovering who deceived whom and he has to fight it alone with her.

'Jannat is still alive. She escaped before I could rescue her from that asshole, Moga . . . This is my business. If I see a single scratch on her you can be sure I will spare no one, I mean . . .' he finally manages to say, trying to control his rage.

'You mean spare no one?' Ranjeet can't take it. This is not just business, this is the whole family hierarchy that is being challenged, and he simply can't let that happen. If Puneet is not going to say anything then he will. 'Oye! Who are you pointing the gun at? Have you lost your mind?'

Puneet finally steps into the conversation, lowering the hand in which his son holds a gun pointing at Ranjeet. 'What's wrong with you, son? He is your uncle? What madness is . . . ?'

Ranjeet stares at Rajveer in anger. The alpha male of the house may change any second now and Ranjeet feels power dripping from his hands like the blood of a freshly slaughtered lamb. Rajveer paces the room like a leopard. A couple of framed photographs of their ancestors stare at them. All of them are brazen men who reigned with power in their respective eras. He inadvertently stares at them. They survived be-cause they took the right decisions at the right time.

Puneet pats Rajveer in consolation and gently slides the gun into his hands.

Ranjeet walks up to him. He is not calm but he knows he must control his emotions. He guides Rajveer to sit down on the bed. Ranjeet sits next to him.

'Listen son, Jannat is too dangerous. She has used you, made you vulnerable. She always had an agenda. I also found out she has been visiting the families of those people we cleared . . . she is a serpent . . . '

'Cleared' is the word he uses to mean brutally killed for money. Only now does Rajveer notice this subtle word trick. All these years he was made to think that commis-sioning a murder is just business. Money comes in, money is paid to hired guns and you don't dirty your hands ever. This is like any other commerce. In every business somebody profits at the cost of somebody else, here it is a matter of some lives. Simple. Everybody dies.

'Jannat has enough information to nail us, especially after the kidnapping. She certainly has been to the police to gather information, by now she has made some friends inside the system. She is not one of us. She's partly English, and they like to involve the police in any little incident. We have very little time. If we don't clear her now we lose everything. Name, fame, fortune and family. And for what? For some girl you met a few days ago and whom you hardly know. What's with you? Your power, your passion, your diehard attitude, your commitment to business all down the drain for some deceitful pussy who walks into your path. I can buy you . . . ?'

Rajveer clenches his fist and punches the wall.

Ranjeet is blasé. 'Think about Bittu, your *chachi,* your mamma, your ageing father. Will you put them through living hell for the rest of their lives? Because what's going to happen once the business is in the hands of the police is that you and I will be hanged, your dad may be spared if we call a powerful friend in time, but all the money and the property of the family will be taken away by the greedy bureaucrats and politicians.'

Rajveer now knows this is a mess he never imagined. He could punch through the ceiling into the sky and disappear into a black hole.

'Do you want to die and make your old parents live lives of misery?'

Ranjeet lets a minute pass before he continues talking again to make sure the message is sinking in. 'Son, am I not making sense, try to . . . ?'

Rajveer is evidently hurt, torn between loyalty and love. Ranjeet's words are indeed sinking in his brain, slowly and painfully. This is the house, the family and the world that he has grown up with. This is where he belongs first and foremost. He gets up, walks to his father, takes the gun from him, shoves it into his pocket, then turns around and looks at Ranjeet.

'Let's go.'

Ranjeet puts on his denims and a dark brown jacket.

Puneet is taken aback. He was playing neutral. This is not what he expected from Rajveer. He tries to intervene. 'Son, you are making a mistake you will repent, don't . . . '

They ignore him and walk off like two war heroes who have an enemy to finish.

Puneet is powerless, defenseless. He crawls to his room in complete despair. His gloomy eyes stare at a golden-framed photo on the wall. It's a picture of their family-himself, his wife and Rajveer, when he was about five, such a carefree, serene child.

His wife appears behind him and, for the first time in years, without the need for him to say a word, she hugs him. She understands, she knows everything, and she is ready to stand by his side whatever decision he makes. This is a thought, a feeling that is somewhat reassuring for Puneet who had thought he had lost his wife to parties and socialites a long time ago. A wife who once read out the Bhagwad Gita to her toddler son. He is overwhelmed by his trail of inquiries.

'Does life always come to a full circle? Once a wise man said nothing?'

29

In the middle of the night Jannat runs through the streets of Jalandhar, trying to re-member the landmarks she noted on her way to the Khannas. The dark night has changed the physiognomy of the city many times over the last hour. The people who were crowding a small square laughing and singing have left, leaving behind an empty space, much larger than Jannat remembered, surrounded by trees and with a shrine in the middle.

The streets seem much broader now that they are not clogged with the fast cars that are trying to get home before the dark night falls. Stray dogs have appeared out of nowhere. The houses on one side of the road stand apparently deserted. The office buildings wear a look of the devil in disguise.

The leaping flyovers stretch into infinity. So poetic!

Everything is more frightening now that she learnt that the person who promised to love and protect her is actually the one who wants to kill her. So poetic!

As she walks quickly, with the hood pulled over her head to disguise herself, Jannat shudders.

I never trusted men before. My father barely knows where I am, guys in college wanted to simply ejaculate, even with Andy it took ages before I told my story, before I opened myself . . . With Rajveer everything came naturally. He was there, he was genuinely interested, he listened, I talked, he felt me, I enjoyed it. For what? To serve me as a lamb for slaughter?

She walks fast. She is petrified of being alone at night in the empty streets of Jalandhar, more so now that she knows that an entire gang of killers is after her. This is not real.

When she finally finds herself in the neighbourhood where Kawaljeet lives she breathes a sigh of relief. She feels that now things can only improve. In less than ten minutes Jannat finds Kawaljeet's house, a small house, one of the last ones, surrounded by buildings that seem to be growing overnight all around the neighbourhood.

As she walks into the porch, shaking off the cold that weighs over her like an ice coat, she is warmed by the soft light Kawaljeet keeps on during the night in the white-washed porch and by the smell of dry flowers and lemon zest in a plate by the door. This is a woman's touch, but there is no sign of a woman around, men don't think about these things, maybe he has a girlfriend. She surprises herself as she gently scratches the door with insecurity.

But then she remembers how he was snoring when she left and how he might get re-ally wild at her for sneaking out. She is standing in the porch with a lamp hanging above her head-she could be spotted from a million miles away. If she hasn't been found yet it is only because she got a small advantage thanks to Puneet and because, quite evidently, no one has thought of looking for her here. Otherwise they would have found and killed her. The sound of a bullet ringing in her ears out of sheer deli-rium gives her the creeps.

The thought of being shot in the head makes her shudder and she knocks more firmly on the door. She can freeze to death right on the porch before she solves the 'Khanna Killers' mystery.

She breathes heavily. The knocks become bangs. After a few minutes Kawaljeet appears on the doorstep with his eyes still closed. As soon as he realizes who it is and where she actually is he is dumbfounded.

Jannat hops from one foot to the other to keep warm, and as soon as the door opens she is engulfed by the cosiness and warmth of a bonfire that Kawaljeet lights every evening despite owning heaters. She pushes Kawaljeet in to jolt him out of his slumber and enters and warms herself by the fire. She feels a sting in one of her knee that was hurt. She collapses on her knees and gets her face closer to the fireplace.

'Jannat? Where were you? Holy cow . . . I was . . .'

'In a matrix, like somebody else is playing a simulation game, it all seems so fabricated. He dances with me, then he makes love to me, then he makes me meet his mother, she blesses me, then he gets me kidnapped, then he wants to kill me, his father saves me from him, does he . . .'

'Jannat please, who are you referring to?'

'Rajveer... he knows everything. He's part of the syndicate. I don't understand, how could I be so stupid, I have . . . ?'

'Jannat... calm down!'

'I can't believe he probably killed Preet, bast . . . !'

'Who?'

'Rajveer. And Preet's husband and the other

guys . . . the syndicate . . . they're all murderers!'

Kawaljeet shakes off the last of his sleep-not going to happen tonight, I guess-and goes closer to Jannat. She removes her woollen scarf and throws it on the last few pieces of ignited coal. She gets up and paces the room hysterically, mentioning names and places that, unless she tells him the full story, will not make sense to him.

'The modest cabin you know? His family business's outhouse... and then what? Oh yeah sure, plays the harmonica to wake me up, makes me ginger tea . . . Why didn't he stab me there and then, dog . . . ?'

'Jannat, relax . . . '

'And the ball . . . the first time we met, we danced so close. How could I be so stupid, he is a . . .?'

Kawaljeet walks over to Jannat and hugs her tightly so that she can feel his heart beating close to hers and finally calm down. As he does she bursts into tears, a long over-due cry. She sobs inconsolably for a few minutes and Kawaljeet never lets her go. He is there for her, it might have not seemed that way at the beginning but he's not going to let her down now.

Jannat extricates herself from the policeman's arms for a second, and with her eyes still wet with tears she simply tells him: 'I feel hollow inside. Not only did I trust the man I also slept with him! And now I want to see him behind bars. In hindsight, I came all the way to India to nail Preet's murderer and he tricked me into falling in love with him!'

She can feel a sense of shame scorch her even as she speaks. Of course she blames Rajveer but she's also aware that she did nothing to avoid it. She allowed herself to fall into a fast-flowing river that could have drowned her. And most of all she is ashamed at her powerlessness. She just let things happen because she felt . . . comfortable . . . she let loose for once with a man who was different.

'Listen, you have to leave. Go back to the UK, do you understand, before . . . ?'

'No . . . I have to talk to Rajveer first, he needs to . . . '

'Damn it Jannat, you don't understand!

'But Jeet, I have enough evidence on my video camera that I have just shot . . . '

'If you stay they'll kill you. And at this point of time, to erase all evidence, they'll make me disappear too.'

'I have proof of their illegal firearms . . . '

'But there will be no confessions, no witnesses and the case will shut forever.'

'There is a list of NRIs who have ordered the killings . . . '

'The syndicate have minted money in these jobs and they will go to any lengths; they can buy lawyers, politicians, cops, it could be the Lord of Demons himself and they would still erase him!'

'To make love to life one must first seduce death. Jeet you are a cop . . . '

'But I care for you, Jannat. They will bury me first and then what about you?'

'But what if Raj is just a pawn in the whole thing, he was so . . . '

Kawaljeet places his hands firmly on Jannat's shoulders with a sad look in his eyes. She looks at him and nods her head in agreement. In the end he has put his life in danger for her and he'll stay behind, trying to see all the Khannas behind bars. Jannat has no right to put him in any further danger.

'This is Punjab, Jannat, the legal system sucks. You may not be allowed to leave the country if you are framed falsely. I am not a coward. I am worried about you. You will get trapped. You have evidence against Harry, but he is a British citizen. He will fly away before you can spell his name aloud. Just go back to the UK and get him arrested there for Preet's murder. If we take action here he may not even see the prison building; he's too rich for that. Plus the syndicate here works hand in glove with power brokers and politicians. Back in England once Harry is under arrest he'll name everyone who is involved in this operation. People who collaborate get deferred sentences; he'll want that if he's smart, because I don't know your legal system but in any other country this degree of premeditation leads you straight to the death penalty. Remember you are an honest journalist and you need to get this story published. Jannat, you have a job!'

Kawaljeet is infatuated by her purpose. If she were an Indian reporter he would go on his knees right now and propose to her. But Jannat comes from a different planet.

Their worlds will never meet.

'What a shame! Jeet, I am running away from my own native country to fight for the truth.'

'Greed is a curse, Jannat.'

'No, helplessness is the biggest curse.'

'Wait! Do you have all the evidence files, where is . . . ?'

'Shit, my iPhone is completely ruined. It broke when I swam across the pond . . . I think . . . '

'What about . . . what about the backup you saved, where . . . ?'

'What back up?'

'Your pen drive?'

Jannat's hand immediately reaches to her neck-hanging from it is the chain with the bullet shaped pendant; she opens it and pulls out the pen drive. For the first time since she got back to the house Kawaljeet and Jannat exchange a hopeful glance.

Jannat inserts the pen drive into Kawaljeet's laptop, a few seconds later all the files are successfully retrieved and saved, ironically, in a file named 'lost love'.

'If anyone searches your computer they'll never think of looking in here.'

'Ah, you'd make quite a spy, Miss Gill, or should I say Jannat Bond?' They both sigh with relief and hug, and then Kawaljeet takes the chain and puts it back around Jannat's neck.

'Guard this with your life. Let's go! Where's your passport?'

'At Naseebo *dadi's* house.'

Kawaljeet reaches for his phone and dials a number, a few seconds later a kind voice answers.

'Amritsar Airport, Air India Ticketing Desk. How may I help you?'

'This is SHO Kawaljeet Deol. I need an

emergency ticket to London on the next available flight. When does it leave?'

After having taken care of the guard outside Rajveer and Ranjeet stealthily enter Na-seebo's *kothi* through the main door that she had left unlatched because she knew there was a cop outside. Ranjeet puts on the torch on his phone while Rajveer has his gun pointed. They enter Naseebo's room and see her fast asleep. There's no need to wake her up for the moment. They tiptoe into a couple of other rooms till they find Jannat's. They barge in and find the room empty.

'I can't see Jannat. I guess the guard outside was here just to protect the old lady . . . '

Jannat's laptop is open on the table where she left it only yesterday morning. Before his uncle can do something crazy, or stupid, Rajveer turns it on and goes through all the documents but can't find any relevant files. He is puzzled. Meanwhile Ranjeet rummages through the paperwork and finds a handwritten note.

He moves closer to the window and reads in a whisper, 'SHO Kawaljeet Deol, residential address: BMC CHOWK, Lane #Five, House number 47.'

As soon as Rajveer's SUV pulls out of the driveway with a roar Kawaljeet's car pulls in. If they had arrived a minute earlier or the other two had left a minute later they would have certainly bumped into each other. Jannat hears the sound of an engine and for a moment she's paralyzed; but after considering that the sound is getting farther away she reassures herself.

Once they are in Jannat's room she takes all her stuff and shoves it in her bag. She reaches under the mattress for her passport. Naseebo appears in the doorway of the room. She says she heard noises and decided to pretend she was sleeping but when she heard Jannat's voice she got up knowing this may be the last chance to say good bye. They hug a tearful goodbye.

'Jannat *puttar,* till your flight takes off I will be in the sacred company of *Guru Granth Sahib ji.* You must be scared to . . . '

'To embrace life you must first embrace death,' Jannat's parting words puts back the same sparkle in Naseebo's eye that had made her late husband fall in love with her.

Meanwhile, Kawaljeet, who is enjoying a moment of tenderness in the warmth of Naseebo's *kothi,* is receiving an unexpected visit from unwanted visitors back home. Rajveer breaks the door with a kick and barges in. They are so focused on finding Jannat before she talks to the cop that they forget to wear gloves or hide their trail.

The house is empty and he's with her. Rajveer feels the agony of jealousy stabbing right into his guts. Jannat may want to screw them, she may be an investigative journalist or whatever the hell that she is, but this . . . being with another man in the dead of night . . . He can't take it and has to fight back an expression of rage. Ranjeet, who hasn't stopped looking everywhere, finds a small piece of paper by the phone. AIR INDIA Flight AI 111 Amritsar airport, Departure at 10.30 am.

As they get in the car Ranjeet calls Moga.

Moga is the kind of person who always seems to be ready for action. A minute after the call his car is roaring on the road to the airport too.

Several cars are queuing in front of the once black and white bar waiting for the train to pass so that they can proceed to their destination. A lot of them are going to the airport. Kawaljeet taps his forefinger on the wheel. He does it casually, but to Jannat it is clear he is worried. Stopping like this for several minutes without knowing who is in the cars behind or ahead is always dangerous.

Moga gets out of his car and checks how many cars are queuing and if he can spot Rajveer's SUV. Ranjeet is clear, if he has a good shot at the girl and the cop is not around, he must shoot. They can't afford to kill a cop; in an accident yes, no problem, but shooting a cop point blank is suicidal. So

Jannat can only die if the cop isn't around. Not easy, considering the two are in the same car...

A *sadhu* braves the bitterness of the winter and gets up to walk past the cars with his bowl. This is the only way he survives and he has developed a mental scheme on how long he can spend in front of each car. The passengers in the first few cars don't even look at him and he walks past them fast, but when he gets to Jannat, he sees her fair face. A *firangi,* this is worth spending a few seconds, foreigners usually like *sadhus.*

Jannat sees him and smiles. She has a few five-rupee coins left that she won't be using anymore. She rolls down the window and drops them into his bowl. Suddenly Moga's attention is caught by the *clings.* There she is. But as he walks back to his car to get his phone, or at least the gun, the train passes, fast and metallic, covering all sounds, and in a second, Jannat, the cop, the *sadhu,* disappear behind the swarm of cars driving in opposite directions.

This time Moga calls his boss, Ranjeet.

In the car filled with a chanting music that no one is really listening to but that has been turned on to muffle the tension, Ranjeet picks up his phone. He is serious but for the first time Rajveer sees a hint of a smile on his uncle's face.

'Great. Spot her car and finish her off. It's going to be tough if she reaches the airport. And needless to say, be discreet!'

Then looking at his nephew he says, 'Moga just spotted Jannat in Kawaljeet's jeep on this very road. That means she is headed to Amritsar Airport.'

A chill runs down Rajveer's spine. They must find her first.

In Kawaljeet's car, unaware of what is right behind them, Jannat keeps sneezing and searches for a tissue in her bag. She rummages without really looking until her hand hits something hard, small and of an odd shape. She takes it out and she's breathless to find Rajveer's talisman, the stone ring that rolled off his finger that night at the cabin. *Is this a sign?*

As Rajveer devours the road in his black SUV, Ranjeet pulls out a small satchel from the back seat, extracts two guns and silencers and sets them up. He places six bullets in the drum and one in the cane, ready for the kill.

Ranjeet then cleans the gun and hands it to Rajveer as if offering a piece of cake. Ranjeet's sharp gaze cuts through Rajveer's foggy thoughts. Rajveer takes the gun, his chest out, his shoulders leaned backwards only the warrior's vest is missing-and hides it in one of the inside pockets of his leather jacket. His lips are sealed, his breath resolute.

Meanwhile, driving towards the airport, Kawaljeet looks at Jannat to comfort her, he enquires about Jannat's office to distract her from the fear, but with the ring her brain is elsewhere.

'I wear this ring for protection. My mother thinks that as long as I have it I won't die . . . '

I remember the conversation on that crazy night. Time is getting so blurred and confused . . . But if I have his ring, he . . . Superstition? A wise lady's illusion? I can't bring myself to hate him . . . How is that possible? He is after me, to kill me, and I, here, with his ring . . . I fear for his life . . . is he safe, I can't bring myself to think that he's part of this. But what if he's not?

With all these thoughts in her head Kawaljeet's words are muffled. Jannat slips the ring on her finger, as if to remind herself to give it back when she bumps into Rajveer, if she does.

Kawaljeet swerves the car into a *kachcha* road off the highway. Jannat looks at him, unsure what to think; right now she feels she can trust no one.

'Short cut. The perks of being a cop.'

All three cars are speeding individually but neither Moga nor Rajveer can catch up with Kawaljeet's jeep since he is on another road. Crossing a water pond the jeep's rear tyres get stuck in the mud. Kawaljeet curses his shortcut and

Jannat grows tense. What if she misses the flight? When will the next one be? But Kawaljeet is no fool. In less than a minute the car is out of the muddy patch and running again.

Jannat lets out a big sigh of relief, 'I thought twists and turns are only part of a film . . . life is so much more dramatic!'

Meanwhile, the other SUV is also stopped by a herd of cows wandering on a narrow bridge. Ranjeet curses and tries to scare them off, screaming, Rajveer honks, and both men stop as they hear Rajveer's phone ring.

It's five in the morning. So it's Moga telling them he has finished the job, finally it's over.

Rajveer looks at the screen of the phone, MP Bansal.

'Shit!'

'Hello, Mr Bansal, what a . . . '

'Cut the crap kid. My party secretary called in distress . . . A gentleman called Harry Randhawa, from London, complained about your work. There is a glaring loophole. If he gets trapped in a shithole, we drown in the same shit. We don't want to disappoint a wealthy Britisher, do we?'

'I'm on it, sir.'

'Don't be on it, finish the bloody job or we are

all in deep trouble. I don't like trouble, am I making myself clear?' says the politician in the crudest tone Rajveer has ever heard.

'Short cut. The perks of being a cop.'

All three cars are speeding individually but neither Moga nor Rajveer can catch up with Kawaljeet's jeep since he is on another road. Crossing a water pond the jeep's rear tyres get stuck in the mud. Kawaljeet curses his shortcut and Jannat grows tense. What if she misses the flight? When will the next one be? But Kawaljeet is no fool. In less than a minute the car is out of the muddy patch and running again.

Jannat lets out a big sigh of relief, 'I thought twists and turns are only part of a film . . . life is so much more dramatic!'

Meanwhile, the other SUV is also stopped by a herd of cows wandering on a narrow bridge. Ranjeet curses and tries to scare them off, screaming, Rajveer honks, and both men stop as they hear Rajveer's phone ring.

It's five in the morning. So it's Moga telling them he has finished the job, finally it's over.

Rajveer looks at the screen of the phone, MP Bansal.

'Shit!'

'Hello, Mr Bansal, what a . . . '

'Cut the crap kid. My party secretary called in distress . . . A gentleman called Harry Randhawa, from London, complained about your work. There is a glaring loophole. If he gets trapped in a shithole, we drown in the same shit. We don't want to disappoint a wealthy Britisher, do we?'

'I'm on it, sir.'

'Don't be on it, finish the bloody job or we are all in deep trouble. I don't like trouble, am I making myself clear?' says the politician in the crudest tone Rajveer has ever heard.

30

As Rajveer devours the road in his black SUV, Ranjeet pulls out a small satchel from the back seat, extracts two guns and silencers and sets them up. He places six bullets in the drum and one in the cane, ready for the kill.

Ranjeet then cleans the gun and hands it to Rajveer as if offering a piece of cake. Ranjeet's sharp gaze cuts through Rajveer's foggy thoughts. Rajveer takes the gun, his chest out, his shoulders leaned backwards only the warrior's vest is missing and hides it in one of the inside pockets of his leather jacket. His lips are sealed, his breath resolute.

Meanwhile, driving towards the airport, Kawaljeet looks at Jannat to comfort her, he enquires about Jannat's office to distract her from the fear, but with the ring her brain is elsewhere.

'I wear this ring for protection. My mother thinks that as long as I have it I won't die . . .'

I remember the conversation on that crazy night. Time is getting so blurred and confused . . . But if I have his ring, he . . . Superstition? A wise lady's illusion? I can't bring myself to hate him . . . How is that possible? He is after me, to kill me, and I, here, with his ring . . . I fear for his life . . . is he safe, I can't bring myself to think that he's part of this. But what if he's not?

With all these thoughts in her head Kawaljeet's words are muffled. Jannat slips the ring on her finger, as if to remind herself to give it back when she bumps into Rajveer, if she does.

Kawaljeet swerves the car into a *kachcha* road off the highway. Jannat looks at him, unsure what to think; right now she feels she can trust no one.

'Short cut. The perks of being a cop.'

All three cars are speeding individually but neither Moga nor Rajveer can catch up with Kawaljeet's jeep since he is on another road. Crossing a water pond the jeep's rear tyres get stuck in the mud. Kawaljeet curses his shortcut and Jannat grows tense. What if she misses the flight? When will the next one be? But Kawaljeet is no fool. In less than a minute the car is out of the muddy patch and running again.

Jannat lets out a big sigh of relief, 'I thought twists and turns are only part of a film... life is so much more dramatic!'

Meanwhile, the other SUV is also stopped by a herd of cows wandering on a narrow bridge. Ranjeet curses and tries to scare them off, screaming, Rajveer honks, and both men stop as they hear Rajveer's phone ring.

It's five in the morning. So it's Moga telling them he has finished the job, finally it's over.

Rajveer looks at the screen of the phone, MP Bansal.

'Shit!'

'Hello, Mr Bansal, what a . . . '

'Cut the crap kid. My party secretary called in distress . . . A gentleman called Harry Randhawa, from London, complained about your work. There is a glaring loophole. If he gets trapped in a shithole, we drown in the same shit. We don't want to disappoint a wealthy Britisher, do we?'

'I'm on it, sir.'

'Don't be on it, finish the bloody job or we are all in deep trouble. I don't like trouble, am I making myself clear?' says the politician in the crudest tone

Rajveer has ever heard.

Then he hangs up. He gestures to throw the phone through the glass windscreen and smash his escalating anxiety, but the cows have dispersed and the SUV can restart its quest.

The airport is finally in sight. Kawaljeet leaves the car as close as he can to the entrance and escorts Jannat in, looking around suspiciously. They arrive at the ticket counter. He flashes his police card to the stewardess. 'Get her on that flight, now!'

The lady smiles politely, as she would at any customer.

Moga, Rajveer and Ranjeet also make it to the airport. The two men hand Moga their guns and go their separate ways into the terminal, each one with the nonchalant air of frequent fliers. Moga, on the other hand, hides the guns in his jacket and then goes towards the back entrance where a 'friend' who happens to be airport staff is waiting. As soon as the thug has jumped over the wall and is inside the premises his friend hands him a uniform and helps him wear it. The man also takes the guns and puts them into his bag of plumber's tools. Moga nods, he's nervous about someone else keeping the guns but there's no other way. As they pass under the metal detector the lights go off. Moga shivers but his friend pulls out the nicest smile when the sleepy police officer appointed to the rear entrance comes.

'Ay . . . all these thugs who clog the toilets in the middle of the night, do you know my friend what it takes to clean all the shit? At this time . . . Argh . . . '

'Okay, I couldn't care less, just go . . . ' says the cop, who evidently wants to go back to his uncomfortable chair for a small nap.

When they are through to the men's room Moga hands the man a roll of five hundred rupee notes and the man smiles greedily. 'Always a pleasure to do business with you, Sunny!'

Moga nods as the man leaves.

'Sunny, hey?'

'In this job the fewer know your real name the better...' answers Moga.

Ranjeet and Rajveer open the flush tanks of the two toilet stalls parallel to each other where they were hiding and start rummaging through the plastic bag to get their guns. Rajveer unwraps his lightweight Glock 17 attached to a silencer while Ranjeet checks on the sound suppressor of his unused Heckler and Koch 9mm caliber. Ranjeet boosts his self-confidence by rubbing the barrel against his chin. This German beauty will never fail. They both exit with light tinted shades to mask their faces. Rajveer wears a baseball cap while Ranjeet puts on a fur hat.

Now that they all have their guns their disguise is accurate. They leave again and dis-perse around the airport to find Jannat. They spot her in the half empty airport, queuing with the cop. As soon as she has her boarding pass she goes to Kawaljeet, thanks him for everything then asks him to look after her bag as she uses the re-stroom. She senses an odd grumble in her stomach.

The cop stands in the hall with her purse. Moga, who hides behind a pillar, sees Jannat walk by herself towards the restroom. He nods at Rajveer, who's the closest to the ladies room, to prompt him to go inside and finish the job.

Rajveer attempts to enter but right then, a group of schoolgirls cuts across and Jannat enters with some of the girls. They have got to kill her but it can't be a massacre. Jannat exits untouched. A curse slips from Ranjeet's clenched teeth. Rajveer wouldn't want to allow himself to do so but he lets out a sigh of relief.

Jannat bumps into a young Muslim girl. She wears an *abaya* on her head. Her hands let go of a placard that she was holding. She helps to lift the placard and put it back in her hands. Her rambling eyes for once glance at the words on the cardboard cut-out, 'One world, one love, one consciousness.'

She gives the girl an infectious smile and whispers, 'I wish I could be you.'

She goes back to Kawaljeet who is talking to a fellow policeman to ask him to escort her to the plane. He introduces them and the policeman reassures her; his father knew SHO Deol's father, she is in good hands. Suddenly the three men, from their separate corners, see Jannat looking frantically in her white bag, then checking her pockets; her eyes are slightly squint with sleep deprivation and all the tears that she had to hold back. She seems to have lost something important. She seems not to be able to handle another loss, another piece of her that flakes off but suddenly her face lightens up as if all her fears had been wiped off at once. The restroom, that's where she must have left them when she put them down to wash her hands. She runs back.

A pregnant lady exits. Jannat pauses and smiles at the young lady wearing a saree with her head covered. She is moonfaced, genuine, not a conspirator. Jannat lets her pass by and takes a deep breath to cool her nerves. The airport announcer announces her flight boarding. She dashes inside like a bullet.

In a second Rajveer is after her with hypnotic precision. He enters the ladies room and places the 'Do Not Enter, Cleaning in Progress' sign behind him so that no one can enter. He then slips into one of the toilets. She rushes to the washbasin to look for the leather folder that cases her travel documents. A rat squirms on Rajveer's shoe. His eyes bulge out of its sockets. He has a choice, to faint or to fight. He slides his trembling foot like a serpent. The rat scampers away. But it is still in the vicinity and Rajveer can smell its stinking fur. His mind races to go and grab Jannat's hands. 'Ah, the hands of glory,' he smiles to himself.

'This is absurd.' His nostrils flare. He sinks to the ground. He wants to punch a hole in the floor. 'I have to finish the game, hardwired, sorry Jannat!'

His breath is heavy, his heart pounding in his ears, deafening as an explosion, his mouth is dry and his hands slippery. This has never happened to him before. It's happening now because his Her heart spits poetry, ready for the final blow. Romance is not a frantic chase to find love… it's the discovery of the self in the heart of another being.

Still lost in a quantum moment, the one in which she and her love are happy, fused together, she doesn't see Rajveer's hand sliding towards the light switch. He can see a set of reflections of himself since the mirrors are bolted with a pattern. *Who is the real me, Ma?*

Rajveer's fingers shudder, his breath is edgy. *Claustrophobia.*

In a second the bright, obnoxious light of the rest room is off and the air is frozen. A naked zero watt bulb flickers on the side of a mirror. *Ethereal.*

In the split second of stillness that precedes the tempest the hungry hearts of Rajveer and Jannat synchronize. *Serendipity.*

Rajveer senses that his big, powerful heart is not afraid of dying but regrets having led a life that brought him to this point. All that he is giving up, that he has given up, is now tangible. Love, the feeling that his mother always spoke about and which he hadn't considered until this very moment, a stupid thing for bored women, is now a bright mass that pulses inside him, that nudges him to sacrifice his life to save hers. Is this true love?

Jannat, on the other side, looks intensely into his eyes, feels something moving inside her. She almost feels physically sick. She initially blames it on fear, but her brain soon realizes it has nothing to do with fear. Something inside her is twitching. The energy is sublime but sweet. The prey falling in love and ready to sacrifice before her hunter. Why?

Is this karma flowing through many lifetimes? She doesn't know, but her need to be with him is stronger than everything. The yearning has arrived at lightning speed, there have been millions of questions in her head in the last few days and now, sud-denly it's all meaningless. *This is it.*

All she wants is his arms wrapped around her.

She feels trapped like a child in a womb soon to get aborted.

Before she can say or do anything the door slams open. Ranjeet and Moga break in.

Moga closes the door behind him and Jannat closes her eyes. She would prefer to die not knowing who shot her, believing it wasn't Rajveer.

Right after the first shot she throws herself on the floor, then more shots explode showering her with silver glass splinters and the service bulb goes off. The door cracks open again and shuts, more shots are fired.

Jannat lies on the ground, aching but alive, with her eyes closed, counting the seconds to her death. 'Has my heart stop beating? I am losing my breath'

Suddenly everything stops and blacks out, as if she finally fell asleep after a long time with no rest. In the distance she can hear ambulances, police maybe, but it's all so far away, so muffled, that it doesn't really matter anymore. *Mercy.*

As Rajveer lifts his hands in the air, exposing his chest to the bullets but refusing to shoot for fear of killing Jannat, his one and only love, the words of his mother quoted from the *Bhagwad Gita* come back to him now with clarity-'Not any time did I not exist . . . Nor you, nor all these kings and certainly never shall we seize to exist in the future . . .' And at once he feels lighter in his chest. His spirit crystalizes. Amidst the sparks that emit from the silent guns of Ranjeet and Moga he tightens his muscles, takes in a lungful of air, catches the radiance, aims and fires back relentlessly. *Intuition.* He feels like an atom just split open inside his heart. *Triumph.*

31

May's office is spotless and neat as ever. The London skyline that is bright and visible through the huge glass panels brings in a promise of concord with the cosmos. Her pointed stilettos tap on the wooden floor with the rhythm of a metronome. But the noise that fills the room is the news on her TV.

'After three long years the London court has finally convicted Harry Randhawa, an Englishman of Indian origin, and his mother, Kim Randhawa, for conspiring in the murder of Harry's wife, Preet Randhawa, through a murky network of contract killers in Punjab. New Scotland Yard owes this operation to *World Weekly's* investigative re-porter, Jannat Gill, who risked her life in Punjab to uncover the truth behind Preet Randhawa's murder and that of many other victims. The Press Guild will be felicitat-ing Miss Gill with a special award later this month . . . '

A shot of Jannat appears on the screen. It's an extract from her interview. She stares into the invading video cameras. 'Contract killing in India is spreading like a cancer. It's a concealed, complex network and unless the Indian government really tries to invest resources in training men like Police Officer Kawaljeet Deol, who got the most important confession from the vital lead nicknamed-the Messenger-before the New Scotland Yard swung into action. However 'hired for gun' is a supply that responds to a demand, just to put it in economic terms. We can't change the evil in people easily, but we can prevent them from harming others. Your voice, your resolve can save many innocent lives from getting butchered. You could be next. Say NO to contract killing, sign our online petition and support us!'

May switches the TV off. She flings the remote on the Tabriz rug but knows she can't afford to mess. This scoop brought her so much popularity; she doesn't even know how to handle it. She is now on the list of the most powerful women in the United Kingdom. 'Is Jannat a contributor?'

'Send her in,' she says scornfully to Shelley.

May takes a look at her office. Contract killing in India has opened a new frontier of journalism, there's no doubt about it. Jannat has started to speak on talk shows and her book has sold several hundreds of copies. Victim" families have had justice and the murderers who didn't die are now languishing in jail. Jannat is her protégée after all. She and Jannat have never been friends. In fact she assigned Gill to Punjab as punishment, but May has to admit that she really did an outstanding job. In times of bad journalism such news does become the coveted story. Every big magazine has a flag-ship story and this may be the one for her's.

Jannat enters the room and notices roses in a crystal vase kept on the side table. There is a handwritten note on the side. Ahh, bitch is having another affair.

She sits down without any eye contact before May invites her to. She sneezes. Shelley and she, who she's now friendlywith, joke that she must be allergic to May herself.

May glances at the disinfectant spray that she once showered over Jannat but decides against using it again. She'll face the risk!

'There is a new assignment I'd like you to go on. It's rather far away, in another coun-try not so advanced as ours.'

Jannat looks unimpressed and answers in a monotonous voice: 'Okay, right . . . Is that all?'

May's phone rings. The ringtone has changed to the latest James Bond theme song from the movie *Spectre*.

May lowers her breasts and gestures for Jannat to leave. Jannat reaches for the file and is about to get up when May interrupts her. 'I suggest you open the file as soon as you walk out this door.'

May grabs her paper-thin phone but waits for Jannat to exit.

Jannat seizes the file like a warrior pulling out her sword and leaves without a word. As she reaches her desk she drops the file on her table with a thud. She curses under her breath.

'Has to be Syria. May wants me to die so that she can take all the credit for the rest of her life.' She paces around her desk and sips on water incessantly. She chokes on her Fiji water. 'I've made this magazine increasingly popular and this is what I get . . . May, what did I do to you in your past birth?'

She returns to her laptop for her daily dose of BrainHQ, the online cognitive training. Her phone rings.

'Jannat Gill.'

'It's May. I expect a very detailed report on the

conference. Better . . . '

'Waste of paper, I am sorry. Wait . . . What conference?'

'Have you not opened the file yet?'

'Yeah . . . sure . . . ' she quickly opens it and runs through it. For a moment she can't speak.

'Gill? Gill? Well the conference is about international genocide and other murderous crimes against society,' she clears her throat and adds firmly, 'and needless to say, I won't be around, so prepare your speech, well in advance . . . The conference is live . . . just in case you haven't been to one.'

Jannat takes a deep breath, walks to the door of her new office with a big smile, looks at the loudspeaker of her phone and whispers, 'Thank you, May . . . May you always spell fame and glory,' almost sure that Mayhem May had already hung up, but she hears a click on the other side. May has heard her and waited for a minute before hanging up right on her face. Who could have ever imagined she had a heart?

On her desk there is the white file with 'Jannat' written on the top. Inside there are details of the forthcoming American conference on human rights, a plane ticket, a ho-tel reservation and a note from May, 'Do what you do best, talk about contract killing!' ending with a smiley face.

A smiley face? From that viper? Is she on some substance? Ah, must be a big celebrity affair! No wonder she is sending me instead! Is it Daniel Craig? She has an obsession with Bond. She can trap any man with her words? Anais Nin with silicone breasts. Seductress . . .

But her heart can't stop racing. New York City here she comes!

On her way out of the office she buys a vegan roll to celebrate her newly gained Americanness. She calls the nanny and asks her to speak to her son.

'Hey baby, I'll be home soon. Mamma will play with you before shegoes on work to America!'

Rajveer attempts to say something but he's still too young to understand and respond. He mumbles and she can feel the bliss that it attempts to resonate.

Jannat strolling below London Bridge for once feels content. She observes a very old couple locked in a hug. 'Looks like they would be hitting the same grave'. She is hav-ing an internal conversation with starlings.

'Some love stories never begin, they simply float in words . . . some never end, they linger in spirit beyond imagination.'

At home she packs untidily. Rajveer rolls on the bed, his Papa's mouth organ by his side. Jannat looks at him coo and knows that even though he is still young, maybe too young to understand, she still owes him the truth. So what if she has buried the hor-rors of her close encounter with death and disaster. *Raj, how I wish I never met you!*

'Come here my young warrior! Your dad was an amazing man, good at heart, who was led to make bad choices, but who repented at last, for the sake of true love, and de-cided to sacrifice his life to save mine, ours . . . do you understand!'

She sheds a tear while looking at her son who stares back with dreamy eyes. She holds his hands tight. Two hearts melt into each other.

'He didn't know you were inside me and yet something made him believe it was worth saving my life. He shot those who wanted to kill me and got shot in return, but he lives through you. It takes very little to lose oneself, it takes a lot to rediscover who you really are.' But in Raj's case it was quite the opposite she reminisces. It took a lot for him to lose himself but very little to rediscover who he really was.

In that one defining moment Rajveer found himself and stuck to his self-realisation at the cost of his life. The best part about a miracle is that, like love, you never know when it may happen. But it does happen. Raj was ready for another journey, another assignment. His string of *kismet.*

Jannat closes her eyes-thank god it's over. Her son, for the first time, crawls next to her and snuggles, not like a child would hug his mother but like an adult man who would pass on his love to a woman who needs to be loved.

And she whispers, 'To embrace life you must first learn to embrace death.'

A clap of thunder jolts the skies. Raj is dead, with his ashes sprinkled in a country that she will never be allowed to see again. Possibly, he is also here, she ponders, stalking me in a new avatar, barely standing on his short legs, speaking broken words. *Ah, me and my overactive imagination.*

One powerful moment can change one's life. On the accidental night at the cottage, when Rajveer and Jannat sealed their union by making love for the first and last time, they created something beautiful, someone who will keep them alive for perpetuity and who will tell their story, perhaps by example.

She goes to her grandma who is cooking. The old lady, overflowing with love, stands there in a white *salwarkurta* with her white hair creating a halo around her. 'Thanks *bebe,* for taking care of Raj.'

'I have packed some *paneer parathas* for you. Have them on your way to the airport be-fore the Manhattan pizzas kill you with constipation.'

Jannat plants a kiss on her fair cheeks.

'When you don't give in to your desires you change your code of Karma.'

The proud grandma gives Jannat a tight hug, though her hands shiver, weathered with time. 'Somebody taught me that lesson by giving his life, irony rules.'

Her grandma hugs her, 'Jannat, I will take good care of Raj till I am alive, but what about the future?'

'Make love to your fears, it's the best orgasm,' Jannat stands tall, holding her grandma by her shoulders. *Bebe* blushes like a baby.

That night as she turns the light off in the little boy's room sleeping with her grandma Jannat closes her eyes and sighs loudly, trying to fight tears back. But they are not tears of fear, sadness, or desperation like they have been all these years. They are tears that celebrate her new freedom, like the rain flooding her lawn. All her life she feared death, from the very moment her grandma told her that her mother had died very early in her life. And tonight she realizes that having lost the father of her child has erased all fear of death. She discovered she was pregnant; still shocked by her experience in Punjab she carried on her pregnancy and motherhood alone. She managed to keep her job and publish a book. She's not going to give up now.

And it's with this renewed spirit that she goes into her small office. A book rests on the centre of the teakwood desk, the harmonica on the side gleaming with her son's fingerprints on it. She lifts her book as she squats on the wooden revolving chair. The cover has an artistic image of a white chit being passed on by an ugly hand to a hand that wears a black stone ring. The cigarette rolling paper has two words printed in handwritten font 'Kill Gill'. At the bottom of the illustration is the name of the author Jannat Gill.

She pours herself a generous glass of red wine and takes a long swig. She feels her ruf-fled pulse. She opens her scribbling pad with shaky fingers and she jots in her tidy and small calligraphy.

– *Meaning paradise… Paradise, the bridge between life and death'*

The letter is sealed in an empty wine bottle thatshe throws it from the window into the majestic river Thames flowing peacefully before her house. The shimmering bottle against the white moonlight momentarily blinds onlookers, but in a moment the bottle sinks into the dark waters with a dull sound and the great river swallows Jannat's fears, regrets, ugliness, leaving her finally free to live again. She spreads her arms to embrace the galaxy and speaks to the stars above.

'And one day we realise that the entire journey of our life is a single lesson on how to die!'

Amrish is the author of Tiger Mates, the screenwriter of the blockbuster Don2, and the co-writer and creative producer for the international Docu-Drama *Beatification of Mother Teresa*, which was showcased in Cannes.

Amrish began his career in 1995, directing TV shows, music videos and ad films, and worked with Star TV, Sony TV, Reliance Big Pictures, and PVR Pictures.

By practice and passion, Amrish is also a Neuroplastician. He is a Neuroscience Innovator @ *www.supermind.world* and the founder-mentor with an online story foundation called *www.superstoreee.com.*

He is currently working with Farhan Akhtar's Excel Entertainment for a forthcoming film.

Fiction-Thriller

ISBN 978-81-8386-179-3

tara
India Research Press
www.indiaresearchpress.com

₹299 $10.95 £8.99